Krystal Bradshaw

the
ROOT
of All
EVIL

the
ROOT
of All
EVIL

JOYLYNN M. JOSSEL

St. Martin's Griffin

New York

ISBN 0-7394-4337-2

Thank you to my three beautiful children.
Mommy did it, and thanks for allowing me to do it.

Thank you, Nicholas (Boogie Bang) Ross.
Thank you for sacrificing for my sacrifices.
Thank you for the love, arguments, encouragement,
disagreements, and agreements, for they each had their purpose
in the success of my debut novel. I know this now.
I love you and am in love with you.

An extra special thanks to my editor, Monique,
for not letting me go out into the literary
world with my slip showing.

Acknowledgments

I dedicate every morsel of the success of this book and my ability to make a name for myself in the literary industry to the Ross family of Toledo, Ohio. God used them to get me to recognize that support comes in a multitude of forms. A two-hour drive didn't keep them from coming to get the kids so that I could have time to write and go on book signings. Each of your genuine loving and unselfish acts plays the most volatile role in my passion as an author. Grandma Gwen, your powerful brace and character are irreplaceable. Special gratitude to Mama Ross, Aunti Nicole, Tab, NiGayle, Nichelle, Vater, and cousins Chris, Chad, and Bianca for your part in caring for the kids. Thanks to bra-bra Randy (even though after a while you started charging me money to baby-sit). Thank you, Aunt Joy, Aunt Gwen, Ms. Jawan, Ms. Dawn, and Rachel, too. I would've never been able to pick up and go do promotions without your generosity.

Thank you for lending me your angels, God.

. . .

A very special thanks to my agent, Vickie Stringer, and my PR, Earth Jallow. (Who would have thought a couple of chicks from the Midwest would grow up and bring it like this?)

Thank you, ladies.

Thank you, Traci Thompson of the Circle of Friends Book Club's Columbus, Ohio, chapter for your unselfish contribution in getting the word out about this up-and-coming new jack author.

First of All
(Don't Give It Away)

Sipping on an apple martini in a $500,000 condo, a woman would vow, and put it on her favorite auntie's grave, that she would never sell herself. Life is random and lures humanity to unpredictable acts. What a woman pronounces she won't do and what a woman will, in fact, do are two distinct conditions based on the predicament at hand. Let an eviction notice welcome her and her children home after eating Ramen Noodles for two weeks straight. What about the days of choosing between the $1.25 school lunch for the kids or the orange empty fuel light on the car? Or better yet, let her have to boil water to do a warm wash-up because the gas is shut off. See if she doesn't stamp a price tag on her forehead.

The same woman who turns her nose up at a chick who has to do what she has to do to make ends meet is the same broke-ass woman fucking for free. It's funny, isn't it? She can't even keep her cable on, but got some man laid up next to her, getting his nut off. And it's that same woman who is sleeping with every Tiwan, Slick, and Kahari for free that's tampering with the game of women who fuck for needs. Although it's probably not exactly what Iyanla Vanzant meant in her bestselling book, she was right. Don't give it away! This soon became Klarke Taylor's motto.

Klarke's stomach ached every time the phone rang. She was just shy of being three months behind on her truck payment, the same truck that broke down every other week it seemed, costing her more money in repairs and towing than it was worth. She hadn't paid her student loan since Columbus set sail. All of her credit cards were maxed, and the payment due dates had long come and gone without being satisfied. Her bank had already returned two cash-advance checks. Hell, the bank was even hounding her for the negative $287 her checking account reflected. She couldn't seem to help using her checks as if they were credit cards.

If something was on sale that Klarke just had to have, she would write a check for it, knowing she had just exhausted all of her funds. But she just had to have it. She knew she wasn't alone, though. People did it all of the time. Yes, the sweater was on sale for twenty dollars less than its regular price, but once the bank charged a twenty-nine-dollar return-check fee and the vendor turned around and tacked on another fifteen-dollar fee, it equaled out to be one sweater for the price of two. The mathematics of it all never stopped Klarke, though. Her checks might as well have been in a marathon. Whichever one made it to her bank account first was the winner.

She got into the most trouble if her daughter, twelve-year-old Vaughn, and her son, ten-year-old HJ, accompanied her on her sprees. They unknowingly acted as Klarke's justifiable accomplices to her bad spending habits. She refused to let them know how broke she was. Whatever they wanted, she somehow managed to get it.

Last winter she wrote a check for three hundred dollars over the amount that was actually in her bank account. The children had spoken endlessly about wanting a computer for Christmas. While in Best Buy they pleaded with Klarke to buy them one. She put the salesman to work like she really had money for the Compaq. He carried the computer to the register for her as she stood in line sweating bullets. She prayed that CheckRite didn't run her account and put a stop to her madness. Even more so, she was hoping the clerk didn't try to put her on Front Street if she was found out. She knew she was about to commit a crime by writing that stale check. But when it came down to it, she didn't care. She'd do anything for her children to make sure that they had whatever it was that their little hearts desired. She lucked up that time though. The next evening she won the 50/50 raffle at her company Christmas party, for which the pot was $527. She stopped at an ATM and made a deposit that very same night.

Recently the dates for all those damn credit-card deferments Klarke had charged to her debit card were coming around to kick her straight in the ass. Being something of a fashion guru, she couldn't help but shop the catalogs that frequently showed up in her mailbox. At the time of placing the order for that suede faux-fur-collared coat and two pairs of shoes from Chadwick's of Boston, the one dollar that was held on her debit card didn't do much damage. But four months later when the other $299 was deducted, it buried Klarke deeper into debt than she already was. She didn't have the money when she placed the order, but she prayed her luck would turn over the next few months and that the money would be available by the time the balance became due.

Klarke was always hoping money would miraculously appear. Every day when she got home from work she anxiously thumbed through the mail in anticipation of a surprise check. Maybe she had overpaid her taxes and Uncle Sam was throwing her a few ends. Maybe it had gone unnoticed that her mortgage escrow account was overpaid and the error had finally been discovered. Maybe someone had died and named her the heiress of a million-dollar estate. Klarke didn't give a damn where the money came from as long as it had her name on it. But every day Klarke was greeted by the same old acquaintances: Bill, Bill, and Bill.

The past three years had been hell for Klarke. It was three years ago when Harris, her husband of a thirteen-year sentence, decided to leave her for his *so-called* cousin. Klarke never saw it coming.

She and Harris had enjoyed two years of courting prior to their nuptials. She met him one afternoon while out window-shopping. Harris, almost eleven years Klarke's senior, appealed to her inno-cent youthfulness. And Harris dedicated their two years of court-ing to molding Klarke into the perfect woman for himself. And for the next thirteen years, Klarke committed herself to him and their children.

Klarke's parents were both living at the time she and Harris wed. It meant everything in the world to Klarke to have her father walk her down the aisle. He had been battling diabetes for years and had had some close calls. A year later he lost the battle. Shortly thereafter, Klarke's mother lost her will to live and allowed herself to fade away. But they had each lived long enough to see Harris take their daughter's hand in marriage. He had promised them that he would honor their daughter and take care of her. This gave them priceless peace of mind.

During their marriage, Harris provided a very comfortable life for Klarke and the children. He had been employed on the assem-bly line at Jeep for nineteen years, and made decent money once he was promoted to foreman. Although Harris would have liked for them to live modestly, Klarke never had a budget to adhere to. Anything she wanted she could have.

Their three-story home was part of a new housing development on the outskirts of Toledo, Ohio. Harris had wanted to purchase a base-model home so that he could customize it to his liking. The first thing he did was have a swimming pool built in the shape of a heart, to represent what Klarke meant to him.

He couldn't live without her and he wanted to make sure that Klarke was the envy of all. It wasn't because he was afraid that some young buck was going to come along and steal her away. He felt she was entitled to everything he could give her. She was, after all, his creation.

Before Klarke, Harris had mostly dated women his own age. But none of them could ever hold a candle to Klarke's sophistication. She was young in years, but intellectually mature.

Klarke never disrespected Harris's manhood. She never questioned his decisions for the family's well-being, choosing to silently correct his errors and always without argument. She just didn't find it necessary to bring his inaccuracies front and center.

It wasn't a difficult task for Harris to mold Klarke into his tailor-made queen. It was as if she had been born just for him, anyway. Knowing how to please a man came naturally for Klarke. Everything, that is, with the exception of one minor thing. The ability to give head. Getting his dick sucked was Harris's shit. Klarke, on the other hand, couldn't fathom wrapping her lips around a man's urine repository.

When Harris and Klarke were *just kickin' it*, Harris had even paid for oral sex here and there. It was nothing but a thing for him and a few of his cats to roll up to Club Diamond after work and pay for a private dance. Once the girls got to shakin' that ass, he'd tip them two Hamiltons and get three minutes' worth of head. The women there weren't the finest in town, but it was the only place he could get a decent dick suck for twenty dollars.

The Naked Glass had some dimes dancing up in there, but those pretty bitches would solicit a fifty spot before they would even consider going down. The audacity! Pretty girls know they can't suck no dick. They're too busy trying to be just that—pretty. Harris could do without the drama, but on occasion he would visit the bar. All he wanted was a good hardy blow job, but those pretty wannabe actresses and music video rats would be looking at him, trying to be sexy while doing that annoying fake-ass moan ("umm . . . umm . . . umm"). Harris was happy with an okay chick just getting down on her knees and doing her thing, slurping, slobbing—the works.

It would take eleven dates, a gift basket from Bath and Body Works, three failed attempts resulting in Harris having to masturbate, and a weekend trip to King's Island theme park before Klarke would give in to his request for oral sex. Even then, her performance was modest at best. Eventually, however, just like everything else Harris asked of Klarke, she would master it to his liking.

She even learned how to hang over the edge of the bed on her back while Harris stood over her so she could deep throat him. Klarke had read in a magazine that when a woman deep throats in that position the semen just flushes straight down her throat. No gagging, no clumps, no nothing . . . just a straight shot. If there were an Olympic category for dick sucking, Klarke would be awarded the gold on word of mouth alone (no pun intended).

Klarke did everything for Harris except breathe for him. When he came home from a solid day's work and didn't have a taste for what was on the kitchen table, Klarke never hesitated to whip him up something that would please him.

Harris got back rubs when it was Klarke's back that was aching. Klarke pampered Harris with foot massages when it was her feet that were tired. She took delight in every minute of it, though. It was her way of showing Harris gratitude for his role in allowing her to spend her days with their children instead of working a nine-to-five.

By the time Harris walked through the door in the evenings, the children's homework would be complete. Their clothes for the next day, along with his, were ironed and laid out. The children had been bathed and were ready for bed. Klarke kept the house immaculate, so it was always clean when Harris walked through the door, and the shower was running at his desired temperature. Dinner would be hot and dessert would be in the fridge. What Klarke came to find out, however, was that what she thought was keeping her husband honest, loyal, and committed was actually what made him the man of another woman's home.

When a man enters his home, he has the need to feel needed. As far as Harris was concerned, the only thing his home needed was his paycheck. He had often joked to his buddies that his wife's pretty titties hid an S. Although Klarke was exactly the woman he programmed her to be, her perfection made him feel less than a man. His castle was being reigned just fine by the queen.

Take the average married man, for instance, who is cheating on his wife. The other woman damn sure isn't as pretty as his wife, and nine times out of ten she's on Section 8. Her car is an older model that needs a new part each month, and her kids don't have a fit male figure in their lives. That's where his need to be needed is fulfilled. The man's shaft tingles when his pager goes off and it's the other woman needing him to come pick her up because her car broke down. She *needs* him to give her the money to get it fixed. His penis becomes erect when the other woman *needs* him to get her kid's school clothes out of layaway. He outright ejaculates when the other woman *needs* him to help her move from her Section 8 apartment to her Section 8 house.

Most of the time a man's unfaithfulness isn't even about sex. The man doesn't go to the other woman so that he can get his sexual needs fed. He goes to her to get his ego fed. It's called *eating out,* and that's just what Harris ended up doing.

Tionne was Harris's baby cousin. Not a blood-related cousin or even a cousin by marriage. The kind of "cousin" who grew up with the family and therefore qualifies as family. In short, the kind that it's okay to sleep with.

Klarke was never aware of the fact that Harris and Tionne had something going on. It wasn't out of the ordinary for Tionne and Harris to spend time together. Tionne was over at the house on a regular, and at Harris's mother's house for Sunday dinner after church. Klarke liked Tionne. Tionne was only a couple of years older than she was, and the two had even gone out together on several occasions. By the time Klarke found out that Harris was a clandestine adulterer, he and Tionne's love-child was going on one year old.

The affair completely shattered Klarke. When Harris told her the truth about his relationship with Tionne, she took to her bed, and it was weeks before she would regain the strength to get up again. Harris might as well have been Ike Turner and beat her ass for the past thirteen years because that's just the kind of pain Klarke felt consumed by. Her body literally ached all over. She wanted to die. She knew she had to pull it together for her children, but inside she just wanted to die.

It's a wonder she didn't get bedsores because all she did was lie in the bed crying and contemplating suicide. The house became a neglected mixture of clutter and filth. She couldn't even muster up the strength to take out the garbage. The stench had been horrible.

For the children, it had been the next best thing to being at Disneyland. Chores were on hold indefinitely, and they were left to fend for themselves, which meant a diet of ice cream, potato chips, and an array of other junk foods. Vaughn, was very mature for her age, so she kept herself and HJ situated.

Klarke wouldn't answer the phone or the door. She had changed the locks to keep Harris out and her voicemail was full of messages from well-meaning friends and family who genuinely cared about how Klarke was doing, but at the same time were itching to get the scoop. She was too humiliated to oblige them. She herself didn't understand what had happened. She certainly could not explain it to others.

Klarke was the nova of her family and friends. What everyone was working so hard to obtain had seemed to be handed to Klarke on a silver platter. On the outside looking in, she had it all: a beautiful daughter and handsome son, gorgeous home, nice vehicles, expensive housewares, designer clothes, and a few boast-worthy pieces of jewelry. Above all, it appeared that she had an admirable and faithful husband.

How could this have happened? Klarke had thought as she lay in bed crying. *I thought a woman always knew. What the fuck happened to my intuition?*

It sickened Klarke when she thought about the times she had welcomed that woman into her home, her life, and the lives of her children. She had babysat for Tionne and Harris's baby! After five weeks of not being able to eat, sleep, think, drink, or function there was only one thing Klarke could do to kick the bitter feelings and anguish behind her. . . . KICK THAT BITCH'S BEHIND!

Prior to this ordeal, Klarke had pretty much been a nonconfrontational individual. She never made a big deal over trivial matters. She respected that there were folks in the world with bigger problems than hers. She appreciated life's challenges and played with the hand she was dealt. But this particular hand contained a wild card.

Klarke didn't bother to run a comb through her matted hair. She didn't bother to secure her 36 Cs with a bra. It was only 30 degrees Fahrenheit outside and she just threw on her Ohio State University T-shirt, a pair of cutoff sweat shorts, her flip-flops, and grabbed the kids and headed over to Tionne's.

After loading her children into the backseat of the Rodeo, Klarke drove calmly to Tionne's Section 8 townhouse. Klarke pulled up and parked next to Tionne's ten-year-old Toyota Corolla and told the children she would be right back.

She wanted to pull a Jackie Chan and kick in the door, which was made of a combination of metal and aluminum with chipped brown paint. Instead she knocked lightly and waited for Tionne to come to the door.

"Klarke," Tionne said, startled, when she halfway opened the door.

"I figured it's about time we talked. May I come in?" Klarke asked in her most amiable voice.

Tionne hesitated before saying, "Sure, Klarke." After another brief hesitation Tionne slowly opened the door for Klarke to enter.

"I don't know what to say to you. I can't even come up with the right words," Klarke said.

"You shouldn't have to say anything. This is entirely my fault. I'm sorry. As lame as that sounds, I truly am sorry," Tionne said with sincerity as she put her hand upon Klarke's shoulder. Klarke looked down at Tionne's hand. It took everything in her to stay calm.

Tionne gestured for Klarke to sit down at the kitchen table and offered her a soda, which Klarke accepted. She didn't know how she managed to swallow. She was so busy visualizing a fistful of Tionne's burgundy microbraids dangling from her hand.

"Where's the baby?" Klarke asked, knowing she couldn't act out if the child was in the house.

"Oh, she's with her fath . . ." Tionne said, her words trailing off awkwardly. For the past five weeks she had finally been able to freely tell people that Harris was the father of her child. It felt good after having to keep it secret for so long.

Just that quick Klarke knew the small talk was over. No *Why? How long? Does he pay your bills?* or *Did he eat you out?* At that very moment Tionne was every woman who had raped another woman of her man and family.

Klarke launched herself out of her chair and on to Tionne and began swinging. She made sure she gave Tionne a hit, kick, punch, smack, jab, sock, whack, scratch, slug, and bite for every sistah out there who had been played. It was a beat-down worthy of pay-per-view.

Klarke knocked Tionne down and sat on top of her. Locks of Tionne's braids filled Klarke's hands as she slammed Tionne's head over and over against the floor.

Tionne managed to buck Klarke off of her. Klarke came after Tionne like a raging bull and Tionne kicked her in the stomach, almost knocking the wind out of her. Klarke hunched over holding her stomach, gasping for air.

Tionne turned over and tried to crawl away, but Klarke quickly recovered and grabbed Tionne's foot and dragged her back. She flipped Tionne over and jumped back on top of her. She pinned Tionne's arms to the floor with her knees and continued to beat the living daylights out of Tionne.

After about ten consecutive blows to the mug, Klarke stood over her while she moaned and groaned.

Maybe she's had enough, Klarke thought to herself. After all, the tramp at her feet was only human. Klarke did feel *some* sympathy for her opponent. But as she stood there looking down at Tionne, she became pissed off all over again.

"Fuck that!" Klarke said and pulled Tionne up from the kitchen floor and began whaling on her some more.

Tionne was a helpless rag doll as Klarke knocked her around the kitchen, breaking a few dishes and a chair along the way. Unfortunately, Tionne didn't have a timekeeper to ring the bell, or a referee to break up the fight and declare the bout a TKO. Klarke pounced on Tionne until the blood-covered whore looked like she was near death. Klarke didn't want Tionne dead, though.

Klarke felt justified and satisfied. Each blow had been her mouthpiece. Before returning to her children, who were waiting for her in the truck, Klarke knelt on the floor next to Tionne. With her lips barely touching Tionne's swollen earlobe she asked the only question that truly mattered to her, "How long have you wanted to be me?"

When Klarke returned home, she put on her Rachelle Ferrell *Individuality* CD, ordered the children to clean their pigpens, and started working on her house. She couldn't believe how much filth and dust had accumulated. Knowing her daughter had asthma, she felt selfish for allowing it to get that bad.

She cleaned as she sang along with Ms. Ferrell. The frantic cleansing of her house was a symbol of the cleansing of her spirit.

As Klarke dusted the bar and stools she couldn't help but

admire all the expensive bottles of wine, champagne, and liquor Harris had collected over the years. Harris was so proud of this bar. As a matter of fact, he had actually taken a week's vacation from work just to customize it. He had installed a black marble floor to host the eight-seater bar and plastered mirrors above the mantel he built.

The high-priced beverages were strictly for show. Harris never intended to actually drink them. It was a silent boast, kind of like that loser who runs around the club all night with an empty bottle of Moët. Just in case everybody didn't see him and his crew sipping on it, he takes it onto the dance floor and dances with it. He thinks he looks like a baller but in actuality he looks like the man from the movie *Car Wash* who carried that bottle around to piss in.

Klarke picked up the gold-trimmed bottle of Cristal in one hand and the opal black-trimmed bottle of Dom in the other, and sang, "Eeney, meeny, minee, moe."

She looked in the mirror panel, raised the bottle of Cristal and toasted aloud, "Happy Birthday, Klarke Taylor," before drinking every single drop. Klarke felt born again. Soon she would no longer be Mrs. Harris Bradshaw. She would be unattached, a gift to bestow unto the world.

After the divorce Klarke would manage to take out a student loan and earn a two-year degree at a local community college. She began seeing a man named Rawling, who was also one of her professors. After only an eight-month courtship, the two married. Six months later, Rawling decided he needed his space, that they had married too soon. Klarke didn't put up a fight or was she bitter. She had married him out of fear anyway, the fear of being alone. They had the marriage annulled.

Klarke's marriage to Rawling was so brief that no spousal

support was awarded to her, and her second marriage had terminated the alimony payments Harris had been ordered by the court to pay. Klarke couldn't believe she screwed up that restitution. She still received child support for the children, but Klarke had become accustomed to a certain lifestyle. She had gotten used to drinking champagne when she should have been drinking lemonade. Eventually she began drinking lemonade, but by then it was too late. She should have been drinking water with lemon wedges.

1

All Work—No Play

"Miss Taylor, you have a call," the receptionist's voice said over the intercom. Klarke hated when she got a phone call while someone was at her desk. It just so happened that her boss, Evan, was standing over her with a rush print order.

Opalescent Press had just placed a print order for one of their best-selling author's books. They needed seven hundred thousand copies of his latest, *Dollar Bill,* in one week. Apparently the author was scheduled to appear on *Oprah,* so bookstores from all over were putting in orders. With Klarke being the executive accounts representative and company liaison, she was put in charge of the project.

Klarke was honored to be handling this account. Opalescent Press was a major publishing house and one of the company's largest clients. They housed some of the top authors in the United States. Klarke had just seen the author of *Dollar Bill* on a late-night television talk show. Klarke recalled that he was single and not bad looking at all. She had even imagined how nice it would be to be the woman by his side to help catch the windfall of dollar bills that he was about to come upon. On top of that, she could say the hell with her job.

She had been working for the company a little over a year and a half, ever since her divorce from Rawling. With no man and no money, Klarke had been forced to get a job.

"Can you put the call to my voicemail, please?" Klarke asked.

"Oh, go ahead and take it," Evan said.

Klarke could tell he wanted to be nosy. Not only that, but catching her on a personal call would give Evan a rise. It had only been a month since she got off probation for excess personal phone usage. Evan seemed to find personal enjoyment in reprimanding Klarke ever since she had turned down his dinner invitation.

Klarke had already pledged not to let her business relationships and her personal life mix. She knew from the moment she stepped into Evan's office for her second interview with him that he was going to test her conviction.

Instead of him coming to meet her in the lobby and interviewing her in the conference room, as he had done on the first interview, she had been instructed to go directly to his office.

Evan couldn't stop licking his lips once he laid his ocean-blue eyes on Klarke's five-feet-five-inch banging silhouette as she stood outside of his office door. He had been so excited and caught up as to the treat on the other side that he couldn't distinguish Klarke's faint knock from his own heartbeat.

He had been looking forward to Klarke's Friday afternoon appointment. Never had a black woman made this all-American white boy cream his Hanes.

Behind closed doors a cunt was a cunt, be it chocolate or vanilla (hell, strawberry and banana too, for that matter). Evan could have cared less about not being able to take Klarke home to meet his upper-class suburban family. He only cared about satisfying his curious chocolate craving.

Klarke was a very sensual woman. It was the way she looked at a man, the shape of her lips when she spoke, the way her bronze-tinted puffy locks rested softly on the nape of her neck. It was the way her Cimmerian skin looked as if gold glitter had been dusted over it.

She made love to herself when she rubbed her legs and arms, or grazed her chin and cheek with the back of her hand. She suspected she was beautiful, yet she wasn't entirely sure. She wore a deliberate, smile that said, If I'm not beautiful, at least I'm happy. Klarke felt that a person had to possess at least one of three things in order to get by in life: money, beauty, or happiness.

As Klarke patiently waited outside the frosted glass door to Evan's sky-rise office, Evan ran his fingers through his moussed blond hair. He loosened his silk tie and undid the top button of his crisp white shirt before clearing his throat to grant Klarke permission to enter.

Since her first interview two weeks prior, Evan had fantasized about throwing Klarke on his desk, lifting her tight miniskirt, pulling her thong to the side, and fucking the shit out of her. Or pinning her up against his glass window and pumping her so hard that her sweaty ass cheeks left their imprint behind. He fantasized about her sucking his erect penis until cum exploded down her throat and dripped from between those almond lips of hers. It was no wonder he hired her and gave her an annual salary of five thousand-dollars more than the white girl she had replaced, who had been there almost seven years.

Normally the administrative assistant, Renée did all the training, but Evan had trained Klarke himself. The standard one-week training lasted almost three weeks and included five lunch sessions.

Klarke always made sure to carry a pencil and pad to lunch as a corroboration of her business-only stance. She knew her boss was feeling her and didn't want to lead him on in any way.

It was their final lunch date when Evan grabbed hold of his balls and asked Klarke out for dinner. Klarke answered him with a simple no. She didn't even give him an explanation. She didn't smile or pretend to be flattered. She simply said no, then took a bite of her turkey club and a sip of her Shirley Temple. From that point on she was no longer the house nigger as far as Evan was concerned. She was back in the field with all the rest of the black folk.

"Kemble and Steiner Printing," Klarke said in her *white* voice. "Klarke Taylor speaking."

She could feel Evan's eyes on her tongue as he listened.

It was the finance company for her Rodeo, calling to inquire as to whether or not she would be making her monthly payment.

Evan didn't even try to pretend that he wasn't paying undivided attention to Klarke's conversation. *He's probably got nut running down his legs,* Klarke thought. *At least I finally made the fucker cum.*

After a shitty day at the office Klarke hopped into her shitty vehicle and drove her regular route home. There had been an accident on I-75, so the traffic on the freeway was at a complete standstill. Klarke's seven-minute drive turned into forty-five minutes.

While sitting in traffic Klarke just happened to look over into the burgundy Nissan Maxima on her right-hand side. The gentleman driving was very nice looking. He was a bald-headed, deep-chocolate brotha. He looked to be the clean-cut type, sporting a short-sleeved, cream-colored henley. He had a thick gold rope chain around his neck with a diamond cross. Everything about him said class and money. He smiled at Klarke. His pearly whites sparkled like he was on a Colgate commercial. Klarke smiled back. He winked. Klarke blushed.

Klarke looked ahead to make sure traffic hadn't inched any. She just knew the guy was going to say, "Excuse me Miss, what's your name?" But he said nothing.

Why won't he holla? Klarke thought to herself. *Hell, it's the new millennium. Why am I waiting on him to make the first move?*

Klarke straightened up in her seat, cleared her throat, then turned to look at the gentleman. As she opened her mouth to speak nothing came out. Staring back at her was a young thugged-out looking dude with a wave cap on his head. His vehicle, a huge black Lincoln Navigator with spinners, had taken the place of the bald-headed deep-chocolate brotha's. The young man was bouncing to the song "Get Low" by Lil Jon and the East Side Boyz blazing from a huge speaker in the tailgate of his vehicle. The young man was singing along with the song word for word. All Klarke could hear was *bitch* this and *ho* that.

When the young fella caught Klarke looking at him he smiled, then licked his lips as if he could have eaten her right up. His grill had been invaded by silver. He probably received radio signals in that mouth. Other than that, he was kind of cute, in a thugged-out sort of way. It was obvious he had a nice hunk of change. If the oversized SUV didn't scream out money, then those two-carat diamond earrings did.

Klarke cracked a crooked smile at him. Maybe he wasn't so

bad. Besides, she hadn't had a good dick between her legs since Rawling. Perhaps Nelly over there could show her a thing or two. Maybe a thug in her life was exactly what she needed.

Klarke imagined being in the backseat of his Navigator, riding his young ass like a mechanical bull. He'd probably be ordering her around with words like *"shake that ass, bitch"* or *"fuck that dick, ho."* A little dirty talk never hurt nobody. Maybe Stella had something going with that getting-your-groove-back shit.

The driver in the car behind Klarke laying on her horn broke Klarke's thoughts. Traffic had begun to move again. Now even the young thug had proceeded down the highway. Klarke had just lost her chance at two men in less than five minutes. She gritted her teeth in frustration.

"From now on I am not waiting around on any man to make the first move," Klarke said out loud. "From this point on, I'm calling the shots. I'm making all of the rules to the game. Never again will I let a man have control of my destiny."

Klarke thought back to how she had been robbed of the lifestyle she had been accustomed to when she and Harris divorced. She got ill thinking about her interlude with Rawling, another man who didn't know what the fuck he wanted in a woman. Although unfortunate for him, the next man in Klarke's life would have to pay for the sins of the others.

The more Klarke thought about it, the more motivated she was to change the current course of her life's path. "Let the games begin."

And Klarke had just the game in mind. She put the pedal to the metal so that she could get home and begin executing her plan.

2

You've Got Mail

"What a day." Reo sighed as he collapsed onto the king-size bed in his suite at the Omni Hotel in downtown Chicago. He wished that for just once his publicist would get her ass on a plane and hit up two or three bookstores. A brother appreciated the seven-figure contract, but damn. After a three-month spell, his body was pleading for a break. Reo wasn't used to all the travel his five-book deal would entail. He had never been on a plane in his life and now, after thirty-three years, here he was committing infidelities on his hometown of Columbus, Ohio's, modest skyline.

Reo's complaints were short lived, however. Every time he thought about his dedicated following of readers that awaited his arrival to their town, Reo's dick got hard. He had finally done it. He had gone from a $40,000-a-year teaching salary to that of a two-time best-selling author's. Up until a year ago Reo had only dreamed of arriving at the independent African American bookstores with a line of people waiting to buy autographed copies of his books. It didn't bother him one bit that over three-fourths of them were beautiful women.

Being a bestselling author had always been Reo's dream. Tales seemed to spill out of him. He had a vivid imagination, and initially he wrote for his own personal pleasure or just to get stuff off of his chest. Then he had shared his writings with his father, who also thought that Reo had true talent.

Reo's father, who taught college English comp and was considered a respected authority in the community, helped him put together his first book, which was a compilation of short stories. In a strictly advisory role, of course. Reo laughed to himself as he remembered an incident in grade school.

Reo's sixth-grade teacher, Miss Willoughby, had accused him of plagiarism on a paper he wrote on the march on Washington, which was worth 50 percent of his grade. The teacher knew Reo's father's profession, which had been high school English teacher at the time, and had accused Reo of having his father complete the paper for him.

The teacher rejected the paper and gave Reo a week's extension to complete another one. Reo had been crushed. One word of dispute would have caused him to erupt into tears in front of the whole class. He simply took the paper back from Miss Willoughby and placed it in his book bag.

When he got home from school he fell into his mother's arms. Reo had held his tears in for two hours, twenty-three minutes, and eighteen seconds. His head was throbbing and his eyes were stinging. He could barely relay the tragedy to his mother.

Mrs. Laroque couldn't sleep that night. She must have rehearsed in the mirror a thousand times what she was going to say to that teacher. How dare someone, anyone, send her baby home in tears!

The next morning, when Reo's mother, who was still fresh with anger, had finished ranting and raving, he begged her to just allow him to write another paper. He didn't know what was worse, being accused of plagiarism or his mother being hand-cuffed and taken off to the jail for laying Miss Willoughby out.

Mr. Laroque convinced his wife to allow him to handle the situation. Reo was relieved. He knew how his mother could be. He remembered his mother clobbering the neighborhood bully's mother for cheering on her son to fight Reo. That was the first time Reo had heard the adage *the apple doesn't fall far from the tree*. But after the way his momma beat that poor woman's tail, he wasn't too sure who the tree was, his mother or the bully's.

Reo was amazed and proud at how his father handled Miss Willoughby. Mr. Laroque turned the table and told her how insulted he was to be accused of having the writing skills of a sixth grader. He then told her how proud she must be as a teacher for producing pupils who could turn out such well-written pieces of writing and how wonderful it must be to brag to her colleagues.

By the time Mr. Laroque finished swelling Miss Willoughby's head, she was inviting the family over for dinner. Reo was permitted to resubmit the same paper. He received an A+ and the chance to read it to the sixth-grade student body during an honors assembly. He had never felt more proud than to be the fruit of his father's tree.

After numerous rejections of Reo's short stories from publishing houses, Reo decided to self-publish his book. Every dime he earned was put toward the writing, editing, printing, distribution, and promotion of his book. He gave his two-year-old, fully loaded Nissan Altima back to the bank and bought a fifteen-year-old Chevrolet Chevette that didn't even have AC. He gave up his suburban German Village studio and moved back home with his mom and dad. He sold his furniture, pawned his jewelry, and even borrowed against his 401K plan.

Reo called in to radio stations to discuss his book. He wrote fill-in articles for newspapers and magazines, which helped to promote his book. He beat the pavement, visiting beauty and barber shops to spread the word about his book. He visited parking lots where conferences were taking place and put fliers about his book on all the car windshields. He drove from city to city and neighboring states doing this. He sold the book from out of his trunk and out of his briefcase. He even gave it away for free.

It was a long, hard sacrifice, but in the end it paid off. In the beginning though, it was a struggle. He lost Meka, his high school sweetheart and fiancée at the time.

Meka and Reo held the record for the longest engagement ever. It was a well-known fact that the engagement ring Reo had presented to Meka, Christmas of 1999, was really a hush ring. That year, every other word out of Meka's mouth had pertained to marriage. It had gotten so bad she had been holding out on sex. She claimed that she felt guilty having sex under the Lord's watch without even the possibility of marriage on the horizon. Reo had to do something to shut her up so he pretty much proposed under duress.

Meka was from a well-to-do family. Her mother was a doctor and her father was a lobbyist for telephone companies. Meka was a dental hygienist studying to become a dentist. She planned to open her own practice. She was the eldest of three daughters, and each of her sisters had married men who were also from well-to-do families.

Meka wholeheartedly supported Reo's publishing efforts. She wanted to see him succeed. Nothing thrilled her more than the idea of being the wife of a successful writer. She had begged him to let her give him money toward the production of his book, but he declined the offer. He had seen *Judge Mathis* one too many times and knew that a gift from a current girlfriend metamorphosed into a loan with interest upon breakup. There was no way some woman, or anybody else for that matter, was going to be able to stake a claim on his talent and success.

Meka went as far as suggesting Reo move into her loft rent-free. There was no way Reo was going to give her the pleasure of being able to put him out of *her* house every time they got into an argument. Lord knows that was a woman's favorite declaration: "This is my house, muthafucker."

Eventually, it became too unpleasant for Meka to roll in a Chevette, and shameful for her to tell people her fiancé lived with his parents. Reo's sacrifices were more than Meka was willing to make. She could not continue subjecting herself to such humiliation.

Of course, once Reo's book dominated the number-one spot on the national bestseller lists for a record fifteen weeks straight, Meka was back on his dick again, literally. As soon as she caught wind of his accomplishment she called to congratulate him.

A simple phone call wasn't adequate for Meka. She invited him to her loft for a celebration dinner with a guest list including only the two of them. With slight trepidation, Reo accepted her invitation.

When he arrived at Meka's loft he was escorted to a candle-lit dining table, where he was greeted by a small feast. Meka had never made him a peanut-butter-and-jelly sandwich before, and yet here she had managed to whip up a meatloaf, twice-baked mashed potatoes, mac'n'cheese, some collard greens, and buttered rolls.

Reo gobbled down the spread as if it were the Last Supper. They conversed while intoxicating themselves on shots of Hennessy. This was surprising to Reo, as he had only known Meka to sip on cutesy drinks such as fuzzy navels and wine coolers. As a special congratulatory token Meka decided that she would be dessert, so she excused herself from the table in order to begin her preparations.

Reo got reacquainted with the leather sofa in the den that he had made himself comfortable on many times before. He managed to flick through a few channels on the big-screen television until Meka entered the den modeling a Frederick's of Hollywood black chemise. Before Reo could even compliment her appearance, she was feeding him her tongue, nipples, and fingertips that bore the color of Cherries Jubilee polish on the nails.

Departing from their regular sexual encounters, Meka did things to him that he had only fantasized about or had seen on a porno tape. Their acts ventured on the verge of obscene. He screwed her in every position they could think of and invented a few new ones as well. He beat up her pussy like it had done him wrong. She fanatically sucked his dick, licked his balls, and allowed him to give her a pearl necklace. In other words, she let him jerk in her face. She grazed the crack of his ass back and forth with her tongue as if she was licking the ice cream from in between an ice-cream sandwich. What tripped him out was the fact that the glossy crimson lipstick on her lips seemed unaffected. He now understood why she had spent excessive amounts of money on those damn Mary Kay cosmetics. They were everlasting.

Reo had cum more in that one night than he had in his whole life. At least that's what it felt like anyway. He was almost certain that his last climax, like a twelve-year-old boy jacking off for the first time, had been dry.

Reo's mind was blown, considering Meka was somewhat of a tightass. Sex with her, for Reo, had been like a cop on traffic duty. Meka had limitations on how far Reo could insert his penis into her vagina. She preferred he be on top and properly centered.

When he was eating her out he couldn't stick his tongue inside her. He could only suck her clit. When it was time for him to cum he had to pull out because she hated cleaning his fluids from inside of her. One would have thought she hired Paula Abdul to choreograph their lovemaking.

Everything about Meka was predictable, from the way she wore her hair in a tight, low-maintenance bun to the white French cuff shirt and navy bottoms she sported. But on that night it was safe to say that Meka had let her hair down. It also explained those shots of Hennessy she had taken. Like a call girl about to take on her first trick, she needed the liquor to both warrant and excuse her conduct.

After their sexcapade, Meka rested on Reo's chest and they both dozed off for a while. When he woke up, Reo slid from underneath the sleeping beauty and began putting his clothing back on. Meka slowly woke up when she heard him moving around.

"Where are you going, sweetie?" she asked with a yawn.

"It's late. I better get going," Reo answered.

"You don't have to go."

"Yeah, I know," Reo said as he sat back down on the couch. "I want to go."

Meka's mouth dropped open as she sat up. "What do you mean you want to go?"

Reo could tell she was shocked and disappointed. Nonetheless he proceeded to put on his socks and shoes.

"It was good seeing you again. Dinner was lovely and dessert was extraordinary. Thank you."

"Whoa. Hold up. Thank you? Thank you? Is that all I get is a thank you?"

Reo ignored her, a smirk on his face as he searched for the keys to his new Escalade. Meka felt disgusted. Here she had done things that were sure to make her sick to her stomach in the morning, things she would deny ever doing on a stack of Bibles, all in hopes of reeling Reo back into her life. But from the beginning Reo saw right through her scheme. She was just too damn predictable.

"You ate my food. You drank my liquor. You screwed me all night long and all I get is a lousy 'thank you.' Hell, I didn't even get to cum."

Reo knew she was getting ready to recite the angry woman anthem *"You can't even fuck. You don't even make me cum. That's why you have a little-ass dick . . . blah blah blah."*

"Well, what were you expecting?" Reo said before she could get warmed up.

Meka just sat there looking at him, dumbfounded. She couldn't very well tell him that she had expected to pussy-whip him back into a relationship with her. She couldn't tell him that she had expected to get back with him and spend all of his new money.

"I don't know, a little respect maybe?" Meka said, putting her clothes back on. Reo couldn't contain his laughter. "What the hell is so funny? Did I just tell a joke? Am I on fucking Def Comedy Jam?"

"Respect . . . that's funny coming from a woman who just licked my ass clean."

Meka could not have slapped Reo any harder without hurting herself. But he saw it coming and braced himself for the impact. He knew he deserved it, but it felt good to finally take charge. Throughout their relationship, just to keep the drama at a minimum, he had allowed her to belittle him and boss him around. It was fair turnabout.

Meka decided to turn on the waterworks. Reo chuckled under his breath as he headed to the door.

"I ate your food because I was hungry. I drank your liquor because I was thirsty. Hell, I screwed you all night long because I was horny. Now I'm leaving because I'm finished. In other words, my dear, you've just been humbled."

The gray marble tabletop clock missed Reo's head by only a centimeter as he closed the door behind him, shattering into a million pieces, right along with Meka's pride.

That was the last time Reo hooked up with Meka. Strange, but he had missed the hell out of her, too, because as far as intimacy was concerned, Meka had been all his body had known for a long time.

Finding female companionship wasn't a challenge for Reo. Women came in droves. But what Reo soon found out was that love didn't come at all. Most women Reo encountered already knew him as Reo Laroque, the national bestselling author. When they were talking to him, they were talking to the dollar signs in his bank account. When they were fucking him, they were actually fucking his wallet. So Reo never took any of the women he had hooked up with seriously. Lately, though, Reo had been truly longing for a genuine woman to call his own. One who could care less about Reo the bestselling author, but care, instead, about Reo the man.

Eventually Reo rolled out of his hotel bed and jumped into the shower. He knew the Omni was very efficient when it came to service, so he decided to wait and order from the in-room dining menu after his shower. He didn't want to risk not hearing the server's arrival.

After scrubbing his five-feet-eleven-inch frame with his Mambo body wash, Reo moisturized his ebony-toned body with the matching lotion. He massaged his scalp and *good hair* with a Carefree moisturizer and edged up his goatee.

After ordering a Cobb salad and a glass of champagne, Reo pulled out his laptop to check his e-mails. His inbox was always full of fan mail, so he had to keep on top of it. Book clubs and bookstores alike e-mailed invitations for Reo to sign and do readings for them. Reo scrolled down immediately deleting the spam. He didn't have time to waste viewing unsolicited long-distance plans or pharmaceutical specials for Viagra.

After reading and replying to several e-mails, Reo then checked his private e-mail address. One e-mail in particular caught his attention, with the subject heading "Boston Airport." Reo didn't even bother looking at who the sender was. He knew it was from his publicist. Whenever a book signing had been scheduled for him, the city in which the book signing was to take place was always in the heading.

"Isn't this just great?" Reo muttered. "Another damn signing. In Boston no less."

From: KAT@myworld.biz
To: RLQ812@sunset.com
Subject: Boston Airport

Hey you!
I hope all is well. I noticed that you had "accidentally" left the business card I gave you on the restaurant table. I'm assuming the rush of hearing the last boarding call for your flight was the reason you forgot it. I had a good time talking to you. I can't believe we lost track of time. Funny how time flies, huh?

I was cleaning out my briefcase and I found the piece of

paper you wrote your e-mail address on for me. I just wanted to drop you a line and let you know that it was a pleasure meeting you. I never knew a layover in the Boston airport could be so exhilarating. I'm referring to my time spent with you, of course. :-)

Once you get settled into your new apartment and office in New York City, perhaps you can call me sometime. I would love to keep in touch. Let me know and I'll give you my number again.

Sincerely,
Your newfound friend

A warm feeling came over Reo. He couldn't explain it. It was as if he wasn't reading the e-mail, but as if the voice of the sender was speaking the words directly to him.

Then there was a the knock on the door. "Room service," a voice called. Reo walked over to the door to look through the peephole. He opened the door. A tall, fair-skinned girl with medium length, dark brown hair rolled in his order. She was checking out Reo so hard that she couldn't keep from bumping into the bureau with the cart.

"Thank you, um, Jheri," Reo said, reading her nametag.

"You are so very welcome Reo—I mean, Mr. Laroque, sir."

"Reo is fine."

"Yes, sir. I mean, Reo."

Reo quickly signed the receipt and handed it to the girl. She took the receipt, but just stood there like she had shitted on herself and couldn't move.

"Do you need anything else from me?"

"Uh, no sir—I mean, Reo."

Becoming a little annoyed by the starstruck server, Reo walked over to the door and opened it for the girl.

"Oh, I'm sorry. Yeah, all I needed was your autograph—I mean your signature."

"Very well. You have a good evening."

Reo couldn't believe the girl just kept standing there. He was hoping she didn't become as bold as the cleaning lady at the Royal Sonesta Hotel in the New Orleans French Quarter. That woman had actually gotten butt-ass naked and laid herself out on the bed for Reo to have his way with her. The little Latino woman hadn't even spoken good English. All Reo understood was *"boom boom."*

"As a matter of fact there is something I need from you," the girl said as she began to dig in her bra. Reo grabbed her arms and pushed her out of the room.

"You are a beautiful young lady with a lot going for yourself," Reo said, his tone scolding. "Don't you dare degrade yourself or your body."

The girl's eyes filled with tears as she held the dollar bill in her hand that she had pulled from her bra.

"I'm so sorry, Mr. Laroque—I mean Reo, sir. I usually never do this, but I just really wanted you to autograph this dollar. I'm in college majoring in journalism and I just really admire your writing style. *Dollar Bill* was magnificent and . . . I'm just so sorry." The girl cried as she hurried down the hall and around the corridor out of Reo's sight.

Reo just stood there in awe before bursting out laughing. "When did I become so vain?" He laughed.

Reo closed the door, returned to his laptop and reread the e-mail that was still on his computer screen. Although it was pretty simple it was sweet. Reo made his living creating fantasy. Maybe this time, instead of creating a fantasy for millions of readers, he could create a little one for himself.

He sipped on his champagne, hit reply, and began to type.

3

Window Shopping

Klarke always wanted what she either didn't or couldn't have. Which was why she and her lady friends, Jeva and Breezy, would spend hours consoling one another's monetary shortages by window shopping. They truly found comfort in it.

It became a third-Saturday-of-the-month ritual for the girls to spend the afternoon window-shopping. They would get up that morning, get their fake workout on (that five minutes they relayed to each other as twenty), chase the workout with a bowl of cereal, shower, then squirm into some little number guaranteed to highlight all the assets—going braless, pantyless, or both.

Window shopping wasn't fun unless the sun was cooperating. If clouds even teased with the threat of rain, their monthly excursion was put on hold. There was something about the sunshine that complemented a woman's scent, her body, and her hair. They knew the sun was the true pimp. Nothing was quite as good at showcasing a woman to her best advantage.

Klarke, Jeva, and Breezy always met at the same location, but Klarke was always the last to arrive. She did it on purpose. She knew she was the finest of the three and loved walking onto the scene like Dorothy Dandridge in *Carmen*. It's kind of like a bachelor party. A couple of modest makeup dolls go shake their ass for a few minutes, and then the main attraction comes out to give the bachelor the time of his life. Klarke was saving the best for last.

Klarke possessed the average 36 C bust, but her legs were her true assets. They went on for days. Her fair complexion was clear and she always wore light makeup.

At thirty-four, Klarke knew it took just a little more effort to be sexy than it had two babies ago. But being average just was not an option for her. Even when she was younger, she always had to be the exception.

Klarke's clothes had to be the best, and always worn with class. She could have on the exact same outfit as both Jeva and Breezy, yet one would never notice it. Klarke liked to be a little different when it came to her wardrobe. She was good for wearing a tie-back sweater backwards, or a long skirt as a tube dress. Her fashion style was a perfect mixture of funky and classy. She always stood out.

Jeva and Breezy were fine as well. Klarke didn't keep company with people who didn't complement her own flavor.

Jeva was a cute half Caucasian, half Hispanic *mami*, Colombian. She was only five feet tall with straight black hair down to her buttocks. Besides her slanted bedroom eyes that drove men crazy, her stand-out feature was her deep dimples that were visible even when she wasn't smiling.

Because Jeva had been given up at birth, she had never known either of her parents. When Jeva turned eighteen she had gone to the Welford Child Placement Agency, the place that handled her initial foster-home placement. She was hoping that there was some information on her biological parents that would allow her to find them. The agency had nothing. As a matter of fact, Jeva's records had been lost. There was no explanation. They were just gone.

All Jeva knew was that her mother was Colombian and her father was white. This information was given to her by one of her many foster moms. That was always one of the first things people wanted to know when they took in her exotic features, her nationality. It was also the reason she would get beat up by the other girls. Boys tended to get soft in the head over a pretty, exotic-looking little girl, but the girls would be hating! No matter where she was she just never fit in, so she was constantly in and out of foster homes.

In the homes a kid was either black or white. Jeva didn't even fall in between with her Hispanic bloodline and features. After so many years of being teased, if Jeva was asked what she was she would reply that she was a honky spic. The sad thing about it was that she would say it with such pride. It was like a little black boy being asked what he was and replying conceitedly, "A *nigger.*"

Going on twenty-nine, Jeva still struggled with identity issues and hated that she would not be able to share much about herself with her own daughter, Heather. She was just happy to be raising her in a two-parent home. Jeva wasn't married to Lance, her husbfriend. But when she wasn't working as an amateur photographer, she was working on getting Lance to marry her. At this point, though, her efforts hadn't even gotten her a hush ring.

Breezy, on the other hand, knew she was all woman and then some. She was a thick, full-figured woman with a cute face. There was no jiggle in her walk. She was more than enough woman for more than one man, which was why she divided her time between two of them, one of whom happened to be married.

Her short, boblike haircut molded her round face becomingly.

Her men swore she had the most voluptuous ass on earth, and her full breasts could make a grown man cry. Her ghetto vocabulary was a repellent for unwanted conversations with men. But sistah knew how to shut the fellas down with just a few choice words from her ghettosaurus.

You either loved Breezy or hated her. It was as simple as that. She had a fresh mouth and could get real cute sometimes. She really wasn't that ghetto, but she was used to being hard as a way of keeping people at a distance and out of her business. There was only so much of Breezy's life, especially her past, that she was willing to share, even with her girlfriends.

Breezy had worked hard mentally to close a few chapters in her life. She'd dealt with many tragedies, the most devastating being the events that led to the incarceration of her father and her mother eventually divorcing him. Breezy had taken the divorce hard. To this day Breezy and her mother didn't even speak. Breezy blamed her mother for abandoning her father when he needed her the most.

If it had not been for Breezy, her father would have never been incarcerated in the first place. She never spoke of the actual events, but in the back of her mind, she was afraid of loving a man so much and then losing him, the way she lost her father. So, Breezy used men instead. No love, no loss.

When Jeva and Breezy arrived at the Cheesecake Factory they knew that they were going to have to wait the standard thirty minutes for Klarke's arrival. They sat on the patio at their designated table, sipping on drinks and killing time with their latest gossip.

"So, what's been going on with your husb-friend, Lance?" Breezy asked.

"Same old, same old. Still no ring. I give up. I'm just going to leave it alone."

"I've been telling you that for years. He takes care of the baby and he fucks you right. What do you need a ring for? You and Klarke kill me with that marriage hoopla."

"Well, there are some women out there who are still traditional and want more than sex out of a relationship, thank you very much," Jeva said smartly.

"You mean there's actually more to a relationship than sex?" Breezy joked. "Oh yeah, how could I forget? Money!"

"See, that's your problem," Jeva began to preach.

"What, what's my problem, Jeva? Don't hate because my kitty is made to purr on a regular."

"Hold up now, Lance can handle his business."

"I know."

"How do you know?"

"I figured he must be putting it down for you to be with him this long as pressed as you are about marriage."

"If getting laid is so important to you, then why do you have all those vibrators, beads, and finger puppets and stuff? I mean, like, I'm surprised you haven't been diagnosed with carpal tunnel."

"Ha, ha. But, anyway, all that stuff is backup," Breezy said, waving a hand. "I've had some doozies before, or—what's that word for a firecracker that won't pop? Oh yeah, a dud. I'm talking the kind where you get down on your knees and just ask God, Why did you only give him five inches? Couldn't you have at least made it fat?"

Jeva laughed. "You're going to hell, Breezy. Straight to hell."

"That's cool with me 'cause I know ain't no fucking going on up in heaven, that's for sure, and I gots to get mine."

"You know what? I'm getting away from you," Jeva said

scooting away from Breezy, "because when that bolt of lightening comes down, I don't want to be nowhere near you."

"Too late for all that," Breezy said. "The Lord already knows that you and I are cut from the same cloth. But like I was saying, there was this one guy that I only did it with once. I swear I couldn't even tell he was inside of me. I can't help but laugh every time I think about it. I mean, this fool knew damn well that he had a little dick. I can't even believe he pursued me the way he did."

"I don't know why men do that. They know they got a little dick and then on top of that they ask you do you think they have a little dick. Why is it a man needs a woman to confirm that?" Jeva asked inquisitively.

"And little-dick men know they talk big shit. Hell, they light-weight scare a bitch off, but at the same time, they leave you curiously hanging on the edge of a wet dream," Breezy said.

"Umm hmm. Already been there and done that. Remember Kent? I thought he was about to tear it up. He came in less than two minutes, no exaggeration. After he came, he licked my cat, my ass, sucked my titties, the works. I couldn't get over the size long enough to concentrate on any trick he pulled out of his hat. It was like sitting in a lecture hall in school trying to hold in a laugh. The kind of laugh that you know once you get started, there ain't no stopping. The condom was even baggy." Jeva laughed.

"Oh, girl, not the baggy condom."

"Yes, the baggy condom."

"See, FUBU sleeping on that one. They should come out with the platinum baggy condom," Breezy said, laughing.

"You know," Jeva said, agreeing, "I was afraid it was going to come off inside of me. I had never clinched my pussy muscles so tight in my life trying to grip that little muthafucker."

Jeva and Breezy high-fived as they tried to contain their laughs. Then Klarke finally arrived.

"Did I miss something?" Klarke asked, hanging her purse over the back of her chair and taking a seat.

"Nah," Jeva answered still laughing. "Just one of our short-short man stories."

"Don't dog out the short-short man," Klarke stated with authority in her tone. "They are some of the nicest men out there."

"Yeah," Jeva said. "They don't mind spending that extra dollar bill either."

"Shit, they don't have a choice but to be nice," Breezy said, rolling her eyes. "They have to wear their wallet on their dick in order to make up for the missing inches. The same reason why ugly people have to be nice . . . how you gonna be mean on top of ugly?"

The girls laughed as Chauncy, their usual waiter, came over to take their orders. The girls decided on their main entrées as well as an appetizer. Jeva couldn't peel her eyes off of Chauncy's butt as he walked away.

"He's sooo cute." Jeva sighed.

"He's sooo a waiter," Klarke added.

"I'm not into white boys, but he is a cutie," Breezy said with an attitude.

"What's the matter with white people?" Jeva asked.

"Oh, Lord, here we go again," Klarke and Breezy said in unison, slumping down into their chairs.

"Now see, there you go. I didn't say anything about white people. All I said is that I don't do white boys," Breezy said, knowing she was hitting a sore spot with Jeva. "I don't have anything against white people. Hell, I even had dinner with a white man when I was in Vegas."

Jeva took offense. "Basically you are saying that you are prejudiced. What's the difference between a black man and a white man, hell, a Latino, Asian, or Indian for that matter?"

"About three to four inches," Klarke joked to break the building argument between Jeva and Breezy.

The girls laughed and things relaxed a little.

"You always get so serious," Breezy told Jeva.

"Ah, you know how she is," Klarke said. "She got that identity crisis thing going on."

"Will somebody pleazze help Orphan Annie over here find her real parents?" Breezy said loudly as if she truly wanted a response from the other patrons.

"Y'all stupid," Jeva said cracking a smile. "You never know. Maybe someday I just might find them."

"Yeah, and maybe your father reads," Breezy said.

"And betcha your mother sews," Klarke replied.

Klarke and Breezy continued together in song as they butchered part of the chorus from a song in the movie *Annie*.

"Maybe she's made you a closet of clothes."

Jeva blushed. "The hell with the both of youse."

"You know we love you, girl," Klarke said as their shrimp cocktail appetizer arrived.

The girls nibbled on their entrées just enough to satisfy their buds, but were careful not to overstuff themselves. They still had to hit the mall and couldn't be weighed down.

The girls left Chauncy his regular 15 percent tip, touched up their faces in the ladies' room, and headed toward the mall to begin their window-shopping excursion. Klarke stopped outside Structure and looked in the window.

"Umm, I'll take that right there," she said, pointing toward a rack of linen short outfits.

"Too cheap," Breezy said and tried to pull Klarke away in order to proceed to the next store.

"Hold up. Let me go see for myself." Klarke broke free of Breezy's grip and entered the store. She made her way over to a rack of linen shirts and shorts. The gentleman who was standing at the rack couldn't help but notice Klarke as she stood there in her hot pink chiffon dress that hit just below her knees.

"Linen is nice," the gentleman said in a baritone voice. "It's soft, but a tad craggy."

"Yeah, that's what I like about it too," Klarke said, looking up from the linen shirt she was caressing. She couldn't help but notice the gentleman's extra thick eyebrows. They seemed to be growing together.

"Shopping for your husband?" the gentleman asked, trying to determine if he had any chance in the world at hooking up with Klarke. Klarke didn't hear him, though. She was so taken by his woolly unibrow. She just couldn't manage to take her eyes off of it. It looked like a big coochie sitting right in the middle of his forehead. The sound of his voice grew farther and farther away as she stared at his coochie face. She couldn't fight the urge any longer. Klarke raised her hand to finger his brow, but not before Breezy stepped up and grabbed her.

"Hey, the men went to get the car. They're going to pull around and pick us up at the door so we better get going," Breezy said.

"Oh . . . well, excuse me, ladies," the gentleman said. "And by the way, your men are quite lucky." He walked away.

"Oh my God, did you see that?" Klarke asked Breezy, still slightly dazed.

"Yes, I did, and did I not try to warn you about Sasquatch?"

"All you said was that he looked cheap. You didn't say anything about him having a crotch on his face."

. . .

"This is the best Cinnabon I've ever had," Jeva said, licking her fingers. "We ought to come window shopping twice a month."

"Not if you had witnessed what Breezy and I just did," Klarke said.

"What happened?" Jeva asked, looking at them.

"I'll tell you after you finish eating. I wouldn't want it to ruin your appetite," Klarke said.

"Come on, tell me," Jeva insisted, her tone childlike.

"We just saw a man with a coochie," Klarke blurted out as she and Breezy fell into hysterics.

"I can't take you two anywhere," Jeva said, shaking her head.

"Oooooh-wee," Breezy said, interrupting. "Look over there in Nordstrom. I gotta have that. Ladies, follow me." Breezy led the girls over to the store. There was a huge shoe sale going on, so there was quite a crowd.

"Excuse me, sir," Breezy said tapping on the male clerks shoulder. "Do you have this in my size?" She held up a chestnut pair of boots with spiked three-inch heels.

"What size are you?" the clerk asked politely. Breezy was captivated by his immediate attentiveness, not to mention his fine-ass physique. He wasn't too buff, but cut just right. He had wavy black hair that was slicked back, and beautiful brown skin. He had a tight shaved mustache and beard. Breezy imagined using her toes to play with his facial hairs. Each hair tingling her toes, arousing her.

"I'm not sure. What size do you think I am?" Breezy said seductively, smiling at him.

"Hmm, why don't we just get that shoe off and take a measurement?" he asked, returning her smile.

Breezy sat down as Jeva and Klarke checked out the shoe selection.

The clerk removed Breezy's strappy sandal with sensuous ease. He delicately placed her foot on the foot measurer. She looked up and thanked God that her feet were freshly pedicured. She had just visited the walk-in Super Nail shop around the corner from her house. Her toenails sported a water marble design that cost her an *extra fifteen dolla*.

"Umm, a nine and a half," the clerk said.

"How ironic. I was thinking that same thing about you," Breezy said, looking at his crotch.

"Excuse me?" he said, his tone suddenly outraged.

"That you're probably about a nine and a half, too." All of a sudden it was like the clerk turned into Sybil. He stood up, popped his neck, and snapped his fingers in circles as he checked Breezy.

"Nuh uh, Miss Thang, no, you didn't. No, you did not just go there, okay?" the clerk said.

"My fault. I'm sorry. Calm down, *Chanté*."

"Oh, you got jokes. Listen up everybody. The lady here got jokes."

It only took seconds for the manager to hurry over. Klarke and Jeva joined the roundup, too.

"We apologize for our friend," Klarke and Jeva explained, using their mother-hen voices as they pushed Breezy away. "She sometimes doesn't realize what she's saying. We do apologize."

"Don't apologize for me. Hell, he should be flattered someone like me tried to hit on him," Breezy said, smacking her lips and rolling her eyes.

"Girlfriend, please," the clerk said, sucking his teeth. "Women like you kill me."

"Look, let's just go, Breezy," Klarke said, continuing to push Breezy away.

"Women like what?" Breezy asked, getting louder.

"Women who think they can turn somebody like me out," the clerk told her, rolling his eyes.

"You are taking this to a whole 'nother level, trust!" Breezy shouted.

"Yeah, yeah, yeah. Say that, but you are just afraid that if I had your man in a dark room after two drinks he might let me please him better than you can. I know your kind," the clerk said.

"Oh, my goodness!" Breezy said in her Shanae-Nae voice. "No, he didn't! Oh my goodness! You really need to calm down. All of this is not even necessary. I'm sorry that I mistook you for a man."

"Oh, no problem, dear heart. I'm sure people mistake you for a lady all the time until you open your mouth," the clerk said.

"Okay, see, Chanté, now you are hitting below the belt. I would return the blow by hitting you below the belt, but it probably wouldn't even have an effect on you, now would it?" Breezy said.

"Let's get out of here," Klarke said, and this time she and Jeva succeeding in removing Breezy from the store.

"That raggedy queen," Breezy huffed when they were finally out of the store.

The girls sat down on a bench outside the store, Klarke and Jeva relieved that they had gotten Breezy out before she managed to catch a case.

"He wasn't raggedy when you were about ready to let him lick your toes," Klarke said. "And he wasn't raggedy when you were screaming *Ooooh-wee, I gotta have that!*"

"You have to keep in mind that gay men get flak all the time," Jeva said, calmly. "He just had his guard up, that's all. His anger wasn't aimed at you, Breezy. It was for all the ignorant folks he's had to deal with on a regular."

"Is that you talking or that shrink you used to see?" Breezy asked, glaring at her.

"Go to hell," Jeva said, about to get loud too.

"Will you two stop it?" Klarke shouted. "I'm so sick of this shit. What are we doing? I mean really. Once a month we get dressed up, come to the mall, and hope we apprehend our very own Donald Trump. We're so frustrated with our imperfect lives that we're even starting to take it out on each other."

"Well, what do you suggest?" Breezy said sarcastically. "Next month we pack a picnic basket and take a trip to the Land of Oz? Oh, I know, and you can be Dorothy."

"That fly-ass mouth is going to get you in trouble one day," Klarke said, glaring at her.

"Well, you had your Donald Trump," Breezy said, smacking her lips.

"Yeah, and I lost him to a woman like you," Klarke replied, snapping her neck.

"Please, Klarke's right. This is crazy," Jeva said. "Why don't we just join a book club or something?" Klarke and Breezy paused and gave Jeva a disbelieving look.

"Is her dumb-as-rocks routine for real?" Breezy questioned and the three began to laugh. "Don't book clubs have men in them?" Breezy said. "Meeting up with a room full of women every month, and at the rate I'm going with men, them hoes might start looking good to me. Coochie must be the thing any-way. We done met two men with coochies in one day."

"You are just plain ignorant." Jeva laughed.

Klarke's laughter faded and tears filled her eyes. "I'm sorry for snapping at you, Breezy," Klarke said with watered eyes. "It's just that shit gets so hard. I can barely keep my head above the water, you know? This is supposed to be the time when we make fun of our have-nots and love lives and lack thereof. Shit ain't supposed to seem so bad. My misery just hasn't been up for company lately, I guess," Klarke said.

"Harris didn't deserve you and neither did Rawling," Jeva told Klarke. "Your true Prince Charming is going to find you one day. He's searching for you just as persistently as you are searching for him."

"Well, I'm about to give his ass a little help," Klarke said suddenly determined.

"Sounds like you've got something up your sleeve," Breezy said, licking her lips, eager to get the 411.

"It's in the works. But I don't want to jinx myself so I'm keeping it on the low-low for now," Klarke said, winking. "Let's just say that computer I bought the kids last Christmas is coming in handy."

"Well, I'd like to think I've found my Prince Charming, but I don't know," Jeva said, uncertainly. "Lance just isn't feeling the marriage thing. He won't go back to school and finish college. He's content with his lifestyle. I just want so much more."

"Besides," Breezy added. "You done gave him almost five years of your life. If that man died tomorrow or even if he just walked out of your life, you wouldn't get a dime. An investment with no return. At least with Klarke, she *was* getting money for herself and she got the house and stuff."

"Yeah, but paying the mortgage, utilities, and all the other luxuries that come along with being a homeowner is another story," Klarke said with a sigh. "Whoever said owning your own home was an asset is a liar."

"You need to get yourself a sugah daddy like me," Breezy bragged. "Klarke, I know you have a problem with the fact that one of the men I'm seeing is married, but hell, I got bills. He takes care of them."

"Aren't you the one who swore back in the day that you would never be with a man just because he had money? There's just so many men out there who are not married who will take care of you, Breezy," Klarke said.

"Who? Where they at? Do you mean men like Chanté over there?" Breezy said, pointing at Nordstrom.

"Yeah, Klarke," Jeva said. "No offense, but you've lived the good life. You at least know what it tastes like. You lived it for thirteen years. That's more than Breezy and I can say."

"And she can live it again. Next time just don't fall in love with the fucker. As a matter of fact, you might as well had stayed with Harris in the first place," Breezy said.

"What are you talking about?" Jeva asked in disbelief.

"Love and money are like oil and water. They don't mix," Breezy answered.

"I don't know, Breezy," Jeva said, shaking her head. "I can't back you on that one."

"How could you? Lance ain't got no money. I'm not clownin' on him or anything, but the only way you're going to live the good life with Lance is if he hits the lottery," Breezy said. "He's a tennis shoe hustler. He makes enough money hustling weed to buy a pair of new Jordans, then he's straight until the next style comes out. Hell, he's got to be the last weed man on earth selling nickel bags."

"I don't care about all of that. I guess that's why I'm just not fine with window shopping anymore," Jeva replied.

"Yeah," Breezy said. "You spend the day looking for something that you can't have."

"In the end, though," Klarke said, "when you think about all the headaches you're leaving behind, you wish you could donate all that other shit that you actually did buy to Goodwill."

"Well, I'm going to hang in there with my man for now. In the meantime, I'll think of some way to rope his ass in," Jeva said.

"Just remember what I said," Breezy said in a very serious tone. "Love or money . . . when you seek them both you're seeking a headache. It has to be one or the other, love or money. You can't have both."

4

Part-Time Pops

"Mom, do we have to go?" Vaughn asked, stomping her foot with a broken-up look on her face.

"We're not going through this again, Miss Thang," Klarke told her. "Get your stuff together. Your dad will be here any minute."

"But Dad's never even there. He's always at work and we're stuck with Tionne and I can't stand her."

"I think she's kind of nice," HJ said as he licked the cream from the middle of the Oreo he had managed to separate.

"You only like her because she sneaks your fat butt extra Ho-Hos," Vaughn said, poking HJ in his belly as if he were the Pillsbury Doughboy. They both giggled.

"Mom," HJ said. "What's a home wrecker?"

"Pardon me?" Klarke asked, shocked.

"What's a home wrecker? That's what Vaughn said Tionne is."

It seemed as though every other week, when it was time for the children to go stay at their father's house, HJ had a new word he needed defined, thanks to Vaughn. The last time it was *mistress*, and the time before that it was *Jezebel*.

Klarke and Harris had joint custody of the kids. They alter-
nated living one week with Klarke and one week with Harris.
Joint custody usually worked out so that one parent had the children for six months and the other parent for the other six months.
The court finds this less disruptive for the kids. But since Klarke
and Harris lived in the same school district and they never once
had a problem with arrangements, the courts allowed for their
every-other-week arrangement.

It was always a battle getting the children prepared to spend a
week with their father and Tionne. The children loved their
daddy to death, but Tionne's presence caused tension, not so
much with HJ as with Vaughn.

Vaughn, being the oldest, understood more about the divorce
and the circumstances surrounding it. Still, being a child and not
understanding her father's role in the matter, she placed all the
blame on Tionne. It didn't make things any better when they
found out that they had a little sister, either. Vaughn was crushed
to know that she and her mother were not the only women in her
father's life anymore. It was as if they had both been replaced.
She was no longer Daddy's little girl.

Vaughn had always craved attention. When she had been a
toddler she had refused to accept the birth of her little brother.
Whenever anyone was cooing over the new baby boy, Vaughn
would do something disruptive, like pee her pants, just to turn
the attention on herself. She was no longer the star of the show,
and HJ being a junior was a double whammy. She didn't like it.
Eventually, however, she adjusted, but it had taken a long time.

Klarke decided to overlook HJ's question and ask one of her
own.

"Do you both have all of your schoolbooks? I don't want Tionne
having to bring y'all back here every other day to get something."

The children always managed to leave something behind so that they would have reason to come back to the house before their week was up.

"I think I left my spelling book upstairs," HJ said, and dashed up to his room to retrieve it.

Vaughn waited until HJ was out of sight, then turned to her mother and said, "Mom, I don't want to go this week. Why can't we visit him every other weekend like other kids do?"

Klarke couldn't help but laugh at that one. She walked over to Vaughn and kissed her on the forehead. "I love you, too."

The doorbell rang and Klarke yelled for HJ. She walked over and opened the door. There stood Harris, looking his handsome mature self. Tionne was waiting in the passenger side of the "his" of their "his" and "her" Lexuses. She waved at Klarke and Klarke nodded with a cordial smile, feeling like she was in a Lifetime movie.

"Dad!" HJ exclaimed, bumping past Klarke to get to him.

"Hey, buddy," Harris said hugging him and kissing him on the head. "You all set?"

"Yep. I almost left my spelling book. Oh, and Vaughn," HJ said pointing to a purple duffel bag he had laid at his mother's feet, "you almost forgot your gym bag again."

"What were you doing in my room?" Vaughn said angrily, knowing that HJ's courtesy had just eliminated a trip back home during the week.

"The word is thank you," Klarke said brushing her finger down Vaughn's nose.

"Well, if you two have everything, then let's get ready to roll," Harris told the children.

"If by chance they did forget something, just call me and I'll bring it over," Klarke said. She kissed the children good-bye and watched as they headed to the car. Harris lingered behind.

"So how are you?" he asked in a soft tone, trying too hard to be sexy.

"Good, I'm real good," Klarke replied in a nonchalant tone.

"Are you sure?" Harris said with a fake concern that Klarke saw right through.

"I'm not your responsibility anymore, Harris. I thought that would make you happy, a burden off of your shoulders," Klarke said, fluttering her eyes, waiting for Harris's next remark.

"Klarke, you were never a burden," Harris said, looking into her eyes. "You were anything but a burden."

"Just spit it out. What is it you want to say? Every week you are standing at my door pretending to be concerned about my well-being. What, you gonna take care of me, Harris? You want me to be your kept woman now?" Klarke, knowing that she had gone too far, lowered her head and bit her lip.

"Are we ever going to be friends again?" Harris asked. By this time Klarke could see Tionne getting impatient waiting on Harris.

"You better get going. Tionne doesn't look too happy with you standing here talking to me." They both looked at Tionne, who was sitting in the car with the boo-boo face.

It was always obvious how insecure Tionne was with Harris being around Klarke. Hell, she had won the man, but she still saw Klarke as a threat.

"Just let me know if you ever need anything, Klarke. I do still have love for you."

"So, if I said I still had love for you, too, and fell into your arms with promises to take you back, would you leave her?" Klarke said, batting her eyes.

"In a heartbeat," Harris said, shocking Klarke.

"No wonder your girl is sitting out there looking so insecure. Does she know she don't have her shit locked down? Does she know that you still love me and would come back to me if I'd take you?" Klarke asked, knowing what his answer would be. Harris just stood there without words. "Men. You are all the same and you never change. Get your sorry ass off of my doorstep."

Klarke closed the door as Harris walked away. God knows she wanted to say, "Baby, I do love you. Come back home where you belong." But she refused to ever give him the chance to hurt her again. Even if she would have loved to fuck him just to spite Tionne.

Klarke missed the lifestyle Harris had given her. She just couldn't go back to Harris, not after the way he had hurt her. Besides, she had her mind set on fresh bait, something bigger and better.

5

Meow

"So, how is the Opalescent job coming along?" Evan asked Klarke as she poured her afternoon cup of coffee.

"The shipment is going out today and I'm going to track them on Thursday," Klarke answered.

"Make it Wednesday," Evan said, grabbing himself a cup of coffee as well.

"Whatever you say, boss," Klarke said enunciating the *b* and letting the *s* sound roll off her tongue.

"Is there a problem with Wednesday?" Evan asked, almost daring Klarke to say yes.

"No, not at all. As a matter of fact, I always say, why put off until Thursday what you can do on Wednesday?" Klarke walked away, putting a slight switch in her ass.

She knew if Evan was going to even try to get the last word in, that swing in her hips would shut him up for sure. She sat down at her desk and prioritized her assignments as she did every Monday afternoon. Her Monday mornings were spent checking her voicemail messages and e-mails. She got out her follow-up list and took a sip of her steaming hot coffee. No sooner than she could put the cup back down, Evan was at her desk.

"Klarke, can I see you in my office, please?" Evan asked.

"I'll be right in," Klarke responded. She placed her cup of coffee on her electric coffee warmer with a sigh. Evan loved tearing her away from her work for some dumb shit.

Just as Klarke approached Evan's office she could hear her phone ringing. She knew the call would go to her voicemail, so she continued into Evan's office.

She hated being in his office alone with him. Every time she set foot inside he was trying to get to her. Besides, she could have had on a snowsuit with a floor-length parka and still would have felt butt ass naked with the way Evan stared at her. Evan wasn't a bad-looking white man by far. If a sistah was going to get with a white dude, he'd be the one.

Evan was about six foot even with beautiful ocean-blue eyes ringed with black. He had shiny light blond hair, his roots just a shade or two darker. He was well built and quite fashionable. The three thousand dollars' worth of dental work gave him a near perfect grill. His breath smelled of the Altoids he kept on him at all times and last, but not least, his pockets were deep.

None of this mattered to Klarke, though. The fact that Evan was non–African American didn't even play a part in her decision not to get with him. She was firm about not dating anyone she worked with, especially her boss. She simply felt that mixing business with pleasure was begging for trouble.

When Klarke got to Evan's office he ordered her to close the door behind her. As she did Evan's phone buzzed and the receptionist's voice came over the speaker.

"Mr. Kemble, is Klarke in your office by any chance?" the receptionist asked. "She has an emergency phone call. It's about her daughter."

Klarke felt her heart begin to race. She quickly picked up the phone. "I'm here, I'm here. What happened?" Klarke asked frantically.

"Your daughter's school called," the receptionist said. "Apparently she had a serious asthma attack and had to be taken to the hospital."

Klarke could hardly breathe herself after hearing those words. She raced out of Evan's office, grabbed her purse from her cubicle, and dug for her truck keys. She rushed through the office lobby and out to the elevator doors. She pushed the Down button continuously, but the elevator was taking its sweet time coming. Klarke opted to take the stairs down to the parking lot.

When she got outside, Klarke frantically searched for her vehicle. Her mind went blank. She couldn't find the Rodeo anywhere. She tried to calm herself down so she could think straight, but that didn't work. She had to have walked up and down every single aisle in that parking lot, but still the truck was nowhere in sight.

Klarke ran back inside the building. The window at the receptionist's station had an aerial view of the parking lot. She had a better chance at spotting her vehicle that way. The receptionist was puzzled to see Klarke coming back.

As Klarke came through the lobby doors Renée was coming around the corner with Evan right behind her.

"More trouble with the truck?" Renée asked. "I saw the tow truck racking it up and taking it away."

Klarke knew she hadn't scheduled for anyone to pick her truck up for repairs. Then it dawned on her what had happened. Of all the times in the world the finance company decided to make good on their threat to repossess her vehicle, they picked now, when she needed it most.

Klarke's eye flooded with tears. She just stood in the lobby trying not to cry.

"Let me grab my keys," Evan said. "I'll take you to the hospital."

By the time Klarke made it to the hospital, Harris and Tionne had already been there over an hour. Another damn accident on 75 had held Klarke and Evan up. Evan let Klarke out at the emergency-room entrance. She went straight to patient information to find out where Vaughn was. The nurse saw how distraught Klarke was and called for a candy striper to show her to Vaughn's room.

Klarke felt as though she was lost in a Roman maze garden with all the twists and turns the candy striper took her through. One more turn and she was going to yell at him if he even knew where the fuck he was going, but within seconds she saw Harris and Tionne standing in the hallway outside of Vaughn's room.

About three Mississippis before Klarke reached Harris and Tionne, the doctor approached the two. The doctor grabbed Tionne's hand and said, "Your daughter is a strong girl. She's going to be just fine."

As if things weren't bad enough, Tionne attempted to take pleasure in the moment by thanking the doctor, but Klarke stampeded onto the scene.

"I'm her mother," Klarke said almost out of breath. "My daughter, she's going to be fine?"

"Klarke," Harris said as he hugged her. "Our baby's going to be all right." Klarke fell into Harris's arms with tears of relief.

"You two don't know how lucky you are that her school was aware of her asthma condition," the doctor continued. "They knew exactly what was going on and called nine-one-one immediately. They saved your daughter's life."

"When the school called me," Tionne said, "they said that she started getting short of breath. She told the teacher that she had left her inhaler at her mom's house."

Klarke planted her forehead in the palm of her hand. She knew Vaughn had deliberately left it in order to have a reason to come back home. All of this was becoming far too much for Klarke to bear.

"Can we see her?" Klarke asked the doctor.

"Yes," the doctor replied. "Don't be alarmed when you see her. She has tubes to assist in stabilizing her breathing, but she's just fine."

They all entered the room and upon seeing her baby girl in such a condition, Klarke almost fell to her knees. Instead she just pulled up a chair beside Vaughn's bed and held her daughter's hand for the next couple of hours.

Harris and Tionne tried to get her to go down to the cafeteria with them to grab something to eat, but Klarke refused, almost becoming aggravated by their pestering.

"I need to be here when she wakes up," Klarke said.

"Honey, she's going to be all right," Harris said to Klarke.

"She needs her rest. Go home, get changed up, get some rest, and come back in the morning," the nurse said with authority. "If anything changes, anything at all, I promise we will call."

"Thank you," Harris said to the nurse. They gathered up their things in order to leave. "HJ is at Momma's. We have to swing by and pick him up. Klarke, are you okay to drive?"

"Oh, man," Klarke said as she had forgotten all about her lack of transportation, "I got dropped off here. The truck is gone . . . well, it's a long story. I'll tell you about it later."

"We'll take you home," Harris said.

"No, thank you. I have no desire to take a backseat to her again," Klarke said, pointing at Tionne, and exited the hospital room.

Klarke decided to pay a visit to the ladies' room before calling a taxi. She went back over to the patient information desk in the emergency room lobby and asked where the pay phones were. The receptionist pointed Klarke in the right direction, and as Klarke headed over to the pay phones she saw Evan sitting in the waiting area flipping through a magazine.

Klarke couldn't believe it was him.

"Evan," Klarke said walking up to him. He immediately rose to his feet.

"Klarke, how is she? How is your daughter?"

"She's fine. She's going to be okay. Evan, what are you still doing here?"

"You didn't think I was going to let you walk home, did you?"

It was pouring rain when Evan drove Klarke home. Initially Klarke just sat there and traced the raindrops down the window with her index finger. Her mind was full of so many things—first and foremost, Vaughn's health. But the scene at the hospital had aggravated her situation with Harris and Tionne all over again.

"Why do men cheat?" Klarke asked Evan suddenly.

Evan remained silent, not sure if Klarke was just thinking out loud or if she truly wanted him to answer.

"Why?" she asked again.

"Because we can," Evan said calmly. "Not me personally," he added quickly. "I've never cheated on a woman."

"Please, you're with a different woman at every company affair."

"But none of them are my wife."

"Here we go with that male way of thinking."

"No, seriously. I didn't take vows with any of those women."

"Yeah, but a woman assumes."

"Then they shouldn't," Evan interrupted. "No one should ever assume anything."

"That's not right, Evan, and you know it," Klarke said.

"What's not right is women thinking they can dictate how the male population is supposed to act, how we're supposed to feel, and how we're supposed to think. Men and women do not think alike." There was a brief silence as Klarke pondered over Evan's words.

"I would have rather not known," Klarke said.

"What?"

"I would have rather not known that Harris was cheating on me. As crazy as that might sound, I wish things could have continued on as they were than to go through all the pain and devastation I've had to go through. I'd still be the good little wife, and Harris would still be screwing around behind my back. But at least I was happy."

"Women are always saying how they want honesty," Evan said. "You swear you can handle it and you dig for the truth. Y'all dig in our pants pockets, in our cell phones and e-mails for the truth. Some women even go as far as checking the mileage on a man's car for the truth. They want to know why, if he was just going around the corner to get a pack of cigarettes, there were thirty miles put on the car. Now, when a woman starts questioning a man about the passenger seat being reclined, it's time to let her go." Evan laughed.

"I didn't have to look for the truth. It smacked me right upside the head. Harris just flat out told me one day. It was eating him up, he said."

"Well, women are always saying they'd rather hear it from the man than find out some other way. That's bullshit. It doesn't matter if the bullet hits you close range, three feet, or six feet. Once it hits, it's going to hurt either way."

"Turn here," Klarke said pointing. "My house is right there. The brick house on the right." Evan pulled up in Klarke's driveway and put his car in park.

"Are you going to be all right?" Evan asked in a sincere tone. It was a tone he had never addressed Klarke with before.

"Yeah. Thanks for the ride, Evan. I don't know what I would have done . . ." All of a sudden Klarke broke down crying. Evan, not knowing what to do or how to comfort her, just looked at her with sadness.

"Klarke, I'm sorry all of this is happening to you," he said. "I know I've been an asshole. And I know that you know I've been an asshole on purpose. It's just that, when you rejected me—oh, man. That cut like a knife. You're a class act, Klarke."

"I've been called a lot of things, Evan, but never in my life have I been called a class act." They both began to laugh.

"I guess that was quite white of me." They laughed again.

"Well, thanks again," Klarke said.

"Sure, any—" Klarke's sweet peck on Evan's lips put a halt to his words. The kiss shocked Klarke herself just as much as it shocked Evan. Quickly Evan returned the kiss with one of his own, and then another one, followed by yet another one, each one deeper and sweeter than the last.

. . .

Klarke was up bright and early the next morning. She showered, dressed, and put on a pot of coffee. She wanted to hurry and get to the hospital to see Vaughn, but she also had to contact the finance company to discuss getting her truck back. She planned on being at the hospital all day and didn't want to call them to discuss it there. She dug through some paperwork and collected all the information she would need before making the call.

She poured herself a cup of coffee and walked around the island that separated her kitchen from the living room. She placed her coffee by the phone on the end table, sat down on the couch and proceeded to put her documents in some kind of order. Once she located the phone number of the finance company, she picked up the phone to make the dreaded call.

"This is Klarke Taylor, and I'm calling to discuss my account. Yes, it's account number 555 . . ."

"Good morning. Oh, I'm sorry I didn't realize you were on the phone," Evan said, coming down the staircase and entering the living room.

"Oh, good morning," Klarke said, quickly hanging up the phone.

"Is everything okay?"

"Oh, yeah. Everything is fine. Finance company," Klarke said, gesturing to the phone, then hanging it up.

As Klarke sat there looking into Evan's eyes, which she had never allowed herself to notice were so hypnotizing, all she could think was, What have I done?

Klarke's body quivered as she remembered how Evan had popped one of those famous Altoids of his in his mouth and then proceed to lick and suck her. The curiously strong mint's coolness had provided a delightful delayed reaction. Even after Evan made her climax, her clitoris had still been tingling. Klarke had then proceeded to lay him on his back and take out years of sexual frustration on him.

Klarke had been on a couple of dates since her stints with Harris and Rawling, but she had never gotten close enough to anyone long enough to sleep with them. She was so busy trying to regroup and get her life together that sex had simply not played a starring role. Of all the times for it to make a cameo appearance, Klarke couldn't believe it had been with her boss.

Klarke got up from the couch to go into the kitchen to fix Evan a cup of coffee, giving him a quick, nervous kiss on the cheek on her way. Evan accepted it for what it was and smiled.

As Klarke poured the coffee Evan took her place on the couch and fingered through the papers she had left by the phone.

"You have a nice home," Evan said, making conversation.

"Thanks," Klarke said as she carried the cup over to him.

"Thank you," he said taking it from her.

"Well, I don't want to rush you out of here or anything, but I really need to get to the hospital," Klarke said as she wiped her sweaty palms on her jeans.

"Oh, no problem," Evan said taking a sip of his coffee and placing it down on the table. "I'll take you."

"Oh, no, that's okay. My girlfriend is coming over to pick me up," Klarke said nervously. "You sit right there and finish drinking your coffee."

Just then she heard Breezy pull up. She raced to the door and held up her index finger to let Breezy know to wait a minute, that she'd be right out. There was no way she was going to explain to Breezy the white man sitting on her couch.

"Well, that's her," Klarke said, panicking as she grabbed her purse and her keys off the key hook Vaughn had made in woodshop class. "Uhh, towels and washcloths are in the closet in the master bath. Anything else you need I'm sure you'll find easily. You can just push this bottom lock and let yourself out, okay? Okay then, I gotta go. Good-bye."

Klarke detested leaving Evan alone in her home, but it was either that or deal with Breezy. Just as she closed the door behind her, Breezy got out of her car.

"Whose cat?" Breezy called, referring to Evan's money-green Jaguar in Klarke's driveway.

"Shhh," Klarke said, waving her hand in a shushing motion. "Are you trying to wake up the whole neighborhood? Come on, let's go." The two then got into the car and pulled away.

"How's Vaughn?" Breezy asked.

"She's well. I called the hospital this morning and she'll probably be released this evening."

"I can't believe she left her inhaler at your house."

"Yeah, me neither."

"She just won't get used to the arrangement you and Harris have, huh?"

"Vaughn's just stubborn. You know how you Leos are. It's either your way or you make a way."

"That's how us lionesses are." Breezy smiled and patted Klarke on the leg. "It's going to be okay. Everything is going to work out for you."

"Yeah, it better," Klarke said, deep in thought.

"What is this master plan you've got cooking?" Breezy asked, her curiosity getting the best of her. "You act like it's going to change the world."

"It is. My world."

"Well, spit it out."

"It's nothing really. I just decided that sometimes even divine order needs a shove here and there. Breezy, this lifestyle just isn't me. I mean, sure I have the house still, but this working and try-ing to make ends meet shit is for the birds. It frightens me that I'm feeling this way."

"Why? You're not embezzling money from your job or any-thing like that, are you?"

"No, girl, because you know me. I've always been happy with what I have. It just so happens that now I want more. Knowing that there are people doing far worse than I ever will has always kept me grounded and humble. I mean, I don't have the bug as bad as Jeva, but I want the fairy tale, too. And Jeva was right. I had it. I had it fist-tight and yet it still got away. I swear, if I could do things over, this time around, I don't care if he moves the ho in our house like she's Shug Avery from *The Color Purple*. As long as he's taking care of my children and me, I'll have no complaints. He can do whatever his heart desires."

"Who is this he?" Breezy asked.

"The answer. Just as long as everything falls into its proper place, he is my answer to a secured life. I just hate that it has come down to this. Me, Klarke Annette Taylor, being crafty. Who would have thought it?"

"Sounds like you're convinced that your strategy is airtight. But whatever happens, don't sweat it, mama," Breezy said. "It's like I told you. Yes, you probably should have just stayed with Harris in the first place. Women bounce from man to man before they realize that it's the same shit, different man. Harris, no doubt, took care of you. But you'll get a different man who can give you the same shit. Granted, you are still going to have drama, but at least you'll have shit. You know what I'm saying?"

Klarke looked at Breezy as she drove, an intense and serious look on her face. Breezy took her eyes off the road momentarily to return the acknowledgment. They both started laughing.

"I don't know where you come up with half the material that comes out of your mouth," Klarke said smiling.

"It flows like a gift from God, baby."

"Umm, I wouldn't go giving God credit for what comes out of your mouth." They laughed and continued on to the hospital.

"Hey, baby girl. You feeling all right?" Klarke asked Vaughn as she kissed her. "You had me scared to death."

"Yeah, I'm feeling all right," Vaughn answered, then turned her attention to Breezy, who was standing behind Klarke with a gift bag in her hand. "Hi, Auntie Bria."

"How's my mini me?" Breezy said hugging her.

"Fine. Whatcha got in that bag?"

"My lunch for work today," Breezy joked. "What do you think? It's for you."

"Oh, thank you!" Vaughn said as she took the bag and pulled out the latest in the Cheetah Girls book series.

"No problem," Breezy said winking at Vaughn. "Well, I have to get going to work, but I had to stop by to make sure you were okay first."

"Thank you," Vaughn said, flipping through the book excitedly.

"Call me tonight, Klarke, so we can talk about that cat," Breezy said, rolling her tongue inside her closed mouth and pushing it against her jaw.

Vaughn looked up from her book. "Oh, wow! We have a cat?" she asked.

"Bria Nicole Williams, I will call you tonight for sure," Klarke said, using Breezy's full name—as she did whenever Breezy had gone too far, even for Breezy.

Klarke shook her head and sat in the chair next to Vaughn's bed.

"Meow," Breezy joked as she clawed her nails down the air and walked away.

"Are you and Daddy mad at me?" Vaughn asked.

Klarke looked at her in surprise. "Now why would we be mad at you?"

"Because it's all my fault I'm in here. I didn't take my inhaler to school with me. I had some at Daddy's. I hid them because I wanted to come home for the ones at our house."

Klarke began to smooth her hand through Vaughn's hair. "It doesn't even matter, sweetheart. But now do you see how serious asthma is, girl? People die from attacks like this, Vaughn. It's not like a stuffed nose that comes along with a common cold. We're talking about your ability to breathe." Vaughn put her head down in shame. "I'm not trying to fuss you out. I just want you to know that you can't play with this, okay?"

"I know, Mom. I'm sorry."

Klarke and Vaughn were still embracing when Harris entered the room, dressed for work. Seeing him in his uniform brought back memories. She remembered laundering them every week. She would inhale Harris's scent before throwing them into the washer machine. She felt the heat on her fingertips that the iron expelled as she laid them out for his workday. She remembered how fortunate she thought she was back then.

"How's one of my favorite girls?" Harris said as he walked over and handed Vaughn a teddy bear and bouquet of sunflowers.

"Thanks, Daddy," Vaughn said. "Oooh sunflowers! They're so beautiful."

"They're strong like you, Princess," Harris said as he kissed Vaughn on the forehead, then turned his attention to Klarke. "How are you doing, Klarke?"

"Much better now that my baby is up and about," Klarke said in a pleasant tone. "Where's HJ?"

"Oh, Tionne drove him to school for me. She'll be up here to see you after she drops him off," Harris said to Vaughn.

"Hey, little chiquita!" Jeva said, suddenly breezing into the room. "Hey Klarke, Harris."

"Hello," they each said.

"How are you feeling, baby?" Jeva said to Vaughn.

"Oh, I really feel great now. Mom got a cat!"

Jeva stayed at the hospital visiting Vaughn with Klarke for a few hours. She had taken a sick day from work only because she had exhausted all of her vacation days. When it was time for her to leave, she offered Klarke a ride home. Klarke accepted. She kissed Vaughn good-bye, promising to call her later that night. The doctor had been in to see Vaughn and was going to release her from the hospital. Klarke and Harris decided that Vaughn would return to his house to finish out her and HJ's week there.

Harris hugged Klarke good-bye, and just as he was doing so Tionne entered the hospital room.

"I'll talk to you later," Klarke said, brushing past Tionne on her way out.

"Excuse me," Tionne muttered under her breath. She smiled when she saw Vaughn. "Hey, Vaughn. How you feeling?"

"Ah, so-so," Vaughn said, turning her back on Tionne.

"Your brother said to tell you hello." Tionne continued her attempt to make conversation with Vaughn. "He was really worried about you."

"Did you give him a Ho-Ho to calm him down?" Vaughn asked smartly. "I know how him and Daddy both are really fond of *Ho-Hos*." Vaughn exaggerated her pronunciation.

"Tionne, how about some coffee?" Harris asked, in an attempt to referee. "Let's go down to the cafeteria and grab a cup."

"Sure," Tionne said. "Vaughn, would you like anything?"

"Daddy, would you bring me back some Skittles?" Vaughn said, ignoring the fact that it was Tionne who had made the offer.

"I'll check with the nurse and make sure it's okay," Harris replied.

"Thanks, Daddy."

As Harris and Tionne exited the room Tionne could hardly keep her composure. She had been waiting for an opportunity to let her feelings be known.

"I know Klarke has her acting that way toward me," Tionne said angrily.

"Please, Klarke's not like that. She'd never badmouth us to the kids. Those kids mean more than anything in the world to Klarke. Klarke does everything she can to try to make Vaughn happy with our situation. Do you think it makes her happy to send her children somewhere she thinks that they hate being?"

"Well, aren't we all defensive of the former Mrs. Harris Bradshaw?"

"Look, I'm not going through this with you every time you start feeling insecure," Harris said sternly.

"Well, I'm only what you make me," Tionne replied.

"And what is that supposed to mean?"

"If you wouldn't make me feel so unsure of myself when it comes to you and Klarke then we wouldn't have this problem," Tionne said raising her voice. "It's like you do it on purpose. I walk into the room today and she's in your arms."

"Oh, T, come on."

"And yesterday, did you have to call her honey?"

"I didn't call her honey," Harris argued.

"Yes, you did."

"Look, my child is in the hospital and you're worried about me and Klarke having something going on. Go on with that bullshit, T," Harris said angrily. The more Tionne spoke, the more pissed off Harris became.

"Well, do you have something going on?" Tionne said, continuing to push Harris's buttons.

"Damn it, Tionne, stop it!" Harris said through clenched teeth. "I said I'm not going through this with you."

"You can't even say it. You can't even just say that you two aren't fucking because it's true. You're still fucking her. Just say it, Harris. I'm not going to get mad."

Harris paused before turning to Tionne. He had put up with her crazy accusations for three years now and it was time to put it to a stop.

"This isn't about Klarke and you know it," he said, his voice low and intense. "This is about you and how you and I ended up together. What, Tionne? You think Klarke is on some reciprocity kick . . . that she's going to do the same thing to you that you did to her? You want to brand her as some woman focused on trying to rope in a man at any cost. You want to see her as some woman with nothing better to do than to be hugged up on and wait to be called honey by someone else's man. Think about it. It's not Klarke at all you're looking at. It's yourself you see."

Tears filled Tionne's eyes. "I can't believe you just said that to me," Tionne said as she began to cry.

"Look, baby," Harris said holding Tionne's arms and looking into her eyes. "I'm not trying to hurt you. I just had to put it out there. We can't change how our relationship started. It's a choice we both made. We knew what we were getting into when we decided to be together and you have done nothing but carry around a load of guilt. Feeling guilty about a wrong does not right the wrong or make it any less of a wrong. It's time to move on now. Do you understand what I'm saying to you, woman?"

Tionne was too choked up to respond. Harris had read her like the morning news. For the past three years she hadn't allowed herself to fully enjoy being with Harris. She had never wanted God to see her happy with another woman's husband, a man she immorally and maliciously stole from another woman, to say the least. All she could do was bury her head in Harris's chest and cry. He squeezed her tight and they headed for the cafeteria.

6

A Few Good Men

.

Klarke thanked God she lived only a few miles from her office or she might not have been able to afford the taxi fare to work. She hadn't yet found the time to contact the finance company for her truck to make arrangements to get it back. Who cared if it broke down constantly? This was the last year of payments before Klarke would own the truck free and clear. She would be damned if she would give up ownership on the truck this late in the game.

When Klarke walked into the office she felt as if everyone could tell she had slept with the boss. She felt as though any whispering at the water cooler that day would be about her and Evan's sexual encounter. Klarke thought that it was possible Evan had kissed and told, but then again, he probably wanted to keep their escapade just as much of a secret as she did. The last thing Evan would want is for any of his good old boys finding out is that he boned a sistah.

"How's your little girl?" the receptionist asked in a concerned tone.

"She's fine now, thank you," Klarke answered with a smile.

"Is she out of the hospital?"

"Oh, yes. She's doing good."

When Klarke got to her desk there was a bouquet of flowers and a card expressing the sentiments of Kemble and Steiner Printing. She knew Renée had ordered them because Renée always ordered the floral daisies from Kroger for any occasion. It was like her own personal trademark.

Klarke sat down at her desk. She could hear Evan fumbling around in his office and her stomach turned queasy. She wasn't looking forward to her first face-to-face with Evan since having sex with him.

Klarke decided to call the finance company. She followed the correct prompt to reach a live collection representative. She proceeded to give them her account number and held patiently while the rep pulled up her information.

"Miss Taylor," the collection rep said, "how can I be of assistance?"

"I need to know what I need to do to get my truck back," Klarke said.

"Hmm," the rep said punching away at the computer keyboard. "I guess I'm a little confused. My records show that your truck was returned back to the point at which custody was taken. Let me see what the deal is with that. It will be just a moment. I have to change screens."

Klarke was completely baffled at this point. She had no idea what was going on.

"Just one more second," the rep assured Klarke. "Our computers are running a little slow today."

Klarke was becoming a tad antsy. There was nothing more

nerve-wracking than being on a drawn-out personal phone call at work.

"Okay, here we go," the rep continued. "Yep, just what I thought. Miss Taylor, the past due amount was paid by wire, as was the remaining balance on the note. You should receive your original title in the mail within two to three weeks. Is there anything else I may assist you with?" The line was dead silent. "Miss Taylor, are you there?"

"Yes. I'm sorry about that. I'm still here," Klarke said, stunned.

"Is there anything else I may assist you with?" the rep repeated.

"No, I'm fine. Have a good day."

Klarke hung up the phone and sat at her desk, confused. She went to the receptionist's station to look out the window and into the parking lot. Lo and behold, there sat her Rodeo in one of the visitor's parking spots.

"I can't believe he did this," Klarke said aloud to herself thinking about Evan. "That son of a bitch is trying to keep me quiet. Why else would he spend almost four thousand dollars to get my truck back for me?"

"Did you say something?" the receptionist asked.

"Oh, I was just talking to myself," Klarke answered as she began to walk away.

"As long as you don't start answering yourself," the receptionist said.

Klarke smiled at her, hating how people always said that type of stupid shit. That and *Is it cold enough for you outside?*

Evan had more money than he knew what to do with. The thought of him using his money to get what he wanted in life gave Klarke a bad taste in her mouth. It was one thing for a person to have money, it was another thing for a person to have money and throw it around in the face of people who didn't. Now more than ever she wished that she hadn't slept with Evan. It would be difficult, but Klarke would somehow manage to avoid the subject matter as well as avoid Evan himself.

The alarm clock on the mini refrigerator in Klarke's bedroom went off at 6:00 A.M. She sighed, remembering that that same *buzz beep buzz* used to be music to her ears back when she was with Harris. It was her call to get out of bed and be the perfect wife and mother that she was—iron clothes, prepare breakfast and lunches. Of course that was when she was able to be back in bed by 9:00 A.M., too.

When the children first started going over to Harris's, Klarke would hit the snooze button two and three times before finally getting up. Not having the motivation to jump out of bed and get them ready for school, Klarke would try to catch a few extra zzz's. Being regularly tardy for work earned her a written warning. It got to the point where Klarke had to start plugging in the alarm clock across the room so that the snooze button would be out of her reach.

There were many times she tried to drown out the annoying sound of the alarm by burying her head in her down feather pillows. But when that wouldn't work, the purpose for putting the clock across the room in the first place prevailed. She would stagger over to the clock and shut the alarm off. Only once did she return to bed after shutting the alarm off, and ended up oversleeping, so eventually she moved it back over by the bed.

As Klarke reached over to turn the alarm off she knocked over the book she had been reading, *28 Days* by Nina Tracy. It was a collection of true erotic kiss-and-tales that Klarke regularly masturbated to. Unfortunately, the Dixie cup full of water that was sitting on top of the book went tumbling too. "Damn it!" Klarke yelled, sitting up.

She walked into her master bedroom's private bath to grab a towel. She relieved herself, washed her hands, and untied the silk Louis Vuitton scarf she had around her hair. As she proceeded back to the bedroom to clean up the spilled water, she shook loose her curls.

As Klarke soaked up the water she remembered why the cup of water had been there in the first place. It was for the birth control pill she had forgotten to take. Klarke quickly headed back toward the bathroom to retrieve another cup of water so that she could take her pill. Before she could do so the phone rang.

Klarke looked at the digits on the clock that now read 6:10 A.M. "Who died or who is in jail?" Klarke said as she read Breezy's name on the caller ID box.

"Hey, girl, it's only me. I've got Jeva on the line, too," Breezy said.

"Hey, girl," Jeva chimed in.

"What do y'all want at six o'clock in the morning?" Klarke asked.

"Meow," Breezy purred.

"I know you didn't call me this early for that," Klarke said.

"And I know you didn't not call me like you said you would, so that must mean it's something juicy," Breezy said. "That's why I have Jeva on the line. You can just tell us both so you don't have to repeat yourself. Then you can be on your merry little way to work."

"Come on, Klarke," Jeva said. "Spill the beans. Whose Jaguar was in your driveway and how long had it been there?"

"Forget all that. Did you finally get laid?" Breezy asked.

"You two need to get a life," Klarke said.

"Will you just spit it out, damn it?" Breezy stated.

"Okay, okay," Klarke said. "Yes."

"Yes, what?" Jeva and Breezy said at the same time.

"Yes, I got me some," Klarke said bashfully.

Jeva and Breezy couldn't contain themselves. They cheered like Laker Girls. Klarke just sat on the phone, embarrassed.

"Well, who was it?" Jeva asked.

"And was it good?" Breezy added. The girls waited impatiently as silence reigned.

"Hello, anybody there?" Breezy sarcastically asked.

"I'm still here," Jeva answered.

"Not you, dodo. Klarke," Breezy said.

"Ohhh, can't you guys wait until the next time we're at the Cheesecake? We'll have something to talk about. It will be a great conversation piece."

"You expect us to wait that long?" Breezy asked in disbelief. "Now don't make me come over there. Who was it, Klarke?"

"Okay, okay, it was Evan, my boss," Klarke said reluctantly. The girls each screamed at the top of their lungs. Klarke and Breezy could hear Lance in the background yelling for Jeva to keep it down.

"You didn't!" Jeva whispered.

"I knewed it!" Breezy exclaimed. "You gave him some *Boyz N the Hood* pity sex?"

"Evan lucked up on some life-crisis drama sex like Cuba." Jeva laughed.

"What were you thinking?" Breezy asked. "Bitch, Halle

already got the Oscar for screwing a white man, so what's your excuse?"

"I knew I should have never told you two." Klarke sighed with regret.

"Then you should have gone with your first instincts," Breezy said, " 'cause I ain't never letting you live this one down, Lisa Bonet."

Jeva laughed. "I had almost forgotten about that movie. What was it called again? Oh yeah, *Angel Heart*. What about that one with Angela Basset and Robert De Niro?"

"*The Score!*" Breezy shouted.

"Whitney Houston and Kevin Costner in *The Bodyguard*," Jeva added.

"Yes, good one!" Breezy exclaimed.

"All right, already!" Klarke shouted over Jeva and Breezy. "This isn't a game show. This is my life. Now, will you two shut up and let me finish?"

"There's more?" Breezy asked.

"This is getting even better," Jeva said.

"Y'all, the man done got my vehicle back for me. The balance is paid in full." All the girls yelled and screeched with excitement. They went ballistic with joy.

"You done turned your first trick," Breezy said proudly.

"What the hell are you talking about?" Klarke was stunned by Breezy's comment.

"Look at it any way you want to, but when you fuck for a deed or a need, it's just like turning a trick," Breezy explained. "There's a world full of women out there turning tricks as we speak and they don't even know it. Wives, too, for that matter."

"Okay, Breezy," Klarke sighed. "You are not making me feel

any better about this. I had no idea that man was going to pay for my truck."

"Then you are one up on the game," Breezy said. "It's like serendipity. You were going to sleep with the man regardless, right? It just so happens that you got something in return. You got a fuck and a truck." The girls laughed hysterically.

"How was it?" Breezy just had to know. "I mean how was it doing it with a white man?"

"In complete honesty, it was the bomb," Klarke said licking her lips.

"Hmm, so there are a few good white men out there after all," Jeva said dryly.

"Well, now that Breezy done broke the game down to me," Klarke said, "there's always been a few good white men out there. Ben, Andrew, Abe, and all the rest of those fuckers who make the world go round. Sistahs better recognize."

"That's my girl," Breezy said proudly. "That's my girl."

Klarke had just logged off of her computer when Harris dropped the kids off. She could hear them coming in the door, so Vaughn must have used her key.

"Mom!" the kids shouted. "We're home."

"Hey, babies," Klarke said, coming down the steps to give them a kiss and hug. "Hello, Harris."

"Klarke," Harris said, standing outside of the door. Klarke peeked around him to see Tionne waiting impatiently in the car as always.

"You're not allowed to come into the house? I mean, hell, it did used to be your house. Let me guess," Klarke whispered in his ear to keep the kids, who were on their way up the steps, from hearing. "She's afraid you might come inside for a quickie."

Harris sighed. "Klarke, not you too."

"What's that supposed to mean?" Klarke asked sharply.

"Nothing, Klarke. Nothing at all," Harris said, putting his head down.

"Oh, she's been riding you, huh? And I don't mean that literally."

Klarke looked outside at Tionne, who appeared to be holding something in her hand and scrutinizing it. After all these years Klarke still hated the sight of that woman.

"See you next week, Klarke," Harris said, not ready to deal with Klarke's temperament. "See you next week, kids."

"Bye, Daddy!" they yelled from their bedrooms.

Harris returned to the car where Tionne was waiting for him, their daughter was in her car seat, sound asleep.

"What the fuck is this, Harris?" Tionne said, waving in his face what she had retrieved from out of his glove box. "What the fuck is this?"

Harris buried his head in the palm of his hands and took a deep breath. He had some explaining to do.

There was no way Klarke was going to be able to avoid Evan. Today was the monthly departmental meeting. Klarke had even considered calling in sick, but she knew that would only mean Evan briefing her one-on-one when she returned to work.

The meeting actually went quite smoothly. Klarke managed

not to make eye contact with Evan. She made sure she sat on the same side of the table as he did, but a few chairs down. That way she wouldn't even accidentally look at him.

As her luck would have it, after the meeting, Evan asked her to stay behind in the conference room because he had a few questions regarding her monthly accounts.

Klarke made her way over to the pitcher of ice water to pour herself a glass. She waited for her sidebar with Evan as her coworkers cleared the conference room.

"Did I do something wrong?" Evan said, almost heartbroken. "Do you feel as though I took advantage of you? Talk to me, Klarke. I know you've been avoiding me and I just don't want this to start affecting our work relationship. You are the best at what you do." He flinched. "Oh shit, not in bed. I mean, you were good there too, but that's not . . . well, you know what I mean."

"Evan, it's nothing personal," Klarke said softly, looking down at the floor.

"I can finish this one for you: Evan, it's not you. It's me," Evan said coldly. "So, how did I do?"

"What do you want me to say, Evan?" Klarke said, throwing her hands up. "Let's get together the second Friday night of each month and have sex?"

"No, I don't want you to say that. I want you not to treat me as if I gave you an STD or something."

Klarke laughed. Evan stared at her momentarily, then began to chuckle himself.

"I'm sorry, Evan," Klarke said, bringing her laughter to an end. "It's just that you are so melodramatic."

"Well, it must be a white thing," Evan said looking at her with those hypnotizing eyes.

"Don't look at me like that, please, Evan," Klarke said, blushing.

"Like what, Klarke? Like this?" Evan moved in to kiss her. Fortunately the conference room door was closed. The last thing Klarke needed was to be seen getting it on with her boss in the company conference room. "Maybe if you didn't taste so good, not wanting you would be a lot easier. I wish you didn't taste so good."

"Umm, it must be a black thing," Klarke said as she lifted her skirt and sat on the conference table.

Evan felt so good inside of Klarke that she didn't give a damn if he did have the audacity to offer her some sort of purse to keep quiet about their sexual relationship. It wasn't even worth mentioning at that point. Hell, he could pay her house off for all she cared. After experiencing the most heated and passionate one-and-a-half-minute encounter ever, Klarke straightened herself out while Evan buttoned up his pants and proceeded to leave the conference room.

"Evan, wait," Klarke said. "I just want to say thank you for everything, and I do mean *everything*."

"No, Klarke, thank you," Evan said, winking.

Klarke almost broke her leg trying to get to the phone. After four rings it went directly into her voicemail, and she wanted to catch the call before it did so.

"Hello! Taylor residence," Klarke said in a lively tone.

"Taylor residence . . . aren't we perky?" Harris asked.

"Oh, hey, you!"

"Damn, what's his name?" Harris asked.

"Oh, please."

"Oh, please nothing, I know when Klarke's been done up right," Harris joked.

"Stop it! I'm not going to talk sex with my ex. Now, why are you ringing my phone?"

"I was wondering if the kids can stay with you again this week?"

"What's up?"

"Ahhh, nothing, I just have to put in some long hours at work again."

"You haven't had the kids in a month. Harris, what's really going on? Is it you and Tionne?"

There was silence on the phone. Klarke could tell that if Harris spoke at that given moment his voice would have probably cracked. He eventually did speak.

"It's more like me and you," Harris said a bit desperately. "Klarke, just say the word. Rescue me."

"I'm not going to do that, Harris," Klarke said firmly. "I can't do it."

"You can't or you won't?" Harris asked sharply.

"Come on now," Klarke said, trying to stay composed.

"I mean, everything is all wrong. I'm supposed to be with you. Woman, you never even accidentally washed one of my good shirts, that's how perfect you were."

"I'm not perfect, Harris. I never was and never will be. But I loved you so much that even knowing that nobody is perfect, for you, it was still worth trying for all of my life."

"Can I come over just to talk?"

"Oh, no, you don't, mister."

"I'm serious, Klarke. We've never really talked."

"Because there's nothing to say. You have Tionne. You jeopardized everything for her. You got what you wanted. Talk to her."

"I can't talk to her," Harris said sadly. "There's been a lot of tension between us. Besides, I don't want to talk to Tionne. I want to talk to you. The way things are now between us, I never wanted it to be like this."

"Then why did you bother telling me about Tionne? Why didn't you just fuck her a few times behind my back and stay married to me?"

"You wanted the divorce," Harris said in a bold tone. "All I've ever wanted was you. I didn't want to let go of you. You cut me off when you filed those papers."

"Do you blame me? Was I supposed to stay with you after you dropped that bomb on me?"

"I never thought you would leave me. It was killing me inside, having a child outside of my marriage. I was sick, Klarke, both physically and mentally. My doctor told me I had to come clean."

"Oh, your doctor told you, not your conscience. Harris, what do you think you and I could really be? I'm so bitter it's not funny. You had a child with that woman while you were still married to me. I love that child to death and you know it, but I could never accept her like I could any other stepchild."

"She loves her Aunt Klarke, too," Harris said sincerely.

"She is my children's sister. You know I love her. She has nothing to do with this trifling mess but because of that child, Tionne will always be in our lives. You're asking too much of me."

"Just tell me you love me. That's good enough for me," Harris said, almost begging.

"I can't even give you that, Harris."

"Then tell me you don't and I promise, I'm done pushing the issue forever."

"I'm done giving you what you want. I'm done saying what you want to hear. That's another woman's job now."

"I'd die for you Klarke," Harris said passionately. "I'd die for you."

"I'll talk to you later," Klarke said as if she hadn't heard a word he said. "I'll let the kids know they won't be coming to your house this week. Good-bye."

After hanging up the phone, Klarke went into Vaughn's bedroom. She was listening to her headphones and studying from one of her schoolbooks.

"How in the world can you understand what you're reading while singing '*Baby, baby, baby, baby, baby*'?" Klarke asked Vaughn. Then she walked over to her, removed one of the earphones from her ear and repeated herself.

"Oh, Ma, please," Vaughn said rolling her eyes. "You do everything to music, clean the house, take a bath. If you had a boyfriend you'd probably . . ."

"All right already," Klarke said in a firm tone.

"I wasn't even going to say nothing like that," Vaughn said in an assuring manner.

"Well, one never knows when it comes to you. I think I'm going to cut out you spending the night with Breezy anymore."

"You crazy, Ma." Vaughn giggled.

"Crazy about you," Klarke said rubbing her finger down Vaughn's nose. "Your dad called. He has to work long hours again."

"You mean he's still at the hotel."

"What?"

"That's where he goes when him and Tionne are having it out.

They mostly argue about why he hasn't married her yet. She thinks Daddy is still in love with you. If he marries her then he'll never have a chance at getting back with you."

"How is it you know so much?"

"They talk too much around me. Besides, he always works long hours and it never stopped us from going over there before. Think about it, Ma," Vaughn said, putting the headphones back on her head.

Klarke left Vaughn's bedroom and went into HJ's, where he was tracing a picture of Sponge Bob Square Pants.

"Hey, little man," Klarke said to HJ.

"I heard. No Daddy's house again," HJ said sadly.

"I'm sorry," Klarke said, patting HJ on his head.

HJ didn't respond. He laid down on his bed silently.

"Baby, what's wrong?" Klarke asked him.

"I think I owe Vaughn a million dollars and I don't have it to give to her," he said.

"What are you talking about?" Klarke asked.

"Vaughn told me that Tionne and Lil' Sissy would win Daddy, so not to get too comfortable. She said it was only a matter of time before Tionne would put his head in the clouds with a whip, or something like that. I bet her a million dollars that that wouldn't happen. Where am I supposed to get a million dollars, Mom?"

"Come here for a minute," Klarke said to HJ. She sat down on his bed and signaled for him to sit next to her. "Your father would never turn his back on his children for any reason whatsoever. Do you understand?"

"Yes," HJ said looking down at the ground. "I guess."

"You don't have to guess," Klarke reassured HJ. "Your father loves you very much and he always will no matter what."

Klarke kissed HJ on the forehead and hugged him tightly. She wished Vaughn would stop poisoning him with her own bitterness. She couldn't believe that after three years Vaughn was still this bitter. But then again, why wouldn't she be? Like mother, like daughter.

7

The Pretender

From: RLQ812@sunset.com
To: KAT@myworld.biz
Subject: Boston Airport

How are things going with you? I'm not quite used to life in the Big Apple. Everything has been so hectic that I haven't been able to get a phone line yet. I'm at a training site so I have no idea what my office even looks like yet. My only means of communication has been this laptop I'm working from.

What I do know is that it's great to hear from you. I'm so glad you decided to e-mail me. You don't know how many times I've kicked myself for leaving your contact information behind.

I look forward to hearing from you again!

Reo had no idea who KAT@myworld.biz was, but that didn't stop him from replying to the e-mail that she had sent him. *What if KAT is a man?* Reo suddenly thought. It was too late. He had already hit the send key after spell-checking the e-mail. Reo wasn't going to let whomever KAT was think he needed Hooked On Phonics.

He could feel it in his gut that KAT was a woman. Reo receiving that e-mail was no accident as far as he was concerned. That e-mail could have been misdirected to anyone in the world, yet it showed up in his e-mail box. It was pure fate that a slip of a keystroke landed Reo his mysterious penpal. He wasn't going to disregard fate. Besides, what harm could there be in a little game of cyber charades?

Reo thought about the consequences of his stepping on the toes of someone else's hookup. What if KAT had realized her error and had e-mailed who she meant to e-mail in the first place? Well, it was too late now. He just hoped he had gotten to her first.

"Be careful, man," Nate, one of Reo's writer friends, told him as they were playing a game of chess. "I met a freak on the Internet once and couldn't get rid of her."

"It ain't even like that, partner," Reo said as he studied the chessboard contemplating his next move. "The e-mail wasn't even intended for me. It wasn't any of that freaky fan mail or chatroom mumbo jumbo. It was sent to my private e-mail address, not the public one for fans."

"I hear you, dawg. I'm just saying, you have no idea who you are communicating with in the cyber world. It could be some inmate named Bruce."

"Man, you read the e-mail. You know it's straight."

"I don't know nothing. Why do you think I'm telling you to be careful? You need to ask her name, address, social, blood type . . ." Nate went on as Reo laughed.

"I can't ask her name. You know how women are. If you

remember anything about them at all it better be their name and their birthday. She would be offended if I were the person she thinks I am and I don't even remember her name. She would be pissed. Besides, I already e-mailed her pretending to be that person."

"You should have kept it real, man. You should have replied by saying that the e-mail was misdirected to you, blah blah blah. Ain't you got no game, nigga?"

"I guess I just didn't want to take that chance. She might have thought I was some freak. Then I really wouldn't have had a chance with her."

"What makes you so sure she's someone you would even want to kick it with?" Nate said making his next move. "Don't tell me you believe in that fate shit."

"Yeah, I guess I do. You don't?" Reo said, making a not-so-well-thought-out move.

"Nah, I believe in God, so be careful . . . and checkmate."

From: KAT@myworld.biz
To: RLQ812@sunset.com
Subject: Getting To Know You

Hey, you.

I wasn't sure I had the correct e-mail address there for a minute.

Well, I'm glad things seem to be working out for you. I would expect some chaos after such a big move. It's a little slower here in the Midwest (see, you should have relocated here).

Did I tell you how much I enjoyed conversing with you? It's so hard to find a man with something worth listening to to say.

Half of the men I meet don't have anything to say at all. That probably sounded rehearsed, huh? I hate it when men tell me stuff like: "You have intelligent conversation . . . most women I meet are airheads." LOL.

Do you know what? I would love to know more about you. So tell me something, what's your favorite song, movie, book, food . . .?

My favorite song is "Ribbon in the Sky" by Stevie Wonder. My favorite movie is "Love and Basketball" and my favorite book is "Shattered Vessels" by Nancey Flowers. I absolutely love no-bake cookies.

Besides working, I like spending time with my children, my friends and myself. There's nothing like "self time." You know how us women are, a long candlelit bubble bath and a good book . . . we're in our world (LOL).

Write me back when you get a chance.

P.S. Don't wait so long this time (smile).

"Mom, you didn't have to cook all of this grub," Reo said as he kissed his mom on the cheek.

Whenever Reo was in town, he ate dinner with his mother and father every Sunday. It was a tradition. Before he got involved in the literary game he and Meka had never missed a Sunday.

"Good, because I didn't," his mother replied. "Your father cooked today. He put it in the Crock-Pot before we went to church. Which reminds me, you haven't been to church in a while."

"Momma, you know I'm always out of town on weekends."

"Well, you're in town this weekend."

"Mom," Reo said, as if begging for a break.

"I mean it now, Reo. Don't think you got it going on so much you can't come to church and praise the Lord. Sure, you've been blessed with a lot of nice things. You've shared your blessings unselfishly, too. Your father and I are more than grateful for this fancy house you bought us, the maid, cars, and everything else. But remember, son, He giveth and He taketh away."

"Hey, now," Reo's father said as he entered the kitchen.

"Hey, Pops," Reo said as he hugged his father and kissed him on the cheek.

"Is your momma Bible-beating you?"

"She was fixin' to throw a couple of jabs," Reo said as he balled his fist and did some play fighting by punching the air.

"Umm hmm," Reo's mother continued. "Make fun all you want. Remember that pair of pliers that made all that money entertaining folks and then went bankrupt?"

"Momma, what are you talking about?" Reo asked.

"Don't play stupid with me," she said. "Some people relish in monetary and material things and think that they are set for life. Next thing you know, zip, zero, zilch."

"But pliers, Momma?" Reo said.

"You know the guy. He wore them trash-bag pants and had a whole army on the stage with him when he performed."

"MC Hammer," Reo and his father said at the same time.

"Whatever. Y'all know more about that worldly music than I do," his mother replied with an eye roll. "Just don't get too big for your britches. Give praise every chance you get."

"Oh, lay off of the boy," Reo's father said in Reo's defense. "The church isn't always a building with folks trying to outdress one another and speaking in tongues. The church is a man's heart, too, you know."

"Is that how you feel about our holy temple?" Reo's mother asked. "Why do you bother stepping foot in it then?"

"Do you know how many men are up in there specifically

looking for a fine woman like yourself?" he answered. "If I let you go up in there alone I'll end up a single man." He winked at Reo.

"Don't try to flatter me. It's the Lord you need to be flattering," she replied.

"Next Sunday, Momma, I promise," Reo said kissing her on the cheek. "Next Sunday for sure."

From: RLQ812@sunset.com
To: KAT@myworld.biz
Subject: Getting To Know You

You are not going to believe this in a million years. My favorite song is "Overjoyed" by Stevie Wonder. Now my favorite remix ever is Biggie's "Give Me One More Chance." My favorite movie is a toss up between "Love Jones" and "Love and Basketball." My favorite book is "Dollar Bill" by Reo Laroque. I really don't have a favorite food, but I can stand the taste of anything sweet. You're sweet, aren't you?

Did I make you blush? Good, then I'm doing my job.

When I'm not working I enjoy reading and especially writing. Looks like we have a great deal in common. So tell me a little bit more about yourself, KAT (smile).

When is your birthday? What do you like to do for fun? How many kids do you have again? How old are they? What about your family, any brothers and sisters?

I bet you think I'm writing a biography on you (LOL). I just want to get to know you better.

Talk at ya later!
P.S. I hope I didn't make you wait too long.

. . .

"It's a woman!" Reo exclaimed to Nate who had just arrived at Reo's house for a game of chess. "She likes candlelit bubble baths and reading."

"Hmm, a romantic," Nate said as he handed Reo a bottle of J. Roget.

"Man, she's the one," Reo said as he sat the bottle down next to the chess game on his Philippines wood coffee table that had once been a door. Reo admired unique furniture and laced his home with such items. The table was fixed across a sheepskin rug that he had purchased from a French flea market while on vacation with his parents in France.

"Slow down, son. Give me a light," Nate said as he pulled out his hand-rolled cigar and ran it under his nose for a whiff. Nate was one of those cool cats. He dressed crisp clean and sharp. He always smelled good. He carried around a leather flap bag to keep his personals in, versus a wallet. He had the word *classy* written all over him.

Nate and Reo became acquainted via their online writer's group, the Black Writer's Alliance. Reo had been a member for some time before Nate got his membership. When Nate joined, the welcome e-mail that was sent to all the current members showed that he lived in Columbus, Ohio, also. Reo thought it would be cool to have someone local to work with, pass ideas back and forth and edit each other's writings and whatnot. Reo hit him up offline and they'd been friends ever since.

"I just can't stop thinking about her," Reo said.

"She could be tore up, man," Nate said, lighting his cigar with the pack of matches Reo handed him that he had gotten from a club called the Milk Bar while touring in Dallas, Texas.

"Nah, she's one of the beautiful ones. I can tell by her words."

"See, that's why I write nonfiction and you write fiction. I keep it real and you make up shit people want to hear."

"What do you do before you come over to my house? Drink a gallon of hateraide? You never have anything positive to say."

"The truth ain't always positive, nigga. It is what it is. Now get pussy off your mind, get us some glasses, and let me whoop your ass in dis here game."

"Naw, you got it wrong. It's the other way around. I'm 'bout to whoop your ass."

"I didn't hear you talking trash last time you lost."

"Well, this is a whole new game and I damn near got your move sequence memorized."

"But I'm like the L.A. Lakers, nigga. I dominate back to back."

"Well, all good things come to an end," Reo said, lightweight slamming the champagne glasses down. "And stop calling me nigga!"

From: KAT@myworld.biz
To: RLQ812@sunset.com
Subject: More About Me

Hey you,

Hmm, where should I start? Let's see: No, I don't believe in a million years that Stevie Wonder just happens to be the artist of our favorite songs; yes, I'm sweet, very sweet if you'll allow my ego a moment to come out and play; and yes, you did make me blush, so job well done. Remind me to talk to you about a raise.

My birthday is February 12 (you didn't think I was going to offer the year did you?:=) What do I like to do for fun? I'm a woman. Shopping. What else?

I have two children, a preteen daughter and a ten-year-old son. I have two sisters, no brothers. My sisters live in different states. Careers, education and/or a spouse led them there. What about yourself? Do you have any siblings?

Well, Mr. Writer, since you like writing in your spare time, and I like to read, write me something. Write me something I can read during my next candlelit bath. Don't hold back.

KAT
P.S. I just love that nickname (wink).

"That was a nice sermon, Reverend Sandy," Reo said shaking his pastor's hand. Service had just ended and Reo stopped by her office to chat.

"Well, I'm glad you enjoyed it," the reverend replied sitting at her desk. "Three weeks in a row I've seen you out in the congregation. You haven't gone and run out of things to write about, have you?"

"Oh, no," Reo laughed.

"Must be a woman," Reverend Sandy said, getting serious as she looked at Reo from over the top of her eyeglasses.

"Excuse me, Reverend," Reo said surprised.

"You done found yourself a wife, Reo?" Reverend Sandy asked.

"You know what, Reverend? I think I have. The only thing is, I don't even know who she is."

"You're going to have to explain that one to me. You haven't been communicating with that Miss Cleo, have you?"

"No, Reverend." Reo laughed. "It's nothing like that. It's just that I've been communicating with this woman on the computer who I've never met in person."

"Oh, Lord. I would rather it had been some business with Miss Cleo than an Internet rat."

"Reverend, Sandy!" Reo said shocked. "And in the Lord's house at that."

"You don't think I know about all those Big Boob Bambis and Luscious Lip Lindas on those Internet pay sites?"

"Ah ha ha. It's not anything like that either. It's a woman who I connected with sort of by accident. See, she sent me an e-mail that was really meant for someone else."

"And instead of you just deleting it or advising her that she misdirected the e-mail," the Reverend interrupted, "you replied to it and now she has no idea she's not communicating with the person she had originally intended to receive that e-mail."

"Now who's been messing around with Miss Cleo?" Reo laughed.

"If this person is meant to be your wife, then you've already started off on the wrong foot."

"I know, Reverend. I just have to find the right time to work in the truth in our e-mails."

"Don't wait too long. Before you know it you'll bury yourself in lies."

"I'm going to clean it up, Reverend, and I know everything is going to work out. She and I have so much in common. She's like a gift from God. I was just starting to think that I was going to be a bachelor forever. I want what my mom and pops have. I want to come to church every Sunday . . ."

The reverend cleared her throat.

"I mean, every Sunday that I can, with my wife on my arm."

"Sounds good, Reo. I do hope everything works out for you. I'm just going to ask you to remember just one thing."

"Sure, Reverend. What is it?"

"That every gift isn't always from God."

From: RLQ@812sunset.com
To: KAT@myworld.biz
Subject: What's Your Pleasure

What's Your Pleasure?
Stark and startling I appear with all inhibitions flung
Standing before you bold, butt naked, and nicely hung
Verbalizing a sensual verse of late
Watching you bite your bottom lip, drool, and salivate
Figuratively speaking you go into a head spin and do back flips
Anxiously moving about like a cat that craves catnip
With an intensifying urge, that in time, does not ease
Because at a respectable distance my nakedness is a tortuous
    tease
Moving ever closer to you while gettin' my prose on
My nakedness grinds against your body, with all of your
    clothes on
With the inviting vibes that you're throwing, I am a receiver
I touch your forehead, you're hot, you have a fever
Feverously horny you are; my eyes you intently watch
All the while guiding my hand to a now-moist crotch
And while through your clothes, I massage your treasure
In a soft, strong male tone, I whisper, "What's your pleasure?"

I kiss you and massage your crotch a few moments more
You moan and breathe heavily from the passionate outpour

Your pussy in my hand, your tongue in my mouth, this I adore
Suddenly, your clothes magically fall to the floor
Mind opening is the mental/physical erotic ajarment
As I see the floor littered with sexy, girly undergarments
Still with a handful of twat, with a feel of derriere
I see a strapless bra here, pair of panties there
Here we be, as hot as two hot toddies
Two awaiting startling stark naked bodies
Up against one another, grinding away
Each waiting for the other to move beyond the arousing fore-
    play
With my endowed maleness stiffening, the candle is lit
Using the head of my shaft to titillate your clit
Teasing you as I tease myself, teasing measure for measure
As I hold you, and your eyes are closed, I whisper, "What's
    your pleasure?"

At the second asking, there wasn't much in the way of decidin'
Just like your eyes, the gap between your legs widened
Guiding my rod into you slowly, savoring the feel
Letting out a blow as if you're blowing hot oatmeal
We start up a rhythm, let the pace advance
Before long I'm pumping into you, and we start to dance
Backing you against a wall to which your ass, I pin
And your expression is more of a grimace than a grin
With each thrust, and intended pussy pounce
I jar your body and make your titties bounce
As I fuck your lovely femaleness, sweet and tender
We both approach the orgasmic experience to which we will
    ultimately surrender
with a mean look on your face, set like the stones of Stonehenge

Your expression is that of an angry woman out for revenge
Working this groove without a hitch
Instead of screaming my name, you yell, "FUCK ME LIKE I'M
 A BADASS BITCH!!!"

Shocked and amazed at what I was to hear
I get excited and throw it into high gear
Intensity growing hotter and bolder
So much so, you bury your head into my shoulder
One hand grabs my back, the other my ass
Grips and squeezes as I repeatedly impale you with my male
 mass
That makes you groan and utter about
And erotically, fuckingly cuss me out
"UH . . . UH, UH . . . AHHH . . . OOOOOOH!!!"
You jump, you jerk, you twitch, you squirm, you bounce, you
 squeeze, you coo
As I bring you to orgasm, to me your twat convulsions serenade
Making the neighbors blush as I juice your pussy like lemonade
I continue to fuck you with your eyes wide open, feeding my
 sexual consumption
Fucking you, loving you, as the white lava spews from my
 eruption
Slowing the pace, and still hard from these gestures
I'm ready for round two baby, so tell me . . . What's your plea-
 sure?

Once again Reo was back at the Afro-American Bookstop at the
New Orleans Centre Mall. Besides Ujamaa and Zawadi Bookstores in his hometown, they were one of the other few bookstores
willing to host a book signing for Reo when he was selling his

self-published books out of his trunk. The owner even squeezed him in during the Essence Music Festival, when author time slots were in high demand.

Today, though, was Reo's first time signing at the store when he had brought out such a large crowd.

The line stretched from the store down to the main mallway and almost to the food court. There had to be over three hundred people waiting to meet and greet him. Reo felt like the Ali of the literary world.

Of all those folks in line, one woman in particular stood out. She was with her two friends, chatting, then all of a sudden, she was staring right into his eyes.

This woman had to be one of the most beautiful women Reo had ever laid eyes on. Reo sized her up to be about five feet and nine inches tall. She had jet black, shoulder-length curly hair. She had to be about a 38 D bra size, with a waist he could almost fit his hands around . . . and that ass was banging. This chick was Bonita Applebum in the flesh.

As all the other readers in line began to notice that the guest author had arrived, Reo was followed by the crescendo of their applause. He couldn't take his eyes off of this particular woman, though.

He made his way to the table, where he was greeted by the bookstore's friendly staff. He didn't waste any time prepping. He immediately began pen-whipping those books. Some people didn't have money to purchase a book that day. They simply stood in line to congratulate him on his success with promises to return to purchase his book on payday. He thanked them and supplied them with bookmarks and autographed postcards.

It seemed as though Reo had signed a million books before the woman he had made eye contact with reached him. Her two girlfriends, who were in line before her, praised and flirted with Reo. He smiled, nodded, and stared at their lady friend. He couldn't have moved the two groupies along fast enough. Then finally she stepped up to the table. Reo opened the book to the title page and smiled up at her.

"Who am I signing this to?" Reo asked her.

"Tuesday," the woman replied. "You can sign it to Tuesday."

"Is that you?" Reo asked.

"How'd you guess?" the woman asked with a sexy eyewink.

Reo smiled. "Are you from here, Tuesday?"

"Not originally. But I live here now. I was born in Atlanta."

"Oh, you're a Southern girl. With a name like Tuesday I was sure you were going to say you were from the West Coast or something."

"Don't you hear that Southern twang in my voice, mista?" she said, emphasizing her accent even more.

"Stop teasing me. As a matter of fact, don't stop," Reo said, teasing right back.

"How long are you going to be in the Big Easy?" she asked.

"I'm just in town for the weekend," Reo replied.

"Well," Tuesday said, grabbing the pen out of his hand. She dabbed the tip of the pen on her tongue and began writing on one of Reo's postcards. "This is how you can get ahold of me this weekend."

"Let me guess, you want to show me around."

She smiled seductively.

"I can show you a few things. For now though, just watch me walk away."

Tuesday handed Reo his pen back and slowly walked away with book in hand. Her white form-fitting Capri accented her hips. She was shaped like a pear, and Reo couldn't wait to take a bite.

The remainder of the book signing was like a scene from *The Matrix*. Reo was moving as fast as lightning. He moved the line right along, scribbling the standard "Best Wishes" and "Peace and Blessings."

When Reo got to his hotel the first thing he did was phone Tuesday. Of course, it was her cell phone number. She didn't pick up so he left a message. He told her where he was staying and left her the hotel phone number. He checked the messages on his cell phone and then signed onto his computer to check his e-mails.

From: KAT@myworld.biz
To: RLQ@sunset.com
Subject: What's Your Pleasure

Hey you,

What are you up to? Me, I'm just sitting here drying off. I'm still just a tad wet from that poem you sent me (wink). What can I say? You've got skills.

Did you write that poem specifically for me? I hope so. If not, there's a lucky girl out there somewhere. I'd love to write you a poem as well, only I'm not that great of a writer. I guess I'll have to show you better than I can tell you.

Whoa, it's getting hot in herre.

I hope I'm not getting too personal, but there's just something about you that makes me feel as if I can tell you and ask you anything. For instance, what's your favorite position? I like being on top, backwards. There ain't nothin' like a good rodeo show.

You'll have to forgive me. I hope I'm not offending you. I know how some men like to be the sole instigators when it comes to sex, with very little feedback from the opposing party. That's where I'm a little different than most women. I like taking charge every now and again. Maybe someday you'll find out. You never know when we just might run into each other again. It could happen.

KAT

Reo closed his eyes and cupped his pulsing manhood. He envisioned KAT riding him like he was a champion horse and she was the jockey. He decided to go for the full act so he unzipped his pants and pulled out *Simmy*. Before he could get down to business the hotel phone rang, disrupting his groove.

"Hello," Reo said.

"What are you wearing?" the voice on the other end moaned.

"Excuse me?" Reo said.

"What are you wearing? I'm wearing a black trench coat with clear high-heeled open-toe pumps."

"Tuesday, is that you?" Reo asked.

"How many women know where to find you?"

"Besides my mother, only one other woman."

"Then I'm that woman, and you know what, Reo?" she said in her most alluring tone.

"Why don't you tell me, baby," Reo said as he began to stroke *Simmy*.

"I'm right outside your door."

"Stop playing."

"Baby, I don't play. I flunked kindergarten because I don't play."

Reo walked over to the door and peeped out the peephole. There stood Tuesday. He could see the collar of her coat standing as erect as *Simmy* was. Her hair was clipped up with spit curl strands falling about. He could see the glow of her lip gloss that covered a deep path of lip liner around her lips.

"Damn," Reo said out loud.

"You didn't believe me?" Tuesday said looking directly at the peephole as if she could see Reo looking at her through it.

"No, it's not that I didn't believe you. Damn, you look good."

"I must not look good enough," Tuesday said.

"Why is that?"

"Because I'm still standing out here."

"Oh, my fault," Reo said as he put *Simmy* away and zipped his pants back up. He got so goosey acting that he pulled the phone off of the desk, which made the receiver jerk out of his hand. He picked the phone up and placed it back on the desk. "Sorry about that, I'm coming now."

"Don't cum yet. Let me in first."

Reo hung up the receiver and opened the door. There stood Tuesday in a black, three-quarters length trench coat. He followed her chocolate legs all the way down to her clear slippers. She was like a Cinderella right out of *Playboy*.

"Hi," Reo said, licking his lips.

"Right back at ya," Tuesday said as she stepped into the hotel room.

Reo closed the door behind her and began to straighten up the room a little. He walked over to his laptop to log off. KAT's message was still on the screen. He paused for a moment. All of a sudden he felt bad. He felt as though he was cheating on her and here he didn't even know his penpal's real name. Tuesday could detect the change in Reo's attitude.

"Is something wrong?" Tuesday asked.

"Uh, no. Nothing's wrong."

"It looked as though your mind wandered off there for a moment."

"No, I was just thinking of something I forgot to do," Reo said.

"Don't worry," Tuesday said as she pulled a string of condoms from her coat pocket. "I've got you covered." She grinned a naughty grin and started kissing Reo all over as she began to peel his clothing off of him.

Reo remembered that he hadn't had a chance to shower yet. As Tuesday made her way to removing his pants he grabbed both her wrists to stop her.

"What's the matter?" she asked.

"Baby, let me get cleaned up. I just got back from the bookstore and I haven't had a chance to take a shower or anything yet. I won't be long. Why don't you order room service and a movie?"

"That's fine with me. Do you need me to wash your back?"

"You save your energy for other things."

Reo handed Tuesday the room-service menu and gave her the remote to the television. He went over to the closet and grabbed some khaki shorts and a short-sleeved henley, then proceeded into the bathroom. Even though he knew he was about to get down with Tuesday, he didn't want to come out of the bathroom in the buff.

As the water from the shower massager beat on Reo's chest he couldn't get KAT off of his mind. A beautiful damn-near-naked woman was waiting on him in the other room and a stranger occupied his thoughts.

After Reo showered, performed his particulars, and got dressed, he once again joined Tuesday. Room service arrived merely seconds later. Tuesday had ordered some wine, chocolate-covered strawberries, and a cheese-and-cracker plate. They drank a couple glasses of wine, nibbled on the food, and then had meaningless conversation followed by meaningless sex.

"When is the last time you got you some?" Tuesday asked in a joking tone. "My shit is probably swollen. I'm going to have to go home and take a seltzer bath."

"I'm sorry. I thought it felt good to you," Reo said licking his lips.

"Oh, it felt good all right," Tuesday said in a sensual tone.

"Good, now maybe you can give me back my skin from underneath your nails." They both laughed as Tuesday went into the bathroom to clean up. She came back out a few moments later and put on her coat and shoes.

"It's been real, Mr. Laroque. You'll have to make sure you give me a call the next time you're in town. I'd love to do business with you again," Tuesday said, running her tongue across her teeth.

"Fo sure," Reo said.

"Your total comes to fifteen hundred dollars," Tuesday said, holding out her hand.

"That's cute," Reo said getting up and slipping on his shorts. "I'll walk you down to the lobby."

"No, you're cute, Mr. Laroque. Now, just pay your tab and I'll let Benjamin walk me down to the lobby."

Reo couldn't believe he had been bamboozled. He would have never imagined that Tuesday was a call girl. He ended up having to walk Tuesday down to the lobby anyway because he was a few hundred dollars short and the lobby had an ATM machine. There was no need for Reo to try to argue with her. All it would have done was cause a major episode, or even caught him a case. But there was one thing Reo was certain of—he was taking this one to the grave.

Nate would have never let Reo live down the fact that he had been tricked, literally. Reo had to force himself to look at the bright side. Hell, Tuesday could have turned out to be a man instead of a call girl. Reo was cool with the latter.

"Nate, man, I mean all of a sudden I just started feeling guilty," Reo said as he phoned Nate with the details of his latest one-night stand.

"All I know is if you tell me you didn't hit that because of some computer love, I'm revoking your playa license," Nate responded.

"Oh, I hit it all right. I didn't go down on her or anything like that though."

"No foreplay. She must have been a hairy one."

"You got it!"

"Will somebody please tell all these women out here that they will get a man to go down on them more often if they keep that shit bald?" Nate yelled.

"At least fade that muthafucker," Reo added.

"I ain't mad at you, dawg. So what's been up with you and your mystery woman anyway?"

"I'm still diggin' her. She must feel the same about me. We've sent each other a thousand e-mails."

"She must be married."

"Why do you say that?"

"She ain't asked for your phone number, cell number, pager, or nothing. She hasn't given you hers, either. Something ain't right."

"See, there you go. I haven't even asked her for her phone number yet, for your information," Reo said angrily. "If I try to call her then she'll know I have a phone. She'll ask me for my number. Once she finds out that I have a 614 area code she'll know something is up."

"Well, it looks like you are going to have to go to New York just to make a phone call."

"I could get me a New York cell phone and have the calls forwarded to my Columbus phone."

"Okay, you just got two points taken from your playa license. I was just going to let you off with a warning this time, but I see I got to give your ass a citation."

"I was just hypothetically speaking. I wouldn't really go through all of that."

"Well, you thought about it and that's bad enough."

"I just don't know what to do. I have to think of something quick."

"Ride the wave."

"Is that all you have to say? Nothing slick this time?"

"Do you think you might be falling in love with this chick?" Nate asked Reo.

"I know it sounds crazy, but I think so. Well, I think I'm in love with the idea of being in love with her. With her being a mystery to me, I get to make her the woman I want her to be. It's easier to like someone who's not in your face getting on your nerves every day, you know what I mean?"

"Naw, man. My wife's mean ass keeps me rooted. Do you have any idea how many times I might have made some fucked-up decisions if it wasn't for my fear of hearing her mouth? You talk about something sounding crazy, I don't even look at other women the wrong way anymore. I feel guilty when you tell me stories about you fucking."

"Persia got your ass whipped." Reo laughed. "And you haven't even been married a year yet."

"Persia don't take no shit. Out of all the women I have dated, I came to realize why my and Persia's relationship worked out so well. I realized why I never fucked around on her."

"Oh, then you better keep that under lock and key because you've got the answer to the twenty-five-million-dollar question."

"I'm serious," Nate said.

"So, tell me. What did Persia do to keep you an honest man?"

"It's what she didn't do," Nate answered.

"And what was that?"

"Compromise. She never compromised for me."

"What?"

"She never compromised herself. I ain't talking about small shit like I want cheeseburgers and she wants hamburgers so hamburgers it is. I'm talking about stuff other women compromise every day."

"Like what?" Reo inquired on the edge of his seat.

"Well, take a woman whose dude doesn't come home until four o'clock in the morning. His lying ass tells her that he was just out driving around, listening to his music. She accepts it. She knows damn well it's a lie, but yet she accepts it. She might fuss and argue about it, but in the end she accepts it and then her man turns right around and does it again. This time his lying ass talkin' about he went to the Waffle House after the club. She accepts it. She compromises her beliefs and what she knows to be true."

"Okay, I'm feeling you," Reo said.

"Now take the woman who has the potential nigga," Nate continued.

"Who's that?"

"That nigga that ain't got nothing but potential. He ain't got a car, but he has the potential to get one. He ain't got his own house, but he has the potential to get one. Hell, the potential nigga ain't even got a job, but he has the potential to get one."

"Okay, okay," Reo said.

"His woman is letting him drive her car around and live up in her house rent free. When she goes out of town she actually leaves this nigga money to kick it with while she's gone. Now she wants to cry and complain to her girlfriends because she compromised her own shit. A woman should never ever compromise herself for no man. Once she starts, it never stops. It's like letting a man hit her. If she allows it once, he's going to do it again."

"That's true."

"A lot of niggas get confused as to what a good woman is. They think that a woman who is always compromising for their sorry ass is a good woman. They think that her allowing him to get away with so much dirt makes her a good woman. They got it wrong. A good woman is going to keep that ass in check."

"Some men do have it twisted. Because a woman allows for some man to hit on her don't make her a good woman. Because a woman allows for some man to spend all her money up and cheat on her don't make her a good woman," Reo added.

"Like you say in your book, homie. It makes him a dawg."

"That's the most sense you've made in the two years I've known you."

"I'm not the author of *The Rule Book* for nothing," Nate said in a confident tone.

From: RLQ812@sunset.com
To: KAT@myworld.biz
Subject: The Poem

I'm glad you enjoyed the poem. Of course it was written especially for you. You told me to write you something so that is exactly what I did. Your every wish is my command. But on another note, me personally, I like to hit it from the back. I like to lay my prey on her stomach and enter. I like to pin her arms down and plant kisses on the nape of her neck. I like to cum deep. Did you feel that?

This doesn't seem quite fair. I want some reciprocity, some quid pro quo, a tit for a tat . . . write me something. It doesn't have to be publishing quality. Just write me something my imagination can dance to. I want to know more than just what you like. I want to imagine what it's like to be inside of you. So tell me, what's it like?

Also, e-mail me a picture of you. I need a new screen saver.

From: KAT@myworld.biz
To: RLQ812@sunset.com
Subject: The Poem

Hey you,
Imagine this: You ask what it feels like to be inside of me.
Well, with words, it's hard to explain.
Imagine the wind grazing a leaf.
Imagine clouds releasing rain.

And every move you make, like a Broadway production, is cho-
    reographed so well.
Imagine a flower blooming.
Imagine rolling off your tongue a secret you promised not to tell.

It's a desired imprisonment, the weight of your body holding
    down mine.
Imagine the anchor of a glass ferry.
Imagine a cork securing the freshness of a wine.

I anticipate the pliant kisses you apply upon my portions
within your reach.
Imagine the landing of a snowflake.
Imagine the fleecy skin of a peach.

The moisture created between us two when we become one is
passionate and warm.
Imagine mist on a 110-degree afternoon.
Imagine the sticky honey of a comb where bees swarm.

Each time we climb the mountain it's like the first time no
matter how many times before we've reached the top.
Imagine waking up every morning.
Imagine if the Earth's rotation just stopped.

Imagine what it feels like to be inside of me.
Imagine that.

Attachment: Photodoc.1

From: RLQ812@sunset.com
To: KAT@myworld.biz
Subject: Picture

The picture you sent is stunning. You are so beautiful. Your
pretty brown eyes sing songs. I fell asleep to the rhythm.
    The same way I feel like I've known you all of my life, I feel
like I've seen you before. It must have been in my dreams.
    My imagination did more than a jig to your words. Damn,

girl. My water bill isn't going to be nothing nice with all the trips to the cold shower you've sent me on. This is crazy, the way I'm feeling about you. This is crazy!

From: KAT@myworld.biz
To: RLQ812@sunset.com
Subject: Picture

Hey you,

Thanks for the compliment. I'm blushing again.

You have seen me somewhere before, Silly, the Boston airport. Your sense of humor is just another attribute that's making me fall head over heels for you.

I'm glad you liked the poem, but I have a confession to make. I got it out of a book of poetry by Joylynn M. Jossel titled "Flower in My Hair." But just because I didn't make it up myself doesn't mean they weren't my words. I was thinking them, it's just that she beat me to the punch in writing them down.

You never did tell me about your family, if you have children or any brothers and sisters. Mr. Reciprocity, how about a picture of yourself?

KAT

From: RLQ812@sunset.com
To: KAT@myworld.biz
Subject: Hello

I wish I did have a pic to send you right now. I'll have to unpack and find a good one or get one taken just for you. Yeah, that's what I'll do. I'll go out and get one just for you, KAT, to go along with that poem I wrote just for you.

I'm an only child. I don't have any children, although my parents are hounding me about getting a girlfriend to at least get the ball rolling. They want me to give them some grand-children soon.

From: KAT@myworld.biz
To: RLQ812@sunset.com
Subject: Hello

Hey, you.

Well, you answered my next question, which was going to be are you married. One never knows.

An only child, huh? You must be spoiled rotten. But that's okay, I'd love to spoil you too.

From: RLQ812@sunset.com
To: KAT@myworld.biz
Subject: Single

Nah, I'm not married. I was engaged before to my high school sweetheart. It's a long story. I'll tell you some other time.

From: KAT@myworld.biz
To: RLQ812@sunset.com
Subject: Single

Hey you,

Actually, I'm not too fond of hearing about exes. I find that in the future that does damage to a relationship. Frankly, I don't give a damn about her. You're my concern now.

But just so that you know. I've been married before, twice. It's my past. I have no intentions of showering you with details of my ex-lovers. I hope you'll spare me the same.

From: RLQ812@sunset.com
To: KAT@myworld.biz
Subject: Friends

Who do you keep company with? Do you have many friends?

From: KAT@myworld.biz
To: RLQ812@sunset.com
Subject: Friends

I have two best friends, Jeva and Breezy. Breezy and I have been friends the longest, for about ten years now. Breezy met Jeva a few years ago and we've both been friends with her ever since.

What about you?

From: RLQ812@sunset.com
To: KAT@myworld.biz
Subject: Friends

My closest partner is named Nate. He and I have only been friends for a couple of years.

Do you tell your girlfriends about me? What do you tell them?

From: KAT@myworld.biz
To: RLQ812@sunset.com
Subject: Conversation Piece

You're not vain are you (LOL)? You just got straight to the point.

You want to know if you're worthy of girl talk, huh? Allow me to put your mind at ease. You are a great conversation piece. I tell my girlfriends all about you. Of course, they think I'm crazy. They don't understand how I can possibly dig you as much as I do just from communicating mainly over the Internet.

Why don't you call me? My number is 419-777-9311. You can even call collect.

What about me? Am I a good conversation piece?

From: RLQ812@sunset.com
To: KAT@myworld.biz
Subject: Conversation Piece

You are more than a good conversation piece. Woman, I've even talked to my reverend about you.

People think I'm crazy too. Hell, sometimes I think I'm crazy. It's amazing that two people can become so close. The written word is a true gift from God. Look at how much we're learning about one another just by writing each other back and forth. Some married people don't know as much about each other as we know and will continue to learn.

I was with my ex for years and I'm learning more about you than I knew about her. It just goes to show you how one can benefit from being confined to one source of communication.

P.S. That's the last you'll hear about my ex . . . I promise! What do you do for a living besides sit around looking beautiful?

From: KAT@myworld.biz
To: RLQ812@sunset.com
Subject: Work

I do work for a printing company.

From: RLQ812@sunset.com
To: KAT@myworld.biz
Subject: Work

You mean like Kinko's?

From: KAT@myworld.biz
To: RLQ812@sunset.com
Subject: Work

Pretty much.

Reo had to buy himself some time and continue ignoring the fact that KAT had e-mailed him her phone number. Once he researched the 419 area code and discovered that Klarke resided basically in his own backyard, he knew she was heaven-sent. Toledo was only a two-hour drive from Columbus.

Reo didn't know how he was going to get out of not calling KAT. He knew from the moment she provided him with her phone number, every time her phone rang she would be expecting his voice on the other end. If only he knew what would show up, if anything, on her caller ID box if he was to call her. What if it showed up "Ohio Call?" She might think he was some stalker calling from her own basement.

Not wanting to appear as though he was a bugaboo anyhow, Reo stalled on calling KAT. He proceeded with the e-mails as if she had never supplied him with her phone number. They continued e-mailing back and forth and forth and back. He decided that he would wait for her to bring it up again.

8

It Takes Two

Breezy couldn't decide whether to wear her low-cut black Donna Karan dress or her paisley-printed Spiegel skort set. She never knew what Hydrant had in store for her when they went out. One time she got all decked out in her Armani skirt suit and to her surprise he took her on an evening picnic by lantern in the park. It was quite romantic of him, but it pissed Breezy off that she had wasted the most expensive outfit in her closet. Not that she had paid for it or anything like that. It's just the fact that she wouldn't be able to wear it again on a date with him, plus she had wanted to be seen out on the town in it.

On another occasion Breezy decided to sport the hottest little Baby Phat outfit she could fit her body into. The hookup brought out all the flavor in her, but no one ended up seeing her in that outfit either. Hydrant waited until he got to Breezy's house to pick her up for the date to decide he wanted to spend the evening cuddled up. He could be such a softy at times, but damn, how Breezy loathed wasting good outfits, especially that Armani one.

Breezy had lucked up on the Armani garb on a trip to Las Vegas. Breezy's job sent her to an insurance fraud seminar at the Bellagio hotel last winter. All expenses were paid. It only cost her eight hours a day of being bored out of her mind with lectures.

During one of the seminars the lecturer asked a question regarding red flags on fraudulent claims. Breezy raised her hand to answer the question, which she correctly did. She was given a $250 gambling chip. Breezy hadn't really done any gambling that entire trip, but since it was no money out of her pocket, she decided to play the slots. Breezy randomly picked out a $5 slot machine and put in a single coin. Her dad had always told her to find one machine, and if it paid off after the first few spins, stick with it all night.

On Breezy's first spin the son of a gun went jackpot. She couldn't believe it. She was jumping up and down screaming and causing all sorts of commotion. There were jealous onlookers who were down to their last dime and here she came out of nowhere to win five thousand dollars.

Breezy was escorted to the cashier, where she eagerly collected her winnings. She was glowing like a full moon at midnight. This radiance attracted an older-looking gentleman who was playing the blackjack table. As Breezy walked by, he neglected the dealer and did a one-eighty to speak to her.

"Congratulations to the lady," the gentleman said. Breezy couldn't help but notice that he was playing with a stack of chips identical to her $250 chip. She also couldn't help but capture a glimpse of his Rolex watch.

"Good evening," Breezy said.

"Do you think you could step over here so that some of your luck could rub off on me?" the gentleman joked.

"That means I'd have to rub on you."

"Whatever works. But seriously, I'm going broke here. I guess gambling just isn't my thing. While I still have a penny to my name let's say I treat you to dinner tonight."

"Oh, I get it," Breezy said, pretending as though she hadn't noticed his stack of chips or his expensive jewelry. "You just saw me win all of that money and you're inviting me out to dinner. Let's see if I get this right . . . we'll get to the restaurant and you'll say you forgot your wallet and I'll end up paying for our three-hundred-dollar meals. Well, let me save you the time," Breezy said as she stripped her wad of money of three one-hundred-dollar bills and threw them at the gentleman's feet. She then walked away. She knew he wouldn't be far behind. There was no way her sassy ass didn't just make him bust a nut. So she walked away praying he'd bring her back that three hundred dollars.

"Hold up, now," the gentleman said as he signaled for one of the men with him to watch his chips. He leaped from the stool, picked up the three hundred dollars, and went after Breezy. "Don't be so mean, Miss Lady. Here, you dropped something."

He handed Breezy her three one-hundred-dollar bills.

"Thanks," she said, taking it and then turning away to continue her strut.

"Just dinner," he said, hurrying after her. "I'll send a car for you out front in two hours. It will take you to the Stratosphere. Meet me in the line for the restaurant On Top of the World."

"You took a gamble coming after me, huh?" Breezy asked, stopping in her tracks.

"Yes, I did," the gentleman said approaching her.

"In that case, you're right, gambling isn't your thing."

Breezy continued to walk away with a killer grin on her face. The gentleman followed close behind her.

"How do you know I'm even staying at this hotel?" Breezy

said as she once again stopped in her tracks, nearly causing him to run into her.

"Because we all are. I've only been in seminars with you for the past three days."

"Commissioner of the Nevada Insurance Department," Breezy said, realizing who he was. "I'm so embarrassed right now."

Breezy held out her hand to shake the commissioner's hand. His strong grip and mature features sent a faint shiver through Breezy's body. His jet-black hair with strands of gray was very becoming.

"Don't be. You are in Sin City, after all. You can't just be accepting dinner invitations with any ole body," the commissioner said, kissing Breezy's hand.

"I would love to go to dinner with you, Commissioner, but this is our last night here. Look at me. I'm a mess," Breezy said, pointing at her business-casual attire. "The only other outfit I have to wear is what I'm wearing on the plane home tomorrow."

"Hmm, I guess we do have a problem. Here, take this," he said, handing her his hotel cash card. "Stop off at one of the hotel shops. Grab yourself something nice to wear. Charge it to my room. Two hours," he said, walking away.

This was Breezy's lucky day. She would have been a fool to stop off at any other shop but Armani's. She felt like Pretty Woman. The suit she picked out was sharp and the commissioner was pleased. They had a lovely dinner as the revolving restaurant allowed them to see the glittering, flashing beauty of Vegas.

The commissioner didn't even try to push up on Breezy. It might have had something to do with the fact that he had a wife at home. Nonetheless they shared hours of conversation before they parted, with him giving Breezy a simple kiss on the cheek outside of her hotel room door. The next morning upon checkout, a dozen red roses with a card that said *Have a safe flight*, signed by the commissioner, was left for Breezy at the front desk.

Breezy never communicated with the commissioner again. She never forgot him, either. She thought about the commissioner every time she opened her closet and looked at that Armani suit. And tonight was one of those times as she contemplated what to wear on her date with Hydrant.

Hydrant could care less about what Breezy was wearing, but she really wanted to look good for him. Most important, she wanted to look good for herself. Why she tried so hard to impress Hydrant was beyond her own reason. Hydrant was cool people, but he lacked the class that normally attracted Breezy to her men.

Hydrant fooled Breezy by looking so fly the night she met him. The diamonds in his ears lit up the joint. Breezy was certain he had a little *amour propre*. She met him at a First Friday happy hour affair. He was styling a royal blue suit with matching gators that had all the women sniffing behind him.

Breezy loved how he was shooting all the females down with suavity. She felt as though she was looking at the male version of herself. He felt the same way about Breezy as he noticed her putting the fellas in their place.

Breezy, being the intrepid woman that she was, stepped to Hydrant because she had to have him. They ended up exchanging phone numbers and hooking up.

The first few times they got together it had been something simple, like him renting a video and the two of them watching it at Breezy's apartment. Other than that, Breezy would perhaps make dinner and Hydrant would clean up the kitchen afterward.

Breezy had never met a man she didn't have to pick up behind. Most men felt that a woman shouldn't mind cleaning up behind them, or that it was her inborn duty. Hydrant took pride in his surroundings and respected Breezy's dwelling.

Her place wasn't that big anyway, so it wasn't like Breezy would have had to break a sweat or anything if she had to pick up after him. Breezy's apartment was more expensive than her salary as an insurance claim tech could afford. But it was conveniently located near the major malls and theaters. She paid far more in rent than it was worth. Her two-bedroom, two-and-a-half-bath place was nice though. She made sure, during her apartment hunt, to get a two-bedroom, just in case she ever accidentally got pregnant or for whenever her imprisoned father was released from jail, whichever came first.

Tidiness was a must for Breezy. Her mother had been strict with her when it came to cleanliness. Hydrant, having been raised the only boy of six children, inherited most of his tidy habits from his sisters. If Hydrant was drinking a beer and failed to use the coaster, he would grab a paper towel and clean up the mist. He cleaned out the shower after every use and wiped down the sink after shaving or brushing his teeth.

When Hydrant dusted he would even go as far as dusting Breezy's picture frames. Breezy had a picture of herself in a wooden frame engraved with her name that was a magnet for dust. He maneuvered the dust rag through every nook and cranny of the frame. For one reason or another, Hydrant's neatness turned Breezy on even more.

After the sixth or seventh date or so, Breezy slept with Hydrant. That was all it took for Hydrant to lasso Breezy in. She had met her equal in bed. Hydrant was the first man to ever fill her up and satisfy her. As a matter of fact, that's why Breezy gave him the nickname Hydrant instead of using his real name, which was Kristopher Long. She told him that was exactly what his dick resembled, a big ole fire hydrant.

After that, all Breezy and Hydrant did was hook up to have sex, and neither of them thought of their relationship beyond that. What did the two have to offer one another besides some good, down-and-dirty sex?

Once Breezy finally did come out of hibernation with Hydrant, she found him to be, in the words of Eddie Murphy, *just a regular ole cracker*. There was nothing major wrong with him. Breezy just found him not to be her typical flavor at all. Klarke had advised Breezy not to pick up any of those men at First Fridays as they were, in her opinion, nothing more than dressed-up thugs.

Hydrant wasn't a thug, but he wasn't the Mr. Suave she first thought him to be, either. As it turned out, that royal blue suit and matching gators Hydrant had been sporting on the night Breezy met him were his only nice fits. Breezy got so tired of seeing him in that getup every time they went out that she broke in a credit card just for him.

Breezy felt as though she was stepping down from her throne to be with Hydrant, but that in the end, he would be worth it. He was like a starter home, a fixer-upper. Breezy had her work cut out for her, but the dick was worth the effort. He was down to earth and lacked drama, no wife, no ex-wife, no babies, and no babies' mammas. For Breezy, being with Hydrant meant that she would have to get used to not getting what she wanted when she wanted it, which was usually right that damn minute. She wasn't accustomed to a man telling her "wait until I get paid." Those words gave her an allergic reaction. She got this sudden tic every time Hydrant would mouth those words.

Breezy tried giving Hydrant up many times. She stopped taking his calls and answering the door if he stopped by, but by then it was too late. She had grown attached to him. They had spent so much time together that they could finish each other's fly-ass sentences. There were things she did adore about him, like his romantic side and his obsession with pleasing her. Even if he couldn't get her what she wanted right then and there, he would always come through eventually.

Breezy craved Hydrant like a pregnant woman craved ice cream. When she had to be done up just right, she knew Hydrant was the go-to man. It was unspoken, but they sort of fell into being a couple.

There was Guy, on the other hand. Talk about a knight in shining armor. This man didn't even give Breezy a chance to ask him for anything before he was showering her with her desires. Guy's generosity was always right on time.

Money was time as far as Guy was concerned. He gave Breezy money as a substitute for the time he couldn't give her. Guy was one of those career-oriented, loving, devoted husbands and fathers. There appeared to be a shortage of those types of men.

Guy picked up Hydrant's slack, material-wise. Although she did care for Guy, Breezy didn't feel for Guy half of what she felt for Hydrant. Sometimes she got so confused and indecisive between the two that she didn't know which way was up.

Breezy never allowed herself to get caught slippin' though. If she did, she always managed to slither her way out of any farce.

Just last week she was supposed to meet Guy for a drink. After twenty-four hours of a Hydrant fix, she was worn out so she left Guy a voice message on his cell phone saying that her car had broken down and she couldn't meet him. She went on and on about how she was plagued with a headache because of the stress of finding out that her car, which he paid the down payment on, was going to cost over $1,500 in repairs.

Guy stopped by Breezy's house bearing a basket he had made up with Tylenol, chocolate bars, and tea. It was one of Guy's typical sweet gestures that Breezy was hoping he didn't try to pull on this particular occasion. Since he came bearing gifts, Breezy felt obligated to let him hang out for a spell. Guy tried not to push up on Breezy, but he couldn't resist with her gallivanting around in that oversized University of Toledo sweatshirt, panties, and white bobby socks. She looked like a little college freak to him. He had to try to get some. He ended up saying to her what every guy says, but never really means: *Let me just eat you out. We don't even have to do it.*

Guy could eat the hell out of some coochie and Breezy could barely resist the offer. *It won't hurt if I just let him eat me out*, Breezy thought. She gave in to Guy by climbing on him and placing her thick juicy pussy on his face. She had barely straddled him before he sealed his serpent tongue behind his teeth and pushed her off of him.

"What the fuck?" Guy said as he rolled out of bed in rage. Breezy stared up at him, clueless. She thought that maybe she had started her period without knowing. That had happened with them once before.

"I can't believe you are fucking somebody else! And on top of that, you let me stick my tongue in your pussy after some muthafucker's dick been up in it."

"Guy, I don't know what you are talking about, baby," Breezy said, keeping her cool. Besides, she knew there was no way in the world Guy could have known she had just had sex with Hydrant. She figured he was just testing her.

"Next time wash your fuckin' pussy out a little better so that I won't smell and taste the rubber from the condom."

"You're married, for Christ sakes," Breezy said, not fazed that she had been busted. "You fuck somebody else on a regular. Do you mean to tell me that you've never come over here after sticking it to your wife and then stick it to me? You're a goddamn liar if you even try to tell me you haven't. As a matter of fact, you fucked her before coming over here tonight. My pussy is laced with gold, but there ain't no way you just want to eat it unless you done already got you some."

Not only did Guy finish eating Breezy's coochie until she juiced all over his face, he left her two thousand dollars to repair her perfectly running Benz.

Breezy could do no wrong when it came to Hydrant and Guy. They would believe her if she told them that water wasn't wet. She had a way of always turning the dice when it looked like she was about to throw craps. She played men like they were dice. And although she cared for Hydrant, he was one of them potential men, and potential wasn't paying any of Breezy's bills. She would have been stupid to stop fucking with Guy in order to be with Hydrant . . . stupid and broke!

"Damn, Hydrant, you're early," Breezy said in a smart aleck tone, opening the door with only her skort on. "I'm not even finished getting dressed yet."

"It's cool. I was thinking we should stay in anyway. I'll whip up something to eat and get a movie off of pay-per-view," Hydrant said.

"Are you turning into a hermit or something? That's all you want to do anymore is lay up in my house. I've worked hard all week. I want to get out of here and go do something."

"Well, go ahead. Call up your girls. I don't mind," he said in a laid-back tone, kicking off his Timberland boots and flopping down on the couch.

"Then you won't mind taking your ass back home, either," Breezy said sharply, walking into her bedroom.

"Oh, it's like that?" Hydrant asked in a cool voice, following her. "Baby girl, don't be like that."

"Get away from me, Hydrant. I don't feel like playing," Breezy snapped.

"You know you ain't doing nothing but turning me on," Hydrant said, kissing on Breezy as she tried to push him away.

"I'm serious. You are making a habit out of having me get dressed only for your ass to show up looking like a scrub trying to lounge around in my shit."

Hydrant was speechless. It was like those words had been longing to erupt from Breezy's mouth. He left her standing in the bedroom as he went to put his shoes back on.

"I fucked up. I'm sorry," Breezy said, approaching Hydrant.

"Naw, ma, you straight. Do your thang, I'm out."

"Hydrant, don't go. Really, that just came out all wrong."

"I know you well enough to know that nothing comes out of your mouth wrong. Just tell me this, how long have you been feeling like that? How long have you been feeling like I'm just breathing up your air?"

"I don't, baby. I just got mad. I wanted to go out and you keep doing this. I mean, if you don't have the money to take me out then . . ."

"Listen to you, Breezy. Listen to what you sound like. You got a brotha, a damn good brotha, trying to be hugged up under your black ass. You wanna lightweight bitch about me showing up early. I am not one of these *I'm on my way niggas* that got you waiting up all night for me. And fuck going out all the time. You think I give a damn about being seen by the okee doke Negroes in this town? I'm all about you, and you ain't trying to have that. I'm trying to give you me, my time, my heart, and your ass worried about a nigga's pockets. You want to be treated like a hoe, Breezy? You wanna trick? What's up? I can do that shit. Hell, pimpin' ain't easy, but it fo sho is fun, so just let a brotha know if that's what you want in this relationship. We can play games if you want to. I'm cool with that. Just let me know the rules. I'm just here to accommodate you, love."

No man besides her daddy had ever brought Breezy to tears. There she stood before Hydrant, unable to blink for fear the tears would come rolling down. The little voice in her head kept telling her to say something to him, but she was speechless. The little voice told her to get down from her high horse and walk over to that man and put her arms around him. Hopefully by doing so he would put his arms around her and make her feel the way she'd needed to feel for years. Instead she let him walk right out of the door.

"Ahh, he'll be back," she said to herself, knowing in her heart that this was the last straw for Hydrant. They had had that same argument five times in the past four months already. They might have just had it for the last time.

Just needing to be needed and to release some of her pent-up feelings, Breezy decided to call Guy's cell phone to see what his plans were for the night, to see if he could get away.

"Hello," a woman's voice answered.

"Hello," Breezy said, completely stunned.

"Yes?" the woman said, daring Breezy to ask for Guy.

"Is Guy available?" Breezy asked in a cool tone. She couldn't hang up because she was sure her name and phone number was visible on the cell phone caller ID.

"Who wants to know?"

Breezy had no idea what she was supposed to do or say. What if it was Guy's wife? Of course it was his wife. What other woman could have been answering his phone? If she hung up, for certain this person would call her right back.

"I'm wanting to know," Breezy, starting to lose her cool.

"I don't have time to play these games with you bitches. If you are woman enough to call another woman's husband, then be woman enough to identify yourself."

"I'll try calling him another time," Breezy said nonchalantly.

"The hell you will!" the woman exclaimed. "I got your name and your phone number right here on this caller ID screen. All I have to do now is call Pizza Hut to get your address, you dumb bitch. So, you just try calling my husband again. You've been warned."

The phone went dead. All Breezy could do was sit there and stare at the receiver in her hand. No sooner than Breezy hung up the phone did it ring. Guy's cell phone number was on her caller ID box. She let the phone ring so that it would go to her answering machine. Her machine was in her bedroom, so she rushed into her room to see if the caller was going to leave a message.

"Breezy, pick up," she could hear Guy say. "I know you're there. Pick up."

"Guy, what the fuck, yo!" Breezy said snatching up the receiver. "Your wife has your cell phone. You getting sloppy on me?"

"Look, you nasty-ass ho. I'm not going to tell you again to stop calling my cell phone," Guy yelled into the phone.

"Guy?" Breezy said, shocked.

"I told you I didn't want anything to do with you. Do you honestly think I'd jeopardize my wife and family for someone like you? Get over it. I don't want you, so stop calling my phone."

Guy hung up the phone in Breezy's ear. She couldn't believe this was happening. Then she took a deep breath. He was probably saying all of those things for his wife's benefit, but it didn't keep Breezy's emotions from doing backflips. She was heated. She wanted to call him back and cuss him out royally, but she couldn't let him know his theatrics had gotten the best of her. Breezy threw the phone across the room in anger and began to pace the floor.

"That punk!" Breezy screamed. "He doesn't know who he's fucking with. I'll turn his world upside down." Breezy continued to pace. Then she tried to call both Klarke and Jeva to school them on what had just gone down, but neither was available. She left them messages and fell asleep waiting on either to return her call. At about 1:30 A.M. Breezy was startled out of her sleep by a knock on the door. She made her way, bleary-eyed, to the door.

"Breezy, open the door. It's me, Guy," he said in a loud whisper.

"You've got some nerve," Breezy said as she opened the door only as wide as the chain would allow.

"Come on, now. I'm not going to talk to you standing out in this hall. Baby, open the door and let me explain what happened."

"I can put two and two together. You don't have to explain anything to me. You had to impress the missus at my expense. I bet she fell for it and then you two had make-up sex. Now you're here trying to clean shit up with me just like the last time. Well, I'm sick of this, Guy."

"She's my wife, Breezy. You chose to be the other woman."

"Get it right! *You* chose *me* to be the other woman. Don't act like you walked up to me and said, 'Hi, my name is Guy and I'm married. Will you be my mistress?' Shit didn't happen like that."

"Once I did tell you that I had a wife I didn't see you breaking it off with me. You kept right on screwing me, taking my money and accepting gifts. I give you the world. I love you to death, Breezy, but she's my wife, the mother of my children."

"Since when do you give a fuck about having a wife? Certainly not when you're laid up with me. Tell me all of the bad things you told her about me this time. Tell me, Guy."

The neighbor across the hall opened her door to see what the commotion was about. Guy turned to her and gave her an everything-is-okay smile, and she closed her door.

"I'm not going to stand here in the hallway and argue with you in the middle of the night for all of your neighbors to hear. I care about you and I wanted to at least show you the courtesy of coming here to talk to you in person. I'm tired of this shit, too. I can't do it anymore. I can't do this to you. We have to cool it for a while. I have to take care of home. I'm about to lose my family."

Breezy could hear her heart beating in her chest, the sound drowning out anything else Guy had to say. If anything, Guy should have been leaving his wife for her. Who in the hell did he think he was, coming to her door to throw her away like a used-up hussy?

"So you think it's that easy, Guy? Do you honestly think that I'm going to allow you to throw me away like I'm nothing?" Breezy said. "You've got another thing coming. You know me better than to think I'm going to go out like that."

"It doesn't have to be like this," Guy said in a soothing tone. "Don't say things you might regret."

"After all is said and done, you'll be the only one doing the regretting," she said through the cracked door. "Imagine how your wife would react if she just happened to find out every little detail about us. The car, the money, the jewelry, clothes . . . the abortion . . . I wonder who'd be regretting what then."

Guy kicked the door in, catching Breezy off guard, the chain shooting across the room. Breezy backed up toward the couch as Guy lunged toward her with rage in his eyes.

"Look you, little tramp bitch," Guy said, grabbing Breezy's chin with his hand. "You've long been bought and paid for. I don't owe you shit. Your worst fucking nightmare would be to fuck with my family. You got that? Do you?"

Breezy had the heart of a gang member during initiation. She was unaffected by his threats. What she couldn't stand was his hands gripping her pretty face. She went way down in her chest and hacked up a nice-size glob of spit and landed it right in Guy's face.

"Before you go making idle threats you better think twice about all that you have at stake," Breezy said, with her face still in Guy's grip. "Me, on the other hand, I don't have shit to lose. This little stunt of yours—kicking my door in, putting your hands on me—it's already going to cost you."

"Do you think I give a shit about that?" Guy said as he pulled out his wallet and began to lay bills out on Breezy's coffee table. "I waste more money in a month than you net in a year. You could live off of what I throw away, you cheap bitch. You gonna try to swindle me? Is that what you saying?"

Breezy was beyond angry. For the second time in a twenty-four-hour period a man had brought her to tears. Only these were tears of anger. They were tears laced with revenge. The other times when Guy would disrespect her, she knew he hadn't meant it. He had done it before, when his wife got ahold of his pager, and the time she got ahold of his old cell phone. She called every number he had stored in that phone, one of which was Breezy's. She knew he had to put on a show for his wife. But this time his words were swords.

Breezy began to laugh. She laughed hysterically. Guy just stood there watching her as if she were a madwoman escaped from the loony bin.

"Bravo!" Breezy yelled as she began to clap. "Bravo! Encore! Encore!"

Guy was completely lost at this point. He stood there shaking his head in disgust at Breezy.

"I knew I should have never fucked with you," he said.

"Why?" Breezy asked, putting her hand on her hip. "I wasn't worth it? I wasn't worth what is about to happen to your life? You know what? If I were you, Guy, I wouldn't be going out buying a rabbit anytime soon." Breezy snickered in reference to the infamous boiling rabbit scene in *Fatal Attraction*.

"You're crazy!" Guy said. "Look, we're both a little high-strung right now. Let's just cool off and give this thing some time."

"What's the matter, Guy? You afraid I'm going to go kidnap your kids from school or something?" Breezy laughed.

"I'm warning you, Breezy—"

"No, bitch, you've been warned. Now you shut the fuck up and listen to me. Like I said, I don't have anything to lose. You on the other hand have a wife, kids, and a career. None of that means shit to me, but I would like to know what it's all worth to you?"

"You really think I'm going to cave in to your ass? Do you think I'm going to stand by for one moment and let you blackmail me? This is cute, Breezy," Guy said as he headed for the door to leave. "I don't have time for this. You take care of yourself."

"1234 Rinterace Lane, Toledo, Ohio, 46789. Wife, one Eleanor

Gainer; children, one Whitely and Cal Gainer, school . . . ."

"Okay, okay," Guy said, throwing in the towel. "Fuck it. You win, okay? I don't even care. It's not worth it. You're not worth it. I just want you completely out of my life. What do you want? Money, sex . . ."

"Sex." Breezy laughed. "Don't flatter yourself."

"Then, what? What is it going to take for me to never have to lay eyes on you again, to never have to hear your voice or your name? What is it going to take?"

"What's it worth to you, Guy?" Breezy asked greedily. "What's it all worth?"

"Are you okay?" Klarke asked as she and Jeva stormed into Breezy's apartment.

The door was open as Breezy poked and picked at the door chain with a screwdriver. She was going to have maintenance do it, but didn't want to have to wait the entire weekend for it to be repaired.

"When I got your message I thought Guy had beat your ass or something," Jeva said with much concern. "What happened?"

"He tried to play me, so now he has to pay me," Breezy said, smacking her lips.

"What happened this time?" Klarke sighed. "Did his wife get ahold of his pager or cell phone again?"

"You know how sloppy he is," Breezy said as she continued to mess with the door. "He just went overboard this time. He tried to treat me like I wasn't shit to him."

"You know he'll be right back over here next week," Jeva said rolling her eyes.

"He sure in the hell will. To pay my rent," Breezy said proudly.

"And why is that man paying your rent?" Klarke asked glaring at Breezy.

"Because all of a sudden he wants to spare his wife's feelings and shit on me. Nobody shits on me," Breezy said with conviction.

"Wait a minute. Let me get this right," Klarke said, hoping she hadn't heard what she was hearing. "Is this something he's doing to stay on your good side or are you pulling a Michael Jordan mistress stunt?"

Breezy confirmed the latter with the look she gave Klarke.

"Girl, that's extortion!" Jeva exclaimed.

"Not to mention you are talking about this man's family," Klarke added.

"Fuck his family!" Breezy said angrily. "He doesn't care about them, so why should I?"

"Baby girl, don't do this. I know you are pissed right now, but don't do this. You might as well go into the jungle and try to take a male lion's female and cubs," Klarke said in a comforting tone.

"What was that, Klarke?" Breezy said, putting her hand up to her ear. "Did I hear the pot calling the kettle black? Quit acting like you don't have your own little twisted game of ransom going on."

"What I'm into is different," Klarke said in her defense. "It's nothing compared to what you are doing. I'm not breaking any laws."

"What are you doing?" Jeva asked Klarke, her eyes wide.

Klarke paused, then proceeded with her spill. "There's this account at work. It involved an enormous print order for Reo Laroque's book."

"Who?" Jeva said, frowning.

"That fine-ass author that was on BET?" Breezy asked.

"Yeah, that's him," Klarke paused again to gather her thoughts. "I had seen him on television and then the print order for his book landed on my desk. I felt like it was destiny or something. I had worked up this fantasy of being his wife, never having to worry about working for the man or money again. It was like a sign."

"So you called him up?" Breezy asked.

"Not exactly," Klarke said, slowly. "I sent him an e-mail."

"I'm sure he gets e-mails all of the time. What was so special about yours?" Breezy asked.

"It was mysterious." Klarke smiled. "I pretended to be sending an e-mail to some man I had met in a Boston airport. I didn't want him to know that I knew who he was. I mean, like you said, Breezy, I'm sure he gets tons of e-mails from groupies."

"So when he got the e-mail what did he do?" Jeva asked. "Did he respond and tell you that you had sent the e-mail to him by mistake?"

"No, he did exactly what I thought he'd do," Klarke said as a devious grin took over her face. "He pretended to be the person that I met in the Boston airport. And I've been playing the game right along with him."

"Well, have you heard from the guy from the Boston airport?" Jeva asked with great concern.

"Were you not listening, Edith Bunker?" Breezy asked, exasperated. "There never really was a man in the Boston airport."

"Oh," Jeva said, nodding. "Oh, I get it."

"Why didn't you just show up butt-ass naked on his door step? That's what I would have done. You would have left a hell of an impression. I mean, why use the computer? What if he had deleted the e-mail and not have responded?" Breezy asked Klarke.

"That wouldn't have happened," Klarke answered. "I knew the e-mail route would be the most effective in this case. Reo writes fiction, which means he's into a good fairy tale, just like me. He likes a good story. And besides, do you know how many people meet over the Internet and marry? It's today's reality whether you want to believe it or not. Besides, he spends more time on his computer than he does breathing. I know that much about him just from all of the research I did on him."

"Research, huh?" Breezy said.

"Aside from the fact that I've seen him on television and heard a couple of his radio interviews, I've read all his books, I have every newspaper and magazine article that's ever been written on him. Girl, I even know this man's favorite song."

"Is that where you got his e-mail address from?" Jeva asked. "His books?"

"No," Klarke said. "Everybody and their mama has access to that e-mail address. We had his personal information, which included his personal e-mail address, in our system at work for some reason. It was right there at my fingertips."

"Damn," Breezy said. "And I thought I was good."

"We've been corresponding with each other back and forth for about a month now," Klarke said proudly. She then told them how she planned to play upon Reo's sensitivity and his emotional needs. Ultimately, Klarke would catch Reo offguard, get inside of his head and his heart, possess his mind, and then work on the physical aspect once she had him right where she needed him, which was cupped inside her gentle palm.

"So you see, I'm not putting anybody at risk," Klarke said. "What you're doing, Breezy, is putting a man's entire life at risk. What you're pulling could cost him everything."

"Well, his wife finding out the real-deal Holyfield will cost him more than I ever will," Breezy said going back to fixing the door.

"You don't think that Guy might try to get stupid on you?" Jeva asked.

"It doesn't matter what I think," Breezy said. "I got a 9-millimeter in my nightstand drawer that knows he won't."

9

Once Upon a Time

Jeva had already been waiting twenty minutes for Lance to pick her up from work before she called Cassie, the sitter who took care of their five-year-old daughter. This was the second time this week Lance had been late picking her up from work. She had gotten just as used to making the call to the sitter as the sitter had gotten used to receiving it.

"Cassie, hey, it's me, Jeva."

"Lance late again, coming to get you?" Cassie said presuming correctly.

"You know it. He kills me, not answering his cell phone. That means he's on his way and just doesn't want to hear me cursing him out until he gets here." Jeva laughed.

"Don't even worry about it. Your little Heather is asleep anyway."

"Thanks, girl. I'll be there as soon as I can."

"All right, peace," Cassie said as she hung up the phone.

At least once a week Lance was late picking Jeva up from work. They were a one-car family and Lance was always on call for his job as a maintenance man, so he had custody of the vehicle most of the time. Lance's inability to be on time was just one of his flaws that never bothered Jeva for long.

Thank goodness she was blessed with a baby-sitter like Cassie. Cassie lived at one of the properties Lance did maintenance work for. Cassie worked with far fewer marbles than Jeva, but she was great with kids. Klarke and Breezy referred to Cassie as a wigga, a white girl with intentional versus natural-born black characteristics. She was known to get her hair done up in a French roll or even braided and beaded. Lance had gotten her number from the laundry room bulletin board at the property.

Lance did maintenance work for two Eastside Toledo apartment complexes. His work schedule was from 8:00 A.M. to 5:00 P.M. but those hours weren't engraved in stone. If there happened to be an emergency after five, then he was required to go take care of it. He got paid overtime on those occasions.

On the side, he was supposedly a hustler. He was always in the streets making runs to deliver his weed, yet never had anything to show for it. Last year Jeva had to borrow eighty dollars from Breezy to keep her phone from being disconnected. The electric had already been disconnected, but God forbid the phone got turned off. Folks will talk in the dark.

Jeva and Lance had been playing house for about five years. Lance had promised to marry her after her daughter was born. Her daughter would be two years old by the time they planned for a romantic getaway to the Bahamas, during which they would exchange wedding vows.

Jeva had stopped using birth control about three months prior to their wedding date. She wanted to perhaps conceive on their wedding night, which was one of Jeva's biggest problems, she always expected some fairy-tale type stuff to happen. Every step she took in life was supposed to get her closer to that happy ending that all little girls grow up reading about in those damn Disney books.

Lance had really wanted a second child, a son. Making Lance happy was what made Jeva happy. He had been hounding Jeva for over a year to have another baby. Jeva refused to have another child out of wedlock, so Lance knew it was a no-win battle unless he agreed to marry her.

Besides, Jeva had been so caught up in her photography and landing high-profile photo jobs that she couldn't even think of fitting in another baby. This photography thing was new to her and she enjoyed it.

A man she did a bachelor party for back when she used to dance for a living turned her on to it. He supplied magazines and newspapers with photos and articles, mostly fillers. He ended up leasing a studio with state-of-the-art equipment so he could do layouts.

Shortly after Jeva had her daughter, he had contacted her to dance at one of his boy's parties. Jeva told him that she was no longer dancing, but was instead seeking out a new gig.

He had recently decided to hire a couple of independent freelancers and was willing to give Jeva a stab at it. Compared to the fast and easy money she had made dancing, the money from the photography gig was shitty, but it was morally honest.

The gentleman she worked for was now one of the main go-to guys in the industry for fillers in magazines and newspapers. Although most of Jeva's assignments were local, she did well and it kept her busy.

Jeva's exotic look always attracted the male entertainers when she was given a major event to cover, which gave her easy access to photo shoots.

She landed some high-priced photos with her slanted *mami* eyes and petite figure. What would Jeva have looked like being sent off to do a shoot at John Blassingame's *Black Men* magazine anniversary party, for example, big as a house with Lance's off-spring? How would her pop-belly tear the Morris Chestnuts and Nellys away from conversation, and Cristal for a couple of quick camera shots and standard interview questions? Come to think of it, she probably would have gotten more action from the fellas. Men were able to pick up the scent of the wet cream of pregnant pussy like wild animals.

As it turned out Jeva found out she was pregnant a month be-fore their getaway. It wasn't the fairy-tale conception she had mentally worked up, but there was nothing she could have done about it. Let Jeva tell it and she knew the exact night she got pregnant. It was the night she and Lance were supposed to go see Maxwell in concert. Alicia Keys was the opening act.

Maxwell came down with a flu bug and canceled the morning of the concert. Jeva heard the cancellation on the radio while working on a layout. She didn't share this bit of information with Lance, though. They had already booked Cassie's baby-sitting services for the night, so Jeva decided to take advantage of that.

When Lance got in from work, Jeva directed him straight to the shower. He was late getting in so they would have missed Alicia Keys's performance anyway.

Jeva laid out the most elegant picnic setting in the middle of the living room floor. She had spread a Mexican blanket out, which was a souvenir from a trip she had taken to Cancun. The wicker picnic basket, which was a house-warming gift when she moved into Lance's home, was filled with sandwiches, potato chips, and Chips Ahoy cookies. All were freshly packed in Ziploc baggies.

The flare of the apple pie–scented candle flickered off the glasses filled with chilled Asti. Jeva had spread herself out on the blanket in her Daisy Duke denim shorts and checkered haltered top. She had even stopped at a craft market and bought a bale of hay.

When she heard the shower water shut off, she went into the bathroom to retrieve her man. Butt-naked and wet, with only a towel wrapped around his waist, Lance was escorted to the personally prepared indoor picnic.

They made love for what would have been the duration of the concert. It was such a beautiful evening of lovemaking, almost dreamlike. That's why Jeva claimed it as her evening of conception.

Jeva getting pregnant before she and Lance had the opportunity to say "I do" was a lifesaver for Lance. He came up with 101 reasons why they shouldn't get married after all (he wasn't ready, he wanted a big fancy wedding, he couldn't get off work for the trip, etc.). He wanted a baby, a son. He was getting what he wanted out of the relationship, so why take it further?

Jeva couldn't believe he was pulling such a stunt. They argued over the subject matter for months. Jeva felt used and like she had been tricked into thinking that Lance truly wanted her as his wife. She became indecisive as to whether she wanted to give birth to another child without being married. She didn't want to be a breeding ground for any man.

She cried to Klarke and Breezy almost every night. She couldn't believe what was happening to her. She felt like a teen in trouble. For Jeva, there was no feeling worse than the initial pain of discovering someone didn't love her as much as she loves them. Lance's bailing out on their nuptials told her that he didn't feel the way she felt for him.

Jeva thought about getting an abortion. She had actually gone to the clinic to have the procedure done twice, but changed her mind each time. She was finally so far along that when she made up her mind to have it done, she had to go to another city. No doctor in Toledo would touch her with a ten-foot pole.

She told Lance that she miscarried. There was no doubt in her mind that the truth would have sent him packing. After that horrifying experience she felt lucky to have been put up for adoption.

Jeva could hardly contain her anger as Lance drove up. She had stood there over thirty minutes waiting for him. He was acting as if he had just come from the Mardi Gras with the music in the car bumpin' as he rocked his head to each boom of the bass.

Even rugged and scroungy from a hard day's work, Lance still looked good to Jeva. He had dry loop curls that covered his head, and rugged bronze skin. He was six feet, nine inches tall with a medium-cut build. He had appealing brown eyes that he always squinted because he wouldn't wear the glasses his optometrist had prescribed. People always told him that he looked like the guy who played Jason in the movie *Jason's Lyric*.

"I see that somebody needs a watch for Christmas," Jeva said smartly, getting into the car and slamming the door.

"Hey, how was your day?" Lance asked in a pleasant tone.

"Why do you do that?" Jeva asked with a puzzled look on her face.

"Do what?" Lance said, squinting his eyes as he pulled off.

"Act like pulling up almost a half hour late isn't nothing. Why don't you try apologizing for a change, or is that too much like right?"

"And what's an apology going to do? Make the thirty-minute wait feel like fifteen instead?" Lance said, shaking his head.

"You don't have to act like such an asshole, Lance," Jeva snapped.

"Who in the fuck do you think you're talking to? I work hard just like you. Don't even come at me like that. Your ass can walk home next time," Lance said catching a major attitude.

"That's so uncalled for. You don't have to talk to me all disrespectful."

"You're the one who called me an asshole, and it's not the first time. What if I always called you a stripper or a ho?"

"In so many ways you do. Every time we argue that's the first thing that comes out of your mouth: *You were just a stripper when I met you.* How many more years are you going to throw that in my face?" asked Jeva, as if she were sick and tired of Lance's comments. "Every time we get into it it's like you get your jollies off by reminding me about my past. I know what I used to do for a living, Lance. I don't need you to remind me."

Lance turned up the music and continued to drive. He sought pleasure in tuning Jeva out. Her lips were moving. Her neck was twisting. Her head was bobbing. Her finger was pointing and yet he could hear nothing but his music. After several minutes of wasting her breath Jeva turned the music down.

"Do you want to just call it quits, because I'm sick of being treated like a nobody?" Jeva asked.

"Girl, stop talking crazy. You know you ain't going anywhere. What? You going to go stay with Breezy for a week like you always do? You'll be right back home." Lance laughed.

"You think everything is funny. If you don't straighten up, one day you're going to come home and find me gone for good."

"Then why are you with me, Jeva? If you are so determined

to leave me, why are you laying up with me every night?"

"Have you ever heard of that thing called love?"

"Jeva, I'm trying real hard to love you," Lance said seriously.

"What's wrong with me, Lance?" Jeva asked.

"Nothing is wrong with you. You just need to chill out."

"Then why do you make loving me sound like you're training for the heavyweight title of the world? Loving a person should be easy. Loving *me* should be easy. Chinese arithmetic is hard."

"Baby, loving you and dealing with you are two different things."

Jeva was starting to become emotional. Lance knew what this meant. She was beginning to think about her birth parents. That is what always followed their arguments. She would forgive Lance for not loving her because her own mother and father didn't love her. If they had they would not have given her up. Lance pulled into the parking lot of a convenience store and put the car in Park.

"I don't want to keep going through this with you, ma. I know how you feel and before you start telling me that I don't, just listen," Lance said, rubbing Jeva's hand. "I know how you feel because when you hurt, I hurt. I feel the same pain you do. When you close your eyes I see your darkness. Jeva, I know you said that you are giving up the search, but baby, we've got to find your parents. It's eating away at you and it's not good for our relationship. You don't know who you are. We're going to force that child placement agency to locate some type of paperwork on you. It's impossible for them not to have a single document on you or your parents."

"No, Lance." Jeva began to cry. "I already told you it's useless. It only makes things worse getting those letters from Welford Child Placement Agency telling me, once again, that they came up with nothing on my parents. It tears me apart."

"Then we'll hire a private investigator. I'll work longer hours to pay for one. I'll invest in some chronic instead of that weak shit I been pushing and flip my ends. Hell, I'll go find them myself if I have to. We've got to do something."

Jeva looked at Lance. "You'd do all that for me?"

"Did you think I wouldn't?"

"Let's go get the baby," Jeva said as she kissed Lance, and they drove off.

The following two weeks Jeva put the wheels in motion toward finding her biological parents, investing all of her time in just that one task alone.

"When is the last time you washed clothes and when is the next time you plan on washing again?" Lance said as he threw clothes out of the dirty hamper in search of a work shirt.

"Oh, honey, I'm sorry," Jeva said, jumping up off the bed, leaving a stack of letters, envelopes, and stamps behind. "I've been so busy writing letters to the agency and to the media about the agency, as well as talk shows, that I haven't gotten around to washing clothes."

"And you want me to marry you," Lance mumbled under his voice.

"Excuse me?" Jeva said, putting her hand on her hip and rolling her eyes.

"You won't even wash clothes. We done ate out all week. I need a woman who is going to take care of little shit, like her house, and hell, her man."

"You are like Dr. Jekyll and Mr. Hyde, I swear. You are the one who pumped me up to get on top of finding my birth parents and you won't even be supportive."

"If I had known I'd have to wear dirty clothes to work then I would have suggested otherwise."

Jeva stomped away from Lance. She didn't want him to see her cry. She flopped back down on the bed and continued stamping and sealing envelopes. Tears flowed from her eyes as she did so.

"Will you stop crying?" Lance shouted. "You're like a big-ass baby. I don't know who's worse, you or Heather."

Jeva had been nibbling on a piece of pecan cheesecake she had left over in the refrigerator from the Cheesecake Factory. She was so furious and overcome by emotion that, without thinking, she scooped up a mess of it and threw it right at Lance. He had been looking down, buttoning his shirt, but just as the cheesecake flew across the bedroom he looked up. It hit him dead smack in his face.

It was too late when Jeva realized what she had done. She covered her mouth with her hand in surprise. Lance stood there scraping the cheesecake off of his face. Jeva tried her hardest to hold in her laughter but didn't succeed. Lance looked at her and ran over to the bed and jumped on top of her.

"You think that was funny, huh?" Lance said, smearing it on Jeva's face.

"Lance, don't!" Jeva said, laughing.

"Mmm, mmm. I want you to know what it feels like to wear cheesecake."

Lance sat on top of Jeva and pinned her arms above her head. He proceeded to rub his face against hers. When he released her arms, she scooped up some of the cheesecake off of Lance's face with her index finger. Jeva then seductively sucked it off of her fingertip.

"Mmm, it tastes even better on you." Jeva smiled.

"I know where it will taste even better," Lance replied as he gave Jeva a seductive look.

Lance lifted up the white dress shirt of his that Jeva was wearing and pulled down her white Victoria's Secret Body Glove panties. Lance then proceeded to smear his face all over Jeva's pussy. He ate her out until her cream slid down his throat.

Lance planted a hard kiss on Jeva's clit and then on her mouth. He winked at her and then got up and proceeded to go clean himself up.

Jeva watched him walk away, mesmerized. Then she collapsed backward onto the bed and smiled.

"Mmm, I love me some him," she said to herself. "I love me some him."

10

The Check Is in the Mail

"Okay, what did I miss?" Klarke asked as she flopped down into her chair at the Cheesecake.

"If you would stop trying to be the Terrell Owens of the clique," Breezy said, "you wouldn't have to ask that question every time you meet us."

"What does that mean and who is Terrell Owens?" Klarke asked, crossing her legs.

"He plays for the Forty-niners. People think he's always doing things to purposely make himself stand out," Breezy said.

"If you ask me, he can. Hell, he's one of the top five receivers in the league. They need to leave that boy alone, him and Keyshawn." Klarke and Breezy looked at Jeva with squinted faces, repelled that Jeva knew just a tad too much about football.

Jeva shrugged. "I can't help it. Lance and I watch football all of the time together. Anyway, Klarke, Breezy was getting ready to talk about Hydrant."

"What about him?" Klarke said, making eye contact with

Chauncy to signal that he could now bring her a Shirley Temple.

"He still hasn't called her or nothing," Jeva said.

"Can you blame him?" Klarke was quick to ask.

"Y'all, he was laying on the couch all wrong," Breezy cringed. "I just snapped."

"Girl, you stupid." Klarke laughed.

"You know how it is when you just look at a man and get mad? I mean he just be laying there on my couch . . . wrong. It's like he can't do nothing right, not even lay on the couch right."

"You are so wrong!" Klarke chuckled. "And that's just what women like you get."

"I'm not trying to hear you say that shit one more time, Klarke," Breezy said seriously.

"Slow down, baby. That's not even where I was about to take you," Klarke said. "When I said women like you, I meant women who hinder a man. A brotha lets a sistah know his shit isn't all intact, but yet y'all got to have him and y'all got to have him right now. Y'all don't want to wait until he comes through and gets himself together . . . so scared the next chick is going to stick her claws into him. Breezy, if that man is supposed to be in your life, he's going to be in your life. You don't have to hold onto him so tight that you start to suffocate yourself with his presence. Let him go. Let him handle his business without worrying about having to be up under your ass, trying to please you. Do you think that makes him feel good? Do you think that makes him feel like a man?"

"Well damn! I guess you told me," Breezy said, pulling her head back and staring at Klarke. "You think you the funkin shiznit now, huh? Your little scam with Reo Suave is turning you into a philosophizing brute."

"It's taught me a thing or two," Klarke said, smacking her lips. "Not to mention I also went to college and learned a few things there too."

"Oh yeah, miss college girl. I forgot you went to community college. So you completed the thirteenth and fourteenth grade. Big deal!" Breezy joked.

"Have I ever told you how much I hate you deep down inside?" Klarke snarled.

"You know you love me," Breezy said, puckering her lips and making a kissing sound.

"I'm not all that hungry today," Jeva said twisting up her face.

"Me either," Klarke agreed. "What about you, Breezy?"

"I'm not starved or anything like that. I can grab something in the mall if you two are ready to raise up out of here."

"Check please," Klarke called to Chauncy as the women prepared to go window shopping.

"I don't see anything worth admiring today," Jeva said as they walked through the mall.

"Yeah, I could have skipped this, stayed home and watched Lifetime all day," Breezy added.

"Face it, girls," Klarke said. "We've outgrown window shopping. There's no fun in it anymore. It only highlights what we're supposed to be forgetting about."

A quad of men who looked to be younger than the women walked past them and made eye contact. Breezy said hello and the men responded. One of them decided he wanted to take that simple hello to another level.

"Damn, y'all looking good," the idiot boy said as he pranced around. "Woooo, weeee. Do y'all got men? Hot damn! Hell, and if y'all do, are y'all allowed to have friends? You can never have too many friends."

"Come here, baby. Let me tell you something," Breezy said in her most seductive voice.

The men all looked at one another as if they weren't sure who Breezy was directing her words toward.

"Yeah, you," she said, pointing at the idiot boy. "Don't be sceered."

He looked at his crew as if he had just been a made man by the Godfather himself. He held his head high and walked with a slight pimp over to Breezy. She leaned into his ear and whispered, "Men like you are the reason sisters don't speak."

"Excuse me?" he said jerking away, but Breezy jerked him back.

"Baby, let me give you a little bit of priceless advice. From now on, when a woman says hello to you on the street, don't assume she's interested in you, wants to fuck you or even wants to know your goddamn name. Just say hello and walk away. This is the new millennium. If a woman is interested, oh, you'll know. Trust me. But that shit you just pulled, that little crackhead version of the *American Idol* show, it's not becoming of the male species. Now, if any of us had been interested in you, you just blew it. You look quite fuckable, too. Nonetheless, next time, take heed to what I just told you and you might land you some pussy. Now run along and enjoy the rest of your afternoon."

Breezy kissed him on the cheek, wiped her lipstick off of him and shooed him away with her hand. His boys praised him once he returned to their circle, none the wiser that he had just been shut down.

"You are so wrong," Jeva said to Breezy in complete disbelief as they continued walking through the mall. "You done probably scarred the boy for life."

"Women need to start correcting men's behavior," Breezy said as if she was fed up. "When they act like two-year-olds, then they need to be scolded like two-year-olds. I'm sick of it."

"See what I mean?" Klarke said shaking her head. "This is getting tired. I won't be doing too much more of this shit anyhow. Jeva is right. We're going to have to join a book club or something if y'all trying to see my ass every month."

"The girl even has the mouth of a sailor now," Breezy said referring to Klarke. "You must be handling your business after all with the novelist."

"What can I say? I got him, girls," Klarke said as they high-fived each other. "I can just feel it. He's diggin' me tough. He's a busy man. Why else would he spend so much time e-mailing a complete stranger?"

"That shit actually worked? When you go back to work on Monday, flip through them files and get me the e-mail address of a best-selling author. He could be the answer to my caviar dreams and gated-community lifestyle," Breezy said seriously.

"You know," Jeva added, nodding.

"I'm serious," Breezy said.

"This man's e-mails . . . I'm telling y'all. I don't need an erotic book, magazine, a dirty movie, a vibrator, a nothing to get off anymore. His smooth words alone satisfy my pleasuredome and cause me to orgasm," Klarke bragged.

"Then print them muthafuckas out and let me have a look," Breezy said. "My battery expense is more than my damn electric bill."

"So, are you going to meet him in person or what?" Jeva asked.

"Soon," Klarke answered. "I mean we haven't set anything up, but I'm just about ready to pull his ho card."

"Men are so predictable it's ridiculous," Breezy said, shaking her head. "He fell for everything, hook, line, and e-mail, just like you said he would, Klarke. You da bomb."

"I don't see how he's going to possibly agree to meet with you knowing he's not the person you think he is that he doesn't know never existed in the first place," Jeva rambled on.

Klarke and Breezy couldn't make heads or tails out of the point Jeva was trying to get across.

"How does Lance deal with you?" Breezy asked. "You're like Chrissy Snow."

"I swear I was thinking the same thing," Klarke laughed.

"Now that's a scary thought," Jeva said.

"Boo!" Klarke said. "Anyway, I know he's going to agree to meet me in person, then he's going to toss and turn all night trying to figure out what to do. The next day he'll send me an e-mail telling me the truth and my work will be done. I'll meet him, give him a little of this Ill Na Na and be living back in the land of La La in no time. Just like you said, Breezy, men, there're so predictable."

"Klarke Annette Taylor, that's what I'm talking about, damn it," Breezy said giving Klarke multiple hand smacks. "Men have been burning us for ages. It's time we throw a bucket of water on their eternal flame of dawgin' us out. It's our turn to rule the world."

"There is just one thing that could be a minor setback," Klarke said. "My period is a week late."

"Oh, girl," Breezy said like the actress on the cell phone commercial. "You're shittin' me."

"How you just gonna throw that in there like it's nothing?" Jeva asked Klarke.

"Y'all know I take the pill to regulate my cycle. I missed a pill or two and I think my body just got off track," Klarke said, pretending that she wasn't that worried.

"What if you are pregnant?" Breezy said putting her hand over her mouth. "Girl, what are you going to do?

"I'd get an abortion," Klarke said without hesitation.

"I don't know about an abortion for you," Breezy said. "I don't think you could live with that choice, Klarke."

"You and I both have had an abortion before," Jeva said. "Sometimes it's the answer."

"Don't use Klarke's situation to justify ours," Breezy said. "And besides, what I got was an abortion. What you should have gotten was ten to life."

"Breezy!" Klarke said in shock.

"You remember how far along she was," Breezy said in her I-don't-give-a-damn tone. "She had to leave the state. One more week and she probably would have had to leave the country to get it done."

"I know you think your little remarks are cute, but they're not. That's hurtful, Breezy," Jeva said sadly. "And I didn't have to leave the state. I only had to go to another city."

"I don't want to talk about abortion anymore," Klarke said in a regretful tone. "I shouldn't have even said anything."

"Yeah," Jeva said. "Let's not jump to any conclusions. Just make a doctor's appointment and see what's going on."

"I made one for next month. That's the earliest my OB/GYN could get me in," Klarke said. "And I don't trust the accuracy of those home-pregnancy tests."

"Well, I'd be calling every day to see if there are any cancellations," Breezy said. "You don't want to wait too long or you might end up having to leave the state. I mean the city."

"Ha ha," Jeva said.

"Anyway," Klarke continued. "I got to get a handle on this. I can't chance blowing it this far into the game."

"Just make sure you do handle it and I'm here if you need me," Breezy said.

"You are risking something, Klarke," Jeva said sincerely. "I've been thinking about it, about you and Reo. You're taking a risk that you've probably never even thought twice about."

"And do tell," Klarke said opening her hand, giving Jeva the floor to speak.

"Falling in love. You're taking the risk of this man falling in love with you. This could cost him his heart. Or you could fall in love with him. It could cost you your heart."

"Yeah, yeah, yeah," Breezy said, swinging her hand back and forth. "Men don't know nothing about love, not until somebody dawgs them out that is. Hell, Guy's wife has me to thank for his newly devoted monogamous relationship with her. By the time I drain that son of a bitch, he'll wish he had stayed true to his vows in the first place."

"You still taxing him?" Jeva asked.

"I don't look at it like that," Breezy replied. "I took him for a ride, or two, or three or four or five . . . hell, he's just paying the fare."

"Some people grow up Baptist, others Lutheran, some Apostolic or what have you. I grew up Catholic. Breezy, your domination is M-O-N-E-Y," Jeva said, shaking her head.

"It's a very old religion," Breezy said, smiling. "I thought you knew."

"Amen," Klarke witnessed, as she waved her hand in the air.

"You two are tripping," Jeva said. "Money has your minds twisted."

"Don't forget where you came from, Darling Nikki," Breezy said to Jeva.

"Hey, I might have slid down a pole or two back in the day, but I never turned a trick," Jeva said in defense.

"How do you explain Lance?" Breezy asked.

"Well, Little Red Corvette, I met him at the bar I danced at, but it wasn't via sex for hire or anything like that. We just got to talking and formed a friendship. One thing led to another."

"What's with the Prince songs as metaphors?" Klarke laughed.

"Prince done told everybody's life story. If you can't find yourself in one of his songs, then you haven't lived," Breezy said. "I'll be a Little Red Corvette anytime. After my contract with Guy expires, you never know, I just might own one."

"Which one do y'all think I am?" Klarke asked.

" 'The Beautiful Ones,' " Jeva and Breezy said at the same time.

"I guess I am a heartbreaker in the making," Klarke said.

On the way to her truck, Klarke saw Evan coming toward her. There were two other gentlemen with him.

"Mr. Kemble," Klarke said. "Hello."

"Miss Taylor," Evan said nervously.

"Out doing a little shopping?" Klarke asked.

"Uh, yes. Our mother's birthday is next week and my brothers and I decided to hit the mall together to see what we could come up with."

Klarke looked at Evan's brothers, then looked at him, waiting for an introduction. When Evan caught Klarke's subtle hint, he said, "Oh, where are my manners? Klarke, I mean Miss Taylor, this is my brother Elliott and my brother Eric."

Elliott was the spitting image of Evan, only about three inches taller, and Eric was shorter than Evan, with dark brown hair and dark brown eyes.

"Triple E, huh?" Klarke said, shaking their hands. "Well, it was nice to meet you."

"Same here," the brothers said as they looked at her admiringly.

Klarke could see that Evan felt really awkward standing there.

"Well, you all enjoy yourself," Klarke said, waving and walking away.

"Miss Taylor," Eric said, "we could use a woman's touch. Why don't you join us, and then afterward we can all just hang out? You know what I mean?"

From the look in his eyes and the tone of his voice, Klarke knew that Evan had shared their encounter with his brothers. How he explained it was beyond her, but they seemed to have taken it as if Klarke was some free-for-all tramp.

"I don't think so. I've been in that mall a while now," Klarke declined with a smile.

"But you don't have any bags," Eric said.

"Yeah, well, my girlfriends and I did a little window shopping."

"You didn't see anything you liked?" Eric asked as he raised his eyebrows.

"Nah, not really. Thanks for the invite, though," Klarke said, walking away.

"Then what do you say we just skip the shopping and get right to the hanging out?" he asked, grabbing hold of Klarke's arm.

Klarke was starting to lose her patience with him.

"Do you mind?" Klarke said looking down at his hand on her arm.

"Oh, pardon me," Eric said, letting go and backing away.

"You gentlemen enjoy your afternoon," Klarke said, cutting her eyes at Evan.

Klarke walked away feeling the burning sensation of three pairs of eyes on her back. She was so pissed she wanted to cry. No, what she really wanted to do was spit in Evan's face.

As she fumbled for her keys Klarke was startled to see in the reflection of her tinted window a figure coming up behind her. She turned around in panic only to find Evan standing there. She rolled her eyes at him, turned back around, and inserted the key into the door.

"Klarke, I know what you're thinking. My brother just acts that way. He's the youngest and he's in college. He's a little immature," Evan pleaded as Klarke proceeded to climb into the truck and roll the windows down.

"Well, I wonder where he gets it from."

"Klarke, please."

"So, you didn't tell them about us? They don't know that you and I have . . .?"

"No, I didn't tell them, but they know me. I'm sure they could sense that something was up. Why, Klarke? Are we some secret, under lock and key? Are you ashamed of what happened between us?"

"Don't try to flip the script on me, Evan," Klarke said as Evan stood there looking puzzled.

"You're beautiful even when you're pissed off," Evan said, trying to pull a smile out of Klarke.

"You know what, Evan?" Klarke said as she started up the

truck and began to back out of her parking spot. "You're a class act."

Minutes later as Klarke sat at the red light waiting for it to turn, she looked in the rearview mirror at herself and cringed. She had *known* better than to have sex with Evan. Here she had gone to bed with a man she wasn't even in a relationship with. Her vision blurred as her eyes filled with tears.

"If I'm pregnant, I'll die," Klarke said to herself. "I will absolutely die."

She began to sob uncontrollably.

"What's happening to me? You're not me. Who are you?" she said to the mirror. "How in the hell did I go from a housewife to a ho? God, help me. Tell me what to do with myself. Just one word. Please, God."

Klarke was in the basement folding a load of laundry when she heard the doorbell ring.

"Just a minute!" she yelled. The doorbell rang again.

"I'm coming!" Klarke said as she went over to the door and opened it.

"Tionne, what are you doing here?" Klarke said, surprised.

"I've just got to get some things off of my chest, Klarke," Tionne said.

Tionne's chin trembled in an effort to hold back tears. Klarke stood there, waiting for Tionne to gain her composure and state the purpose of her unannounced visit.

Klarke was surprised by Tionne's appearance. Tionne had always made it a point to look her best when knowing that she would be seeing Klarke. But now her hair was pulled back in a dried-out ponytail and it looked like she hadn't run a comb through it in days. She was sporting a wrinkled black jogging suit and some regular white leather Keds with no socks. This was the first time Klarke had ever seen Tionne without makeup on. There were visible blemishes on Tionne's face that Klarke had never known existed under the smoothly applied cosmetics she always wore.

"Look, Klarke, I'll just get right to it," Tionne said, wiping her eyes. "Are you and Harris trying to get back together?"

At first Klarke looked at Tionne, dumbfounded. Then she exploded with laughter.

"You've got some nerve," Klarke said in disbelief. "I honestly can't believe that you've come to my home with this. On a bad day I would tell you to go fuck yourself and have this conversation with your man. And he is *your* man now, Tionne. But since you done drove all this way to ask me that question I suppose I'll answer it. *No*, Tionne. I have no intention whatsoever of getting back with Harris."

"And is that how Harris feels, too?" Tionne asked.

"You've got to be kidding me." Klarke grinned, putting her hands on her hips. "Ask him. I can't tell you how Harris feels."

"Well, you're going to have to tell me something," Tionne said, digging into her purse. She pulled out a piece of paper and unfolded it. "Something's going on, or is Harris just running around paying off people's truck notes now?"

Klarke took the piece of paper from Tionne and skimmed it. Sure enough, it was documentation that Harris had paid off Klarke's truck note. Klarke's mouth dropped in shock.

"I found it in the glove compartment of his car," Tionne said as she studied Klarke's reaction. "Don't tell me you didn't know."

"Honestly, I had no idea Harris was the one who had paid this.

I thought it was my boss," Klarke said still stunned. "Please, Tionne, come in."

Tionne came inside and sat down on the couch. Klarke fixed Tionne a glass of ice water and sat down next to her.

"I don't want to seem cold," Klarke said, "but you and I aren't friends. We are cordial to one another, but that's where it stops. I see you're going through some things and I'm only doing what any decent person would do. I'm listening. I just don't want you to say too much or the wrong thing to me."

"I understand," Tionne said, taking a sip of her water. "This is my karma, Klarke. It's everything I did to you ten times over. I'm sorry, Klarke. I'm so sorry. I'm sorry, not because it's all coming back to me now, but because I knew Harris didn't love me. He didn't love me like he loved you. He cared for me, but that was about it. I knew he didn't want me and I just had to have him. When you filed for divorce and he came to stay with me, do you know how many times I put my ear against the bathroom door and listened to him cry in the shower over you?"

"I don't think I need to hear this," Klarke said, getting up from the couch.

"Even back when I stopped taking the pill and got pregnant on purpose, he didn't want me," Tionne continued. "He went as far as giving me money for an abortion. I took the money, but as you know I didn't get the abortion."

"Tionne, really, I don't think I'm the person you should be sharing all of this with."

"No, you are exactly the person I need to be telling this. Klarke, do you love my child?"

"How can you ask me that? You know she doesn't have anything to do with what went on between you, Harris, and myself. I've never mistreated her and never will," Klarke said taking offense. "My beef has always been with you, Tionne. What's strange is that I probably wouldn't have even been mad at you if you were just *the other woman*. But when you decided to take on the role of my friend—laughing in my face, going out with me, coming over to my house and having me baby-sit your and Harris's love child, you crossed the line. Otherwise my only beef would have been with Harris. Harris took vows and made a commitment to me, not you. You didn't owe me shit. Harris did. I'm not like most women who fly off the handle and set out to beat the mistress down. But you, Tionne, you pretended to be my friend. You played me and that hurt."

"You're right. I think I better go," Tionne said as she walked over to the door to let herself out. "Can you not mention to Harris that I stopped by?"

"No problem," Klarke said. She closed the door behind Tionne.

Klarke recognized that look of devastation in Tionne's eyes. It was that same look that had been on her face when she found out Harris had cheated on her.

"So what's wrong with Tionne?" Vaughn said, coming down the stairs.

Klarke turned around in surprise. "Oh, her and your dad are just going through some things," Klarke said casually.

"Ooooh, did they break up?" Vaughn asked eagerly.

"Come here," Klarke said, sitting down on the couch and patting the spot next to her for Vaughn to join her. "Baby, your father loves you. Your father would love you no matter who is in his life. Do you understand what I'm saying to you?"

Vaughn nodded. Klarke kissed her on the forehead, smiled and got up to go in the kitchen to get dinner started.

"What about you?" Vaughn asked, causing Klarke to turn around and face her daughter.

"What about me?" she asked.

"Will he love you, too, no matter who is in his life?"

11

Your Place or Mine

From: KAT@myworld.biz
To: RLQ812@sunset.com
Subject: Meet Me Halfway

Hey you,
I hope you don't take this the wrong way. I enjoy your e-mails.
I really do. I race to my computer in hopes of seeing your
e-mail address in my inbox.

I honestly feel as though I've known you all of my life (okay,
maybe just for most of it . . . smile) but nonetheless, when it
comes to you everything about me seems to pour out. I don't
hold back with you.

This cyber shit has to stop, though.

I gave you my phone number and it has yet to ring with you
on the other end. Maybe you're not a phone person. If that's
the case, just say so.

I guess what I'm really trying to say is that I won't even be
satisfied with your calling me at this point. I need to see you

again. I don't care when or where. We can meet each other halfway if you like. I just need to luxuriate in your words face-to-face.

I've been waiting for months for you to get around to mentioning that you perhaps wanted to see me again and you never have. So I figured I'd come on out and say it (crossing my fingers that you want to see me too). It's kind of like a couple who's been dating for a while but neither wants to be the first to say "I love you."

Anyway, think about my proposal and let me know how you feel about it.

KAT

From: RLQ812@sunset.com
To: KAT@myworld.biz
Subject: Meet Me Halfway

I'd love to meet you face-to-face. You name it.

"Come on, Dad. You're the only one who can tell me what to do," Reo said to his father.

"You don't need me to tell you what to do. You knew what you should have done a long time ago when the girl first sent you that e-mail," Mr. Laroque said.

"This woman may very well be your future daughter-in-law," Reo said. "She could be the mother of the grandchildren you and Mom have always wanted. You gotta help me out, Dad. Give me some of that *if I were you, this is what I would do* fatherly advice."

"If I were you I would have never pretended to be someone I wasn't. Ain't you got no game, son?"

"Thanks for nothing, Dad," Reo said, frustrated.

"Anytime, son, anytime," Mr. Laroque said, hanging up the telephone in Reo's ear.

Reo didn't know what he was going to do. Hell, yeah, he wanted to meet KAT face-to-face. He had only wanted to do that forever. But either he would have to tell her the truth or he would have to let her go. Or perhaps he could block out her e-mails, ignore them all together. Eventually she would catch on and let him be.

Reo knew it was immature and self-serving of him to continue this masquerade with KAT. He couldn't help it, though. He felt in his heart that KAT *was* meant for him.

He decided to sleep on it. Hopefully the answer would come to him in the morning.

From: RLQ812@sunset.com
To: KAT@myworld.biz
Subject: Confession

Before you tell me when and where you want to meet face-to-face, there is something I need to confess. I'm going to get right to the point as you often do. I know I never used your phone number to call you. I know I've never sent you that picture that I said I would either. It's not that I didn't want to. I didn't want you to find out that I'm not the man you think I am. Literally.

I don't know who you shared moments with in that Boston airport, but ever since you first e-mailed me I've been wishing that it had been me. Through your words, KAT, I've grown attached to everything about you.

Through your words I know how you brush your hair. I know

how you stretch and rise out of bed in the morning. I know that you brush your teeth in circles. I know that you collect figurines of elephants. Damn, you got me, girl. You have truly become a part of me.

I'm going to be sitting on pins and needles awaiting a response from you. If you never want to communicate with me again I'll understand. If that is the case, just hit your reply button for this e-mail with "Return to sender" in the subject line. If that's not the case, 614-576-9322. Ask for Reo.

Reo sat outside his publicist's office, boiling mad. He couldn't believe she had scheduled for him to visit over a dozen different bookstores in one month. She had left him a voice message informing him of his tour schedule and had avoided his phone calls since doing so. Reo decided to pay her a surprise visit.

"Mr. Laroque," the receptionist said. "Carla will see you now."

"Thank you," Reo said as he went into Carla's office.

"Hey, Reo," Carla said as Reo entered her office.

"What's wrong, you can't call nobody?" Reo asked.

"You so crazy," Carla said getting up to close her office door and lock it. After doing so she removed the red-and-black sheer scarf she was wearing around her neck. She undid the top button to the jacket of the red suit she was wearing.

"No, you are the one who's crazy if you think I'm going to spend all of next month packing and unpacking while bookstore hopping. I'm no bookstore ho, Carla."

"What's the problem?" Carla asked. "At first you couldn't get enough of arriving in different cities with a line of women waiting on your ass."

"That was then and this is now. I don't need to do all of this anymore."

"Oh, I get it. You think you're Omar Tyree now . . . or Michael Baisden? Well, let me tell you this, those brothas have been in the game far longer than you have and they are still putting in work. Don't ever think because you hit the best-seller lists that you no longer have an obligation to the readers out there," Carla said as she went to the mirror that was hanging above the couch in her office. She licked her fingertips and dabbed down a piece of hair that was disfiguring her Anita Baker short-short hairdo.

"I'm not saying that," Reo said. "What I am saying is that I don't have to get down that hard in the paint. All of those signings, Carla, in one month. Come on now!"

"Okay, Reo. Let's just sit down and talk about this calmly," Carla said as she grabbed Reo by his tie and led him over to the plush couch in her office. Carla began tasting Reo's lips with a nibble here and there.

"Uh, Carla," Reo said, pushing her away. "I already told you. We are not going there. I'm sorry about that night I came onto you at Marlon Green's book release party. I don't know what I was thinking, but I'm not trying to screw around and mess up our business relationship."

"You don't really mean that. Quit playing hard," Carla said, grabbing Reo's penis through his pants. "Oh, you're not playing. You really are hard."

"Damn it, Carla," Reo said, pushing her hand away.

Just then Reo's cell phone rang. He normally turned it off when he was going into a meeting, but he had been so pissed that it had slipped his mind. He looked down at the phone and the caller ID read "Unknown ID". Reo decided to let it go to voicemail. He pushed the Off button, or at least he meant to, but he had hit the green Okay button instead, which answered the call.

"Damn," he muttered then put the phone to his ear.

"Hello?" Reo heard a voice through the receiver say.

"This is Reo speaking," he said.

"Well hello, Reo speaking," the voice on the other end said.

Reo's heart began to race. "KAT, is that you?" Reo asked.

"I guess you don't have many women calling you, huh?" she said.

Reo dropped the phone down to his side. He closed his eyes and lifted his head up to the sky.

"Thank you, God," he said. "Thank you, heavenly Father."

"Hello? You still there?" KAT said.

"Yes, yes, oh, I'm sorry. Can you hold on one more time?" Reo asked.

"Certainly," KAT replied.

Reo covered the phone with his hand and whispered to Carla, "Just forget it, Carla. I'll do the signings. "I'll do a hundred signings."

Reo jetted out of Carla's office, leaving her standing there in his smoke. Back out in the lobby Reo took a deep breath and then placed the phone up to his ear.

"KAT, I do apologize," Reo said.

"Did I catch you at a bad time?" she asked.

"You couldn't be more perfect. I mean with your timing, that is."

"Hmm, okay. So, do I call you out of your name for having me think, all of this time, that you were someone other than yourself, or do I blow you a smooch through the phone and tell you how flattered I am for you doing so?"

"I would like that very much."

"Which one, to be called out of your name or blown a kiss? Knowing you, you would probably enjoy both."

By the time Reo had made it to his home, he and KAT had

talked and laughed for over an hour. Reo had driven all the way home from Carla's office before he knew it.

They were like a couple of high school sweethearts who had found each other again.

KAT was vague about her previous marriages, but went into great depth with tales of her children and the wonderful relationship she'd had with her parents before they passed. Reo told KAT about his struggle and the sacrifices he had made to become a writer and his relationship with his parents, especially his dad.

"So, we've graduated from e-mail to the phone," KAT said. "Does that mean I'm going to have to talk to you on the phone a few months before we get to actually meet one another face-to-face?"

"I'd enjoy nothing more than verbal relations with you, but I'm shooting for a personal encounter. You say when and where and I'll have airline tickets delivered to your front door," Reo said.

"This 614 area code is Columbus, right?" she asked.

"Yes," Reo said.

"That's only a two-hour drive, max."

"Then I'll send you a gas card, a rental car voucher, or something."

"Why is it you automatically assume I should drive to see you versus you come to see me?"

"I know you, KAT. You wouldn't have a man come to you. You wouldn't play that. No good mother would. I don't see you having that when it comes to your children."

"Yeah, I did right by calling you," she said proudly.

"I take it I gave you the right answer," Reo said, smiling.

"You did. There's nothing more attractive than a man who knows how to respect a woman who has children. Remind me to give your momma a great big hug and kiss for bringing you up right."

"Damn, girl, you already trying to meet my momma? Uh oh, I think that was my other line," Reo said as they both laughed.

"Oh, my, Reo. You are so crazy."

"About you," Reo said on a more serious note.

"Well, I better get off this phone."

"Yeah, but it's been a pleasure talking to you, KAT. But before I let you go, can I ask you something personal, and this is quite embarrassing?"

"What is it?" she said.

"Your name. What's your real name?"

"Klarke. Klarke Annette Taylor."

"I did it!" Klarke exclaimed to Jeva and Breezy, who were at her house preparing to watch *Sex and the City*.

"What are you talking about?" Breezy said. "Did you fart or something?"

"Why are you so stupid?" Klarke laughed. "No, I didn't fart. I mean I did IT . . . I got Reo to arrange to meet me in person."

"I never doubted that you would," Breezy said.

"You a bad woman," Jeva said, smiling. "I don't know how the two of you pull this kind of stuff off."

"Skills, baby," Breezy said. "It's called skills."

"I guess I don't have those type of skills," Jeva said.

"Damn skippy you don't," Breezy said, "or you wouldn't move in with me once a month to get away from Lance, only to keep running right back to him. I'm glad I don't mind my own company. Being alone is all right by me."

"I can't imagine raising my daughter without Lance. It's harder when kids are involved. There is a stronger bond," Jeva said.

"Bullshit, and I'm sick of women using that lame shit as an excuse to stay with a man," Breezy said. "Just because you have a baby with him doesn't mean you love him more than a woman who doesn't have a baby with a man."

"You don't have any kids, Breezy, so you don't understand," Jeva said.

"So you mean to tell me if Klarke had been married to Harris for thirteen years and not had any children by him that your five years with Lance would hold more weight because you two have a daughter? That's crazy. Why don't y'all baby mommas stop using the kids and that bond shit as an excuse to stay in a relationship and be treated like shit?"

"Excuse me," Jeva said dropping the knife she was using to cut the vegetables for the veggie tray. "I'm going to go check on my little Heather."

As Jeva headed up the steps to check on her daughter who was playing with Vaughn and HJ, Klarke went at it with Breezy.

"Sometimes you go too damn far," Klarke said. "You know how sensitive Jeva's feelings are."

"And you know how I am," Breezy explained. "If I'm going to have to tiptoe around her then maybe you two should just hang without me."

"See, now you are talking crazy," Klarke said. "Just try to be a little more diplomatic, why don't you?"

"Whatever," Breezy said as Jeva came down the steps.

"Yeah, whatever," Klarke said.

From: KAT@myworld.biz
To: RLQ812@sunset.com
Subject: Columbus Trip

Hey you!

I booked the rental car. I pick it up next Friday at 5:30 P.M. I can hardly wait. I should arrive in Columbus at about 8:00 P.M.

From: RLQ812@sunset.com
To: KAT@myworld.biz
Subject: Columbus Trip

I'm attaching your hotel itinerary. I got you a suite at the Double Tree downtown. I hope that is okay. If not, let me know and I'll change it to the hotel of your choice.

I'll be out of town from Tuesday to Friday, but my flight arrives back in Columbus at 3:00 P.M. Is 9:00 P.M. an okay time to meet me in the hotel bar? We can enjoy a cocktail and then go somewhere for dinner. I know of a nice steakhouse downtown. Would you like steak? What about alcohol?

From: KAT@myworld.biz
To: RLQ812@sunset.com
Subject: You

Hey you!

I think nine o'clock will be good. Steak sounds great. I don't drink on a regular, but when I do, you know Passion Alizé does the trick for me.

I can't wait to see you, Reo. Which leads me to the million-dollar question: How will I know who you are?

From: RLQ812@sunset.com
To: KAT@myworld.biz
Subject: Me

You just will!

The night Klarke was to meet Reo for the first time she skipped lunch and left work an hour early. She decided to pick up the rental car and load up her travel bags, so that once Harris picked up the kids she could head out straight for Columbus.

Klarke had definitely overpacked, but not knowing what-all Reo had in store for her, she didn't want to take the chance of not having the appropriate attire. Before loading her bags she double-checked the contents one last time. She removed the lingerie from her bag as it didn't coincide with her plan not to give Reo any. She replaced it with a nice long satin gown and robe set.

Hell, I'm not even going to put myself in a position where he sees me in my sleepwear, Klarke thought as she exchanged the long satin gown-robe set for a two-piece, black-and-white Chicago White Sox pajama-short set.

"There, all set," Klarke said to herself as she proceeded to carry her bags out to the car.

As she was coming out the door Harris pulled up and got out of his car.

"So what's taking you to Columbus?" Harris asked, coming up the driveway.

"Business," Klarke said, winking an eye.

"Business, huh?" Harris said, taking the bags from Klarke's hands and putting them in the rental car trunk for her. "I find that hard to believe."

"Well, believe it," Klarke said, slamming the car trunk down.

"Daddy, Daddy!" the kids yelled, bursting through the front door.

"Hey, Vaughn, Junior," Harris said, kissing and hugging them. "HJ, why so much stuff? You act like you don't already have an entire wardrobe at my house."

"This is my PlayStation stuff," HJ said, holding up a red-and-black duffel bag.

"Okay, well, load up," Harris said as the kids gave Klarke hugs and kisses good-bye and headed for their father's car. "Do you have your cell phone on you?"

"Of course," Klarke said. "Vaughn has the hotel information where I will be staying, so if anything comes up just holler."

"Be careful," Harris said. "Traffic is hell."

It was 8:15 P.M. when Klarke checked into her hotel. The bellboy waited patiently as the receptionist at the registration desk informed Klarke of her suite number and provided her with a key. The bellboy then escorted Klarke up to her concierge tower suite.

Klarke tussled with the key card to the suite. It took her three attempts to get the green light to enter the room. She stepped aside and allowed the bellboy to carry her bags into the suite. She dug into her purse for some one-dollar bills in order to tip him a dollar per bag. As she located the money the bellboy approached her, wishing her a comfortable stay. She handed him his tip and proceeded into the suite.

"Damn!" Klarke shouted.

As she walked through the lounging area of the suite, the aroma of scented candles hypnotized her. She turned off the lights to get a better effect. The scene was absolutely dazzling.

There was a basket of fruit and a bottle of her favorite alcoholic beverage, Passion Alizé, on the kitchenette table. As she proceeded to the bedroom she noticed different colors of rose petals covering the floor. The petals trailed to the Jacuzzi that was off to the side.

"I can't believe this," Klarke said, stunned. "Oh, my goodness."

The Jacuzzi was full of water and petals were afloat. Klarke dipped her fingers into the Jacuzzi to make a tiny splash. The water was still hot. On a marbled shelf along the Jacuzzi were a basket of Hershey kisses and a small envelope addressed to *KAT*.

Klarke picked up the envelope and was greeted by its wonderful scent. She swiped the card underneath her nose and inhaled the pleasant odor of what she later learned was Issy Miyake. She opened the envelope to find a message that read, *Let's make it 9:30 P.M.*

Klarke knew that was her sign to get butt naked and enjoy the Jacuzzi before meeting Reo at the downstairs bar.

Klarke's clothing lay on the floor where she had once stood. She had gotten both feet into the water before deciding to go retrieve the bottle of Alizé from the kitchenette table.

Since she was out of the water she grabbed a hair twisty from her toiletry bag and scooped her locks up.

For the next half-hour or so Klarke soaked in the Jacuzzi. She envisioned being able to engage in such treatment on a regular basis. She had to play her cards right with Reo. She just had to.

As Klarke made her way through the hotel lobby to the bar area, all eyes were on her. The gold-sequined gown she wore flickered in the eyeballs of every man, and woman for that matter, that was fortunate enough to catch a glimpse of her. Her three-and-one-half-inch gold pumps with a clear heel made her foot arch high like a Barbie doll's.

The trail of Issy Miyake from the bottle she found in her hotel suite bathroom, along with some other bath and body products, only reminded her audience of the lovely vision that had seemed to vanish too quickly.

As the view of the bar became clear to Klarke, she noticed that all of the men sitting at the bar were white, so she knew none of them were Reo. She had studied the picture of him in the back cover of his novel, but everything on her mind seemed to have gone down the drain right with the Jacuzzi water.

It was 9:50 P.M. when Klarke swallowed the last sip from her Shirley Temple. Reo was a no-show. She kept checking her cell phone to make sure she hadn't missed the call telling her he would be late. Although thirty minutes was the official wait time, twenty had been sufficient, so Klarke scooped up her matching sequined evening bag and left the bar.

Klarke went to the registration desk to see if a message had been left for her. She was hoping that there were no mind-readers in the lobby. As beautiful, calm, and relaxed as she appeared on the outside, on the inside she was pissed the fuck off. Here she had driven two hours to see this man and the asshole didn't have the decency to show up, let alone call her to say he was going to be a no-show. If Reo had, in fact, bitched out on her, to Klarke, that was months of work down the drain (with the Jacuzzi water).

"I'm Klarke Taylor in 2218," Klarke said to the clerk at the desk. "I was wondering if by chance I had any messages?"

"Miss Taylor," a voice called from behind Klarke. "Are you Miss Klarke Taylor?" the voice asked.

"Who wants to know?" Klarke said, turning around seductively, assuming the voice belonged to Reo.

The voice belonged to a man who appeared to be a limousine driver. He had on a black cap, very dark sunglasses and a driver's jacket. "Oh, I'm sorry. I thought you were someone else," Klarke apologized.

"No need to apologize, ma'am," the driver said tilting his hat. "I have a message for you from a Mr. Reo Laroque. Regretfully, Mr. Laroque will not be able to join you this evening. He missed his connecting flight and won't be able to get put on another one until early morning."

Klarke tried to maintain her calm, but her skin tone quickly went from a caramel sundae topping to that of strawberry. *This is just what I get*, Klarke thought to herself.

"Mr. Laroque felt that there was no need for you to miss out on the dinner reservation, so he hired me to see that you get transported and well taken care of," the driver continued.

Although it was a nice cover-up on Reo's part, it was still somewhat of a turnoff to Klarke that he didn't phone her and explain the situation himself. Nonetheless, Klarke hadn't eaten all day and was starved.

"Well, I guess there's nothing I can do about it," Klarke said, trying to emerge as the passive individual she had always been. "I knew I should have taken those flying lessons; then I could have picked Mr. Laroque up myself."

"I'm sure Mr. Laroque would have liked nothing better than to be chauffeured home, via air, by such a lovely pilot."

"Thank you." Klarke blushed.

"Shall we?" the driver said, holding out his arm for Klarke.

"Yes, we shall," Klarke said, allowing the driver to guide her to the limo.

Once the driver got Klarke safely tucked into the limo, he walked around to the driver's side, made a call on the CB, and drove off. The driver rolled down the black-tinted partition that was separating him from Klarke.

"The bar is full for you, Miss Taylor," the driver said. "Please feel free to help yourself. And again, Mr. Laroque sends his apologies."

"Did he say what time in the morning?" Klarke asked.

"Excuse me?" the driver said.

"Did Mr. Laroque say what time I should expect him in the morning?"

"I'm afraid he didn't share that information with me, ma'am."

Klarke sat back in the cushioned leather limo seats, comfortable but extremely disappointed. She had to remind herself that this was business. She looked herself over and could have spit at the fact that Reo wouldn't get to see her in her delectable evening dress.

As the driver watched Klarke through his rearview mirror he could tell she was discontented. Although he was only the bearer of bad news, he felt like he had thrown the knockout punch.

The driver began to make small talk with Klarke in order to get her mind off of Reo's absence. He asked her where she was from, if she was married, and if she had any children. They compared and contrasted Columbus and Toledo, and the driver even gave Klarke tips on where to shop while in Columbus.

They looked at one another's eyes through the rearview mirror, in conversation the duration of the drive. Klarke could barely see the driver's eyeballs but could feel when he was watching her. The driver even swerved a couple of times in an attempt to be attentive to Klarke.

Ten minutes after leaving the Doubletree, the limo pulled up to a quaint steakhouse that was camouflaged by the downtown strip buildings. The driver parked and walked around to let Klarke out of the limo.

"Thank you," Klarke said, taking his hand.

"Right this way, Miss Taylor," the driver said. "I'll see that you are seated properly."

The driver escorted Klarke into the dimly lit steakhouse. There were only a few patrons, but it looked to be the exquisite type of place where crowds didn't lurk. It had a cathedral ceiling with heavy satin drapes that made love to the windowpanes.

"Reservation for Miss Taylor," the driver said to the Maître d'.

As Klarke looked around, she forgot all about Reo standing her up. It was safe to say that he had made amends for his absence with the premeditated hospitality.

The Maître d' asked Klarke to follow him to a table. Klarke was led, with the driver following close behind, to an angelic table setting in the rear corner of the restaurant. A dozen long-stemmed roses were laid across the table, as well as a chilled bottle of Chardonnay.

"Miss Taylor," the driver said, "Everything looks to be in order. I shall wait for you outside. Please take your time and enjoy your dinner."

A saxophone player walked over to Klarke's table and began to blow a smooth melody belonging to one of Brian McKnight's songs. Klarke put her hand over her heart and smiled at the driver.

"Are you sure you want to miss this?" Klarke asked. "I'd hate for you to be sitting out there all alone. Perhaps you can join me. Have you eaten yet?"

"Oh, Miss Taylor, that is kind of you. I don't think my wallet could afford it. But not to worry, Mr. Laroque has taken care of your tab for the night. Do enjoy," the driver said, walking away.

"Then perhaps we can share mine," Klarke said, sad to see the driver walk away. She could only imagine how he must feel, working for peanuts while seeing to it that rich egos got everything their hearts desired.

The driver turned, walked back over to the table, and snapped his finger for the hostess. He removed his hat and began to remove his jacket as the hostess hurried over to take his personals.

"So, I take it you'll be joining the lady tonight, Mr. Laroque?" the hostess said to the driver.

"I certainly will," the driver replied, removing the dark shades and handing the items to the hostess.

Completely astounded and caught offguard, Klarke's eyes filled with tears as she bowed her head at the sight of Reo standing before her. She had to be dreaming. There was no way this was real.

"Baby, don't," Reo said, wiping her tears.

"I don't know what to say," Klarke said to Reo, choked up. "No one has ever done anything like this for me before."

"That's why I'm here," Reo said caressing Klarke's face. "To do things for you and to you that no one has ever done before."

Reo took a small box that was sitting in his chair and handed it to Klarke. Inside was a miniature hand-carved wooden elephant. It was absolutely beautiful. Klarke couldn't hold in her weeping. Underneath that phony limo driver garb stood one of the most handsome men she had ever laid eyes on. Reo's eyes were warm like marshmallows in hot chocolate. His lips were luscious and moist and could only benefit her. His skin was flawless and his manner was that of a veritable esquire.

There Reo stood, not ashamed of the game he played and not afraid of winning it. He went out on a limb and placed his lips against Klarke's. She pressed closer to him and mumbled, "Now I wish I had packed the lingerie."

■ ■ ■

As difficult as it was not to be taken in completely by Reo's charm, Klarke didn't give him any. She had promised herself that she wasn't going to have sex with him the first time she met him face-to-face. She had come this far and refused to mess up now. She wanted to keep him guessing, wanting to know more and more.

Reo's strong hands and mellow touch made it almost impossible for Klarke to keep her panties on. Just the way Reo played with her hair made her panties wet. Yet, she couldn't give her body to him. Not yet.

Klarke and Reo started meeting one another whenever they could. Either she would drive to Columbus or they would meet halfway at a lodge. They had grown so fond of one another that the two-hour distance between them was intolerable.

After several more rendezvous Klarke finally gave Reo the green light to drive to Toledo to be introduced to her children. She felt that the time was right. Harris and Rawling were the only two men the children had ever seen their mother with, so Klarke had been a tad leery. She hadn't wanted Reo to visit until she had her game locked airtight. She didn't want her children to grow fond of Reo only for her to rip him out of their lives, as they had accused her of doing with Rawling.

After her second divorce Klarke realized that when couples parted, it deeply effected the children.

After her divorce from Rawling, Vaughn and HJ had fought a lot with one another and had been cutting up in school. Klarke had had to sit them down and ask what was going on with the two of them. She was heartbroken when they had accused her of husband-hopping—even if they hadn't used those exact words. After that Klarke made sure to never have men in and out of her life or the lives of her children.

Klarke felt that Reo was a shoo-in however. He was so genuine and he enjoyed doing nice things for Klarke because he admired and respected her, not because he was trying to prove something to her.

To get the kids used to the idea of a new man in their mommy's life, Klarke started bringing up her *"author friend,"* Reo's name. She placed his books in the living room and in the bathroom in an attempt to familiarize the children with him.

When Vaughn finally asked if she could meet Reo and interview him for a paper she had to do in school, Klarke had been elated. The timing couldn't have been more perfect. Klarke okayed it with HJ, who gave his two thumbs up, and immediately invited Reo to visit.

Klarke had wanted to plan Reo's visit to the tee. She wanted them to spend the day at an amusement park, go to the movies, eat pizza, and everything else kids love to do, but Reo wasn't hearing it. He told Klarke that he just wanted to spend time with the kids and get to know them because they were a part of the woman he had fallen in love with.

Klarke was so nervous that she was running in circles. Reo was due to arrive at her house any minute and the cake was still baking. Earlier she had turned the oven on before taking her shower but had forgotten to put in the cake.

"Mom, just go put on your makeup," Vaughn told her, exasperated. "When the timer goes off I'll take the cake out."

"Okay, honey," Klarke said as she headed up the stairs. "Set it on the cooling stone and be careful."

"Mom, I just turned thirteen, remember? I know how to take a cake out of the oven."

When Klarke got to the top of the steps, she stopped to check herself out. That was when she noticed a stain near the crotch area of her one-piece white pantsuit.

"What in the hell?" Klarke said, as she suddenly realized that she had gotten her period. At first Klarke didn't know whether to jump up and down because it meant she wasn't pregnant with Evan's child or to be pissed off for ruining her $155 pantsuit. She decided to go with joy.

"Thank you, God," she said looking up at the ceiling. She then hurried to find another outfit to wear for the evening.

No sooner had Klarke run up the stairs than Vaughn heard a car pull up in the driveway. She ran to the window and saw a white Escalade in the drive. Vaughn went over to the door and opened it as Reo walked up the pathway with a bouquet of flowers in hand.

"Are you Mr. Reo?" Vaughn asked.

"I am," Reo said with a smile. "You must be Vaughn."

"I am. Pleased to meet you," Vaughn said, opening the door wider.

"I'm HJ," the little boy said, running over to shake Reo's hand.

"Hello, HJ. It's good to finally meet you both. Your mother has told me a lot about you two."

"Do you have presents for us?" HJ asked and Vaughn elbowed him in the chest.

"Pardon me?" Reo asked in surprise.

After giving Vaughn a stern look HJ said, "Well, in the movies the new boyfriend always comes with gifts. You know? To get the new stepkids to like him."

"You'll have to excuse him, Mr. Reo," Vaughn said, rolling her eyes. "He's an idiot."

"Am not," HJ said, indignant.

"Are too," Vaughn said.

"Okay, you two," Reo said, laughing. "Sorry, little man, but I didn't bring gifts. I'm a rookie at this."

"Ah, that's okay," HJ said.

"Do you have any kids?" Vaughn came right out and asked.

"Uh, no," Reo said with a smile.

"So that means no baby-mama drama, right?"

Reo laughed. "You are too much."

"Those flowers are lovely," Vaughn said, sniffing the bouquet in Reo's hands. "And they smell good. Are they for my mom?"

"As a matter of fact, they are," Reo said, pulling a hot pink daisy from the bunch. "But if I had any idea that you were going to be even lovelier than your mom described, I would have bought you a bouquet, too. Hopefully this will do for now."

Vaughn smiled a genuine smile as Reo tapped her nose with the daisy. She took it from him and gently inhaled.

"Mom will be down in a moment," Vaughn said. "She's putting on her face. Do you want a glass of water?"

"Yes, please," Reo said with a smile.

Vaughn went into the kitchen to get a glass of water for Reo. The timer went off for the cake, so she took it out of the oven and placed it on the cooling stone.

While they waited for Klarke to come down, Vaughn and Reo watched and coached HJ on a video game he was playing. The three laughed and talked for a good while before Klarke came down the steps. The children were enjoying Reo so much that neither of them thought twice about notifying Klarke of his arrival.

"Well, how long have you been here?" Klarke asked as she entered the living room.

"I don't know. I lost track of time," Reo said, rising to hand Klarke the flowers and kiss her on the cheek.

"Thank you, sweetheart," Klarke said, with a huge grin on her face. "I'm so glad you're here. Did you check into the hotel yet?"

"Yeah, I stopped there first before coming here."

"You didn't call me so I guess you found your way okay."

"Sure did," Reo said.

For a moment the four just stood in the room like bashful classmates at a school dance. Klarke wanted so badly to put her arms around Reo and welcome him with a big kiss. Instead, she suggested they all sit down for dinner.

No one could have asked for a more perfect evening. The fried chicken was golden and crispy. The mashed potatoes had not a lump, and the gravy was a creamy, smooth shade of brown. The gravy Klarke had made from the fried chicken grease was just right. The green beans were seasoned to taste, and the rolls were buttery and soft.

The children took to Reo like they had known him all of their lives. He played some more video games with HJ and helped Vaughn ice the cake.

Around eleven Reo decided it was time for him to leave. The children—and Klarke—hated to see him go. He promised them he would return first thing in the morning to whip them up some breakfast.

Klarke sent the kids off to get ready for bed while she walked Reo to his truck. It was the first moment they had alone.

"Looks like they adore you," Klarke said.

"Man, they are great," Reo said. "You are great. You raised some beautiful children, KAT . . . no lie."

"Thank you."

"So, do I need to stop off at the grocery to pick up items for breakfast?"

"That depends on what you are making."

"Do the kids like pancakes?"

"Vaughn does, but not HJ."

"Does HJ like eggs?"

"Yes."

"Okay, a pancake breakfast for Vaughn and an omelet delight for HJ."

"Sounds great, but what about me?"

"For you, I'll really have to exercise my culinary skills. How does a Reo on a stick sound?" Reo said to Klarke, pulling her close to him.

"Stop teasing me," Klarke said.

"That was wrong of me, huh?" Reo said, giving her a peck on the lips.

"Yeah, you know we can't get down this go-round."

"I'm always getting down with you even when you're not around."

"You writers always have some creative shit to say," she said, giving Reo a deep French kiss. "I'll see you in the morning."

"All right, Miss Lady," Reo said unlocking his door. "Oh, what about breakfast? Do I need to stop and get anything?"

"I have everything you need right here." Klarke winked.

. . .

The next morning Reo was at Klarke's door bright and early. She had no idea he would be arriving at 8:00 A.M. She jumped out of bed to look out her window and there his Escalade was, parked in the driveway. Her head hurt and her stomach was queasy, probably because she had jumped up from a deep sleep too fast. She had been dreaming about Reo.

In her dream Reo was away on a book signing and she was vacationing at some ocean-view beach house. She called him and told him how much she missed him as the waves slapped against the shore. The next thing she knew Reo was at the beach house eating her pussy like no one had ever done before.

The dream was so real that as Klarke ran down the steps, she could feel how moist she was between her legs.

She straightened herself up as much as any woman at eight in the morning could do. She stuck a piece of mint chewing gum in her mouth and opened the door.

"Good morning, early riser," Klarke said to Reo, who was holding a bag of groceries in his hand.

"Good morning to you," Reo said, kissing her on the forehead.

"You just had to stop at the grocery store anyway, huh? Man, you are so hard-headed."

"I had to make sure I had my secret ingredients." Reo winked.

"Well, excuse me," Klarke said, clearing the way for Reo.

"You just go on back to bed and let me do my thang."

"Do your thang where? In the kitchen or in my bed?" Klarke teased as she headed back upstairs.

Klarke rested for about twenty more minutes before getting up to get herself together. She could hear conversation downstairs and knew that the children had gotten up and joined Reo in the kitchen.

The aroma of buttermilk pancakes, bacon, sausage, omelets, biscuits, and hashbrowns filled the house. Klarke couldn't wait to get her eat on.

When Klarke got downstairs, Vaughn, still in her pajamas, was pouring glasses of orange juice and HJ, showing off his new Spider-Man sleeper, was laying out the silverware on the huge dining table, which was an old conference room table she and Harris had bought from an auction. She had dressed up the table with a long black runner and placed an Indian chunky wooden candleholder on each end. Klarke couldn't help but smile at the Norman Rockwell scene.

"Good morning," Klarke said, smiling.

"Good morning," the children responded happily.

"I see you had help," Klarke said to Reo.

"Oh, yeah. I couldn't have done all of this without them," Reo replied with a smile. "Everything is ready, so let's chow."

The four hurried to sit down and Klarke, Vaughn, and HJ began to scoop up food onto their plates. Reo sat back and stared at them. Realizing that he was staring at them, they all stopped what they were doing to stare back.

"May I bless the food?" he asked.

Klarke smiled. "Certainly."

Klarke and the children weren't very religious, but they were believers. Klarke almost felt embarrassed that she had never raised her children to take time out to give thanks. Lord knows she should have. Sometimes their meals were indeed a blessing. Klarke felt joyous that someone was in their lives to now teach them about prayer. Better late than never.

From that point on, Klarke and the children always blessed

their food. Vaughn even did it at school. The school had the nerve to phone Klarke at work about it. They felt as though Vaughn could influence the other children with her religious belief.

The day after the phone call, Klarke sent Vaughn to school with a sign she had printed up on her computer at work. Klarke placed it in an envelope and ordered Vaughn to give it to the school adviser who had phoned her.

There was an acknowledgment of the phone call in the envelope. Included was the sign, which read "SCHOOL ZONE: NO DRUGS, WEAPONS, OR GOD ALLOWED."

The next time Reo came to Toledo to visit Klarke and the kids, they shared the experience with him. He told them about the time that his father had to get with one of his schoolteachers. Reo advised Vaughn to continue praying whenever she felt the need to communicate with God.

Reo was so moved by his deep influence on Vaughn and HJ that he took them each out to purchase their first Bible. He gave them a brief overview and went over the first book of the Bible with them. The children enjoyed the lesson and the comparisons to real life that Reo made.

"This is like reading a fairy tale," HJ said to Reo.

"Yeah," Vaughn said, nodding. "This is a good book."

Reo winked. "That's what most people say."

"How's my favorite girl?" Reo said, hugging Vaughn as she ran down the driveway to meet him at his truck.

"Hi, Mr. Reo. Is that HJ's present?" Vaughn asked, knocking on the wrapped gift box Reo was holding.

"It sure is," Reo said, kneeling down infront of Vaughn. "But this is for my favorite girl."

Reo handed Vaughn a mood ring that he had picked up from the Atlanta Underground while in the ATL on a book signing.

"It's gorgeous!" Vaughn said, thrilled.

"Just like you," Reo replied. "Now, where is the birthday boy?"

"He's inside the house playing. Come on." Vaughn said, pulling Reo by the hand.

Reo could tell by all the cars parked outside that most of the guests had arrived. When he walked through the door he saw little boys and girls running everywhere. Breezy was playing Pin the Tale on the Donkey with one group, while Jeva was preparing a tub of water for a game of Bobbing for Apples.

Klarke was in the kitchen talking with one of the parents, while holding a little girl who looked to be about four years of age. Reo's face lit up at the sight of his KAT. Her hair was pulled up in a curly ponytail. This was his first time seeing her in a pair of jeans, and oh how they showed off her figure. Her gray turtleneck sweater fit her like a glove. She was an extremely beautiful woman. Reo had never felt so lucky.

"You must be Reo," Breezy said, holding out her hand.

"Breezy," Reo said, shaking her hand.

"Finally we meet. Though it's not like I don't already know everything about you," Breezy said.

"Same here," Reo said. "Klarke has shown me every last one of her photo albums."

"She didn't narrate the pictures from my twenty-fifth birthday party, did she?" Breezy asked. "I'll kill her if she did."

"Not to worry," Klarke said coming up behind them. "I gave him the edited version."

"HJ will be glad you made it," Klarke said, kissing Reo.

"That's my cue to scram," Breezy said, walking back over to the game of Pin the Tail on the Donkey.

"I've missed you," Reo told Klarke.

"Ditto."

"Who's this cutie?" Reo asked referring to the child in Klarke's arms.

"Oh, this is the kids' little sister," Klarke said, kissing her on the cheek.

"Harris's daughter?" Reo asked, with raised eyebrows.

"Umm hmm," Klarke said, looking down at the little girl.

"Is he here?"

"HJ's actual birthday was three days ago. He had his party for HJ last weekend. Besides," Klarke said in a low whisper, "I'm not so sure his woman would approve of him hanging out with his ex."

"Oh, he's got baby-mama's drama, as Vaughn would say," Reo said, watching for a moment as Klarke rubbed her nose against the little girl's, making her smile. "You are a beautiful woman," Reo said, his voice low and intimate. "And I mean that in every way possible."

"You two going to join the party?" Jeva said, walking into the kitchen with an empty potato chip bag. She threw it in the trash.

"Oh, Jeva, this is Reo. Reo, Jeva," Klarke said introducing them.

"Finally I meet the man who keeps a smile on my girl's face," Jeva said, hugging Reo.

"It's good to finally meet you too," Reo said.

"Where's the birthday boy?" Reo said, looking around.

"Oh, he's somewhere," Klarke said, looking for him as the phone rang. "He's right there getting his picture taken with the clown."

"I've always wanted a picture with a clown," Reo said jokingly and walked away.

"Taylor residence," Klarke said, answering the phone.

Jeva waited patiently as she watched Klarke's mouth drop open. She put her hand on Klarke's shoulder and asked if everything was okay.

"Take the baby," Klarke said, handing the child to Jeva.

Klarke continued to listen to the caller as her eyes filled with tears. "What's wrong?" Breezy walked over and asked, sensing something was wrong.

"I don't know," Jeva said, worried. "Here, take her and let me see what's going on."

Breezy took the little girl from Jeva and rejoined the party. Klarke placed the phone back in it's receiver and stood there.

"Klarke, what's going on?" Jeva asked.

"It's Tionne," Klarke said, her voice filled with shock. "Harris just found her dead. She hung herself."

Klarke didn't feel comfortable going to Tionne's funeral. There had been so much bad blood between the two. She was worried that Tionne's family would be upset if she showed up.

Instead, Klarke cooked and received food from visitors at Harris and Tionne's house while the funeral was taking place. Once Harris and the children, Tionne's family and friends, started arriving, Klarke left.

On her drive home Klarke thought about Tionne's last visit to her house. She remembered how Tionne had wanted her to reassure her of the love Klarke had for her and Harris's child. There had been a desperate devastation in Tionne's eyes. Never in a million years would she have thought that Tionne would kill herself.

Klarke realized that Tionne had chosen the day of HJ's party to do it because none of the children would be home. She didn't have to worry about one of them finding her.

Klarke pulled her car over to the side of the road and gave thanks to God. She thanked him for making her a strong woman. She thanked him for getting her through this devastating time in her life. She asked Jesus to represent her before God by closing her prayer in his name. She wiped the tears from her eyes and continued her drive home.

Klarke had called into work the day of Tionne's funeral and informed the receptionist that she needed to take a funeral day due to Tionne's death. She ended up calling in the day after as well. She just needed time to herself. The day she did return to work, she wished that she didn't have to.

"I heard about what happened," Evan said as he walked up to Klarke's cubicle. "Your ex-husband's wife. I'm sorry to hear that."

"Thanks," Klarke said, not looking up at Evan.

"How are the kids doing?"

"They're fine."

"How are you?"

"I'm fine too," Klarke said, still not looking up.

"So, is this how we are going to deal with this?" Evan asked.

"Deal with what?" Klarke snapped.

"With us. I mean, look at you, Klarke. You can't even look at me. You're ashamed."

"Me, ashamed?" Klarke said, looking up at Evan. "You're the one who tried to act like you barely knew me in front of your brothers, and besides, I don't see you inviting me to Momma Kemble's house for dinner."

"Is this what all of this attitude is about? Dinner? Hell, you can come tomorrow if you like," Evan said, throwing his hands up. "Because this is bullshit. You're treating me like shit has got to stop. I mean, we can go back to me being the asshole white boss and you can be the bitchy black girl if you like, but let's decide what it's going to be."

"Hold it right there!" Klarke said, standing up. She looked around to make sure she hadn't drawn anyone's attention with her outburst, then sat back down calmly.

"No, you hold it," Evan said in a sharp tone. "Look, Klarke, all I want to do is—"

"What? All you want to do is what?" Klarke said with attitude.

"Forget it," Evan said walking away. Evan was tired of saying what he thought Klarke wanted to hear. Yeah, maybe at first being with Klarke had something to do with Evan being turned on by the novelty of being with a black woman. However, he had no idea he would want more from her. Not just more sex, which he wouldn't have refused, but more from her as a person.

Klarke sat at her desk overwhelmed by everything that was going on in her life. She got up and went to the copy room and grabbed some empty Xerox paper boxes. She returned to her desk and began packing up her belongings.

She didn't stop to think of the consequences. She just knew she didn't want to be there anymore.

Once Klarke was finished packing up her desk she went into Evan's office. She didn't rehearse what she was going to say to him or how she was going to say it.

"I'm leaving," Klarke said almost under her breath.

"For lunch, for good, what?" Evan asked baffled.

"For good, I think," Klarke answered confused. "I don't know. I just need some time."

Evan got up to close the door.

"No matter how you feel about me on a personal level, as your employer, I won't let you go. I'll accept the fact that you don't want to have a personal relationship with me, but I refuse to let one of the most valuable assets of the company walk away. Now, I understand you have a lot going on in your life so I'm willing to grant you leave—paid leave—but I won't let you go permanently, Klarke. I won't."

"Evan, why are you making this so hard?"

"You're the one making everything so hard. You're the one who wouldn't even give us a chance. It's obvious we're two very different people from two very different walks of life, but can't we at least start over and try to be friends? We can then just go from there."

"Evan, you and I both know that curiosity got the best of you. You've wanted to climb in bed with me the moment you saw me. You didn't want to marry me, or make me your girlfriend for that matter. You wanted to screw me and so you did. Get over it already. I did."

"You're so cold," Evan said shaking his head. "You're cold and you're wrong. What's happening to you, Klarke?"

"You don't know me, Evan."

"You won't let me know you. You act like I have some hidden agenda."

"You people normally do," Klarke mumbled under her breath.

"Just go, Klarke. You win. Just go. If you are standing here saying hateful things in order to make this easier for yourself because you know you are wrong, then just go. I'll have Renée draw you up some type of severance package. We'll say you were terminated. No need for your kids to go hungry just because their mother wants to be a bitch."

"Or is a severance package your discreet way of trickin'?" Klarke said, storming out of Evan's office.

Klarke carried the Xerox box full of her belongings from work into the house and dropped it right at the door. She slugged over to the couch and threw herself down. Just as she decided to get up and get a glass of Alizé, the phone rang.

Klarke looked at the caller ID and saw that it was Reo's number. She took a deep breath and then answered the phone.

"Hello," Klarke answered.

"I just called your office," Reo said, lightweight frantic. "They said you were no longer with the company. What happened?"

"Baby," Klarke said as her voice began to break up. "I'm tired. There was just so much going on there and . . ."

Klarke began to cry.

"Don't cry," Reo said in a soothing tone. The sound of her tears broke his heart.

"I don't know what I'm going to do!" Klarke cried. "My life is just so crazy! It's always been so crazy. And just when I start to think that everything is going to be okay."

"You don't have to worry 'bout a damn thang," Reo said in a strong, comforting tone. "You've got me in your life now and I ain't going nowhere. I got your back."

12

The Sin Is Pride

In the maternity ward of Columbus Hospital, the doctors on staff were having a hard time with one patient in particular.

"Push! Just one more push," the nurse pleaded.

"The head is out," the doctor confirmed. "Just one more push and you'll be all done. I promise. Just one more push."

"You said that two pushes ago, damn it!" the angry pregnant woman yelled. "This is the last goddamn time I'm pushing. If the baby doesn't come out, then you are going to have to figure out some other way to get it out."

One more push and the baby left its mother's womb. The doctor cut the umbilical cord and offered the new baby girl to the nurses to clean up. The nurse placed the tiny little girl on her mother's chest just long enough for her to take a good look.

The nurse used a nasal suction to clear the baby's throat and nostrils of fluids. The baby girl didn't cry once throughout all the tossing and turning—that was, until they put those darn droplets into her eyes. She had an infant tantrum then.

The nurses seemed rough and relentless as they scrubbed her tiny body clean of her mother's blood. Once the nurses pampered her by shampooing her curly black mane, the little diva relaxed and found some serenity in the entire transition. Nonetheless, if the baby girl had had the strength she would have scratched those bitches' eyes out for fucking up her nine-month siesta.

It was obvious that the young sprout was going to be just like her mother. From the moment the baby girl was rolled into the nursery it was like the other babies immediately fell silent. It was as if she had been born to rule the world.

Others would see her as another statistic, a little black child born without a father to pen his name on her birth certificate. In this case, though, the mother would not have wanted it any other way. She stood to gain more from the father's absence.

"Hey, Mommy's little pot of gold. I can't wait to tell your daddy that you are here," Meka cooed to her new baby girl. "You look so sweet, yes you do. But then again, revenge always has been sweet hasn't it?"

Meka had put her body through nine miserable months of hell in the name of revenge. After her and Reo's lovemaking finale, finding out that she was pregnant was the worse news Meka could have received.

Not only had Reo made her feel like a third-rate slut after a night of explicit sexual acts, but he also thought he had heard the last of her. After that night he never even bothered to call Meka to see if she was still breathing.

Of course Meka, being the kind of woman she was, told everyone that it was she who wanted nothing more to do with Reo. She told her friends and family that success had gone to his head, that he was a changed man. She had even insinuated that he had become violent with her. Everything except the truth . . . that he wanted nothing more to do with her saddity ass.

Meka hadn't been out of the hospital a full day before she phoned her attorney's office. She had had her attorney draft the paternity suit papers against Reo before she had even started showing. Now she wanted to finalize things.

Whenever she would suffer morning sickness or have to purchase bigger clothing, Meka would pull out her copy of the million-dollar paternity suit and know that her discomfort was not in vain.

Reo was going to pay dearly for what he had done to her. He would regret thinking he was Mr. Big Shit.

She had put up with him when he was just a nobody. How dare he settle into a storybook lifestyle and leave her behind? She deserved to be on his arm when he was rewarded the Pulitzer or the NAACP award for best mainstream fiction author. Some trophy tramp would enjoy what she well deserved and was born to be a part of.

Meka never did believe that she was supposed to spend any portion of her life working. It didn't matter how much money her paycheck would be worth, she deemed herself worthy of marrying big money. She had it in the palm of her hands, on the tip of her tongue, at her fucking feet, and she blew it. If only she could have held on for a little longer. But now she was man overboard. The hell with that. She was going to get hers.

"Darling, are you sure you're doing the right thing?" Meka's mother said as the two sat in the baby's nursery while she cuddled her grandchild.

"It's just like you to be on his side, Mother," Meka said. "You don't know the real Reo Laroque. He was just putting on a show for you and Daddy."

"It just seems that something like this could ruin the relationship this little bundle of joy here needs with her daddy."

"By the time I get done with him, Mother," Meka said, "we'll be able to buy her a new daddy."

"You're acting like this baby is more of a meal ticket than your daughter."

"Mother, need I remind you of how you got Daddy to marry you?"

Meka's mother gave her an evil look then got up and took the baby over to the changing table. "You shouldn't believe everything your Aunt Margaret tells you."

"I'm sorry, Mother, but I just hate when I feel like you're against me."

"I'm not against you. I've never been against you. You are my baby. It just doesn't seem right. I mean, you never even bothered telling Reo that you were pregnant. You act as if he abandoned you in the delivery room. I don't understand why you are not even giving him a chance to accept the baby into his life."

"Some things aren't meant to be understood, Mother," Meka said. "Some things are just meant to be."

The doctor had ordered Meka to take care of herself for the next six weeks, but after a week Meka was out and about. She couldn't think straight until she met with her attorney to give the go-ahead on the filing of the paternity suit papers.

"Do you think I should ask for two million?" Meka asked as she lunched with her attorney at the Olive Garden. "I'm sure by now he's got some cute little Barbie he's promising to spend the rest of his life with. The last thing he needs right now is a baby with a touch of baby-mama drama in the equation."

"I work for you," her attorney replied, slinging her butt-length brunette hair over her left shoulder. "You know this Reo far better than I do. What do you think keeping you and your daughter out of his life is worth to him?"

Meka dipped a breadstick in some tomato sauce and nibbled off a piece. She thought about what her resurfacing in Reo's life with a child would do to him.

"Yes, let's go for two million," Meka said, nodding slowly.

"We can negotiate down to a million if all else fails. In the meantime, what you might want to do is take out a million-dollar life insurance policy on your daughter. You never know what could happen between now and then," Meka's attorney said.

"That sounds like a good idea. You are amazing," Meka said, smiling.

"Do you remember that black model guy who started off dancing on that stupid underwear commercial or something like that?"

"The one on the soap opera now?" Meka asked.

"Yes, that's the one. I got the mother of his twins five million dollars," Meka's attorney said proudly.

"Wow, he must have hated her," Meka said.

"No, not really. He hated the idea of his wife finding out about her."

The two laughed. They finalized the specifics of the suit and discussed some interesting ways of serving Reo with the paternity papers.

13

Daddy's Coming Home

The guard frisked Breezy thoroughly. She had gone through the metal detector and had also been subjected to the wand. After visiting her father in the Chillicothe prison for the past fifteen years she was used to the tri-search her body was put through. This could have all ended five years ago, but more time had been tacked onto her father's jail sentence due to his poor behavior.

Breezy didn't mind the depressing atmosphere as she walked through the prison halls. After all, it was her fault he was in there.

"Daddy," Breezy said as her father joined her at the round mint-green table, sticky with leavings of visitors over time.

"Hey, sweetie. How's my little girl?" Mr. Williams said, kissing Breezy, his thick black mustache scratching her cheek. Breezy loved how he had grown his mustache in prison. It made him look refined. Jail hadn't affected his good looks one bit. He still had skin the color and smoothness of honey. A person could melt in the serenity of his hazel eyes. When he had first gone to prison, he had started losing his hair. Breezy had suggested that he shave it bald, so he had. You could see yourself in his shiny head.

"I'm fine. How are you doing, Dad?"

"I'm locked up." He laughed. Breezy didn't find it amusing. "Sorry, honey. How's work?"

"Tiresome. But you know how it goes. We's gots to do our part for Mr. Charlie in order to live in this great land of his," Breezy said in her Kizzy voice.

"Good old U.S. of A," her father said.

"Yep, but I wouldn't want to live anywhere else." She paused. "I hear Ma was asking Uncle Rudy about you."

"Was she?" Mr. Williams said, a smile creeping across his face. "Your Momma is always going to be my girl. Even though she couldn't find it in her heart to wait for me, I love her. How is she and that new husband of hers doing?"

"Beats me," Breezy said huffily. "I hardly talk to her. She don't call me, so I don't call her."

"You can't be like that," Mr. Williams said sincerely.

"I'm like this because you're not. I hate her for you. It was supposed to be until death do you part, not a lousy jail sentence."

"I wouldn't call ten to twenty-five years lousy," Mr. Williams said. "I hate to see my little girl so angry. I don't know where all that hate in you comes from."

"My father is locked up. My mother is off gallivanting with a man half her age. I spend more time working than living. Hell yeah I'm angry."

Mr. Williams put his hand on hers and looked Breezy in the eye. There was something about looking into her daddy's eyes that always made her get teary.

"I know you blame yourself for my being in here, honey. Whether you want to admit it or not, I think that's where a little bit of that anger comes from. I just want you to know that after what that boy did to you, to my little girl, I'd kill him dead all over again," Mr. Williams said, slamming his fist onto the sticky table, causing the people next to them, as well as Breezy, to jump.

"Daddy," Breezy said, looking around to make sure the guards didn't come over and try to end their visit. They had done that a time or two when Mr. Williams had been giving them trouble.

"Listen to me. I don't mind the fifteen years I've spent in this hellhole. I don't mind it at all. If that bullet hadn't killed that boy, I'd happily serve fifteen more years after serving this term because I'd go finish the job."

"I don't want you to talk like that, Daddy. Don't say those types of things. If that's what you said to the parole board, then you can hang up ever getting out of here."

"When you have a child you'll know what I'm talking about. You'll understand this feeling."

Breezy broke out into a sweat as she thought about that unforgettable evening her freshmen year at college. She and a few of her friends had gone to Gino's Pizza and Sports Bar to watch their school's football team play against a rival team. About an hour into the game there had been a disturbance on the field. Some madman had run out onto the field and gunned down the star football player, Judge Callaghan.

It had been gruesome. Judge had been sitting on the sidelines with his helmet off when a bullet entered his head. Brain matter and blood spattered nearby teammates' uniforms and faces. The media had assumed it was rivalry-related as they commentated the event. As the camera zoomed in on the assailant being wrestled to the ground, the person's identity became clear to Breezy. She watched helplessly as her father was handcuffed and escorted off the field by police.

Emergency medical technicians raided the field in an attempt to save Judge, but Judge was pronounced dead at the scene. It was later reported as a vigilante killing. The details of the accused's daughter having been raped by the victim headlined every television channel and newspaper.

The news story brought so much negative attention to Breezy and her family. It was like a tornado funnel had sucked them all in. Their lives had gone under a microscope.

Breezy stayed on top of her father's case every step of the way. She wanted to make sure he was being represented to the best of that public defender's ability. She dropped out of college, and had never gone back. The second-degree-murder verdict earned Breezy's father ten years minimum in prison.

Mrs. Williams, five years after her husband being incarcerated, would eventually lose their home and go on to remarry a couple of years thereafter. She didn't even have the decency to tell her father to his face that she wanted a divorce. She just stopped visiting or accepting his phone calls altogether.

When Breezy's father had received the divorce papers in the mail he had been heartsick. Breezy didn't even know about her mother's intentions. She talked to her every day and never missed Sunday dinner, and not once had her mother mentioned that she intended to leave her father.

Breezy's instincts told her that her mother was seeing someone. Not that her mother wasn't already a beautiful woman, but each Sunday there would be something more and more striking about Mrs. Williams's appearance. One week she had a new hairdo, and the next week she had on a new Sunday's best. Breezy knew a new man was behind the change.

Breezy knew that her mother had needs. She never dreamed in a million years that she would leave her father, though. Breezy programmed her mind and her heart to agree on never forgiving her mother.

After Mr. Williams got over the initial shock of losing his better half to a free man, he gave his wife his blessings to move on. Breezy had had next to no contact with her mother since the divorce.

"So do you know the exact date that you will be getting out of here if the board approves your release?" Breezy asked.

"No, I'm not sure," Mr. Williams replied as he pulled on his three-inch beard.

"I see you got a couple gray hairs in that beard," Breezy said, pulling on it herself.

"Yeah, your pops is getting old."

"You are still the finest old man around," Breezy said. "Remember how all the women in the neighborhood tried to befriend Ma in order to get to you?"

"Now, go on girl." Mr. Williams blushed.

"Please, I take after you so I know you're not a modest man," Breezy said. "Everybody else in here writes letters home asking folks to send them soap, deodorant, and cigarettes or to put money on their books. But you, you want a sistah to buy designer-scented shaving creams and deodorants. You want CK drawers."

"Oh, Bria," Breezy's father said, putting his head down sadly.

"It's almost over, Dad. You'll be free and at home with me before you know it."

"I don't know if I'm going to have to go to a halfway house or not first."

"I don't see why they wouldn't let you come live with me. I've got the spare bedroom waiting for you."

"We'll see, love. We'll see," Mr. Williams said. "Any perspective son-in-laws I need to know about?"

Breezy snickered. "After years of dating, Dad, I've learned the hard way that there is only one man I don't have to tolerate, but just love."

"Oh, yeah," Mr. Williams said. "And who's that?"

"My daddy."

14

The Envelope Please

Jeva was speechless when she went through her mail and found the letter from Welford Child Placement Agency. She knew that inside that envelope was the answer to her questionable life. She stared at it for an eternity before laying it down on the kitchen table.

"Baby, are you okay?" Lance asked, peeking in the kitchen at her.

"It's here. The letter from Welford. It's here," Jeva said, staring at it as if she were hypnotized.

"Do you want me to open it for you?" Lance asked.

"Choca milk," Heather said to her, handing Jeva her favorite sippy cup.

"I'll get it for you, Heather," Lance said, taking the cup from her to rinse it out.

"No, I've got it," Jeva said. "I'll do it."

Jeva decided to see her daily routine through before opening the letter. She fixed her daughter a cup of chocolate milk and started the preparations for dinner. She washed a load of clothes and set a bath for her and her daughter.

Bathtime was mommy and daughter time each evening. It made up for the guilty feeling Jeva had about being away from her daughter all day.

While they bathed Lance mixed the spaghetti noodles Jeva had boiled with the meat sauce she had cooked.

After dinner the family of three watched some television and put together a couple of puzzles with Heather. Once Lance tucked Heather into bed for the night, Jeva made her way back into the kitchen to keep company with the envelope.

"Dear Lord," Jeva prayed. "I know whatever is inside this envelope is what is written for me and my life. No matter how I might feel about it, I know your plan for me is divine. I open my heart and ask that you guide me and give me strength to deal with what is in store for me. I say this prayer in the name of your son and my savior, Jesus Christ. Amen."

Dear Ms. Jeva Price:

We are pleased to inform you that the result of our search for your file has been successful. Your natural parents were located and have responded to your inquiry as to their whereabouts and the possibility of a meeting. Please know that their wishes are just that, and not those of Welford Child Placement Agency.

Your natural parents request that the meeting occur in a public place. This location has been decided by them to be Hollingwood Park in Toledo, Ohio. They will expect you on Saturday, the 27th of this month, at 2:00 P.M. If you are not available on this date and or time, please notify our agency. A new date and time will be mediated for both you and your natural parents.

We do wish you the very best.

. . .

Jeva had arrived at the park an hour early. She didn't want to risk getting stuck in traffic, her car breaking down, or any other obstacle that might hinder her from this moment that she had waited a lifetime for.

Once Jeva got to Hollingwood Park, she took a seat at the first vacant park bench she came to. She watched the parking lot and primped herself every time she saw a car drive up.

Two o'clock had come and gone as Jeva waited impatiently on the bench. It was hard for her to keep from crying every time she thought of the possibility of her parents not showing. She pulled the letter out a thousand times to double-check the date and time. Finally a tall, slender gentleman wearing a black suit approached her.

"Ms. Price, I presume," the gentleman said.

"Yes," Jeva said standing up. She knew this man wasn't her father because he was Oriental. If she knew nothing else about her natural father, she knew that he was white. She smiled nervously and waited for the gentleman to speak.

"I'm Mr. Christian, a representative of the Dawsons."

"The Dawsons?" Jeva said confused.

"That would be the family name belonging to your birth mother and father."

"Is something wrong? Are they dead?" Jeva asked, panicked. "Oh God, they're dead, aren't they?"

"They are very much alive. Ms. Price, they wanted me to share some things with you. Please sit down."

Jeva sat on the bench and the gentleman sat down beside her. He pulled an envelope out of his inside coat pocket and placed it between them.

"Your father is a very positive and powerful figure. Your mother is a loving supporter. You have five younger brothers and sisters who are all either in college or have graduated college and are doing quite well for themselves. There is no history of cancer, diabetes, MS, high blood pressure, or any other serious hereditary disorders." The gentleman babbled on endlessly as if he had a tape recorder down his throat and had hit the play button. It was becoming clear to Jeva that she wasn't going to meet her natural parents that day or any other day.

"Sir, I appreciate all of this information, but all I want to do is meet my parents. I want to look into their eyes to be able to know whose mine are like. I want to hear their voices. I want to ask questions I've never been able to get answers to."

"They were young. They didn't know what their relationship would entail. Their families would have frowned upon such circumstances as an unwed pregnancy. In addition to that, they were from two very different backgrounds."

"Will you stop it already?" Jeva said, her voice rising. "Sir, Mr. Christian, I'm very sorry. I truly am. It's just that you have no idea of how long I've dreamed about this day. Do my parents, or don't they, want to know me?"

"Ms. Price, they are asking that you cease all efforts involving contact or face-to-face meetings with them. They do not wish to know you. They are afraid your surfacing would cause confusion to their lives and the lives of their children."

"My surfacing," Jeva said. "You say that as if they drowned me and my body is now afloat."

"Ms. Price, please understand that three decades ago they were young and lived different lives. They send their regrets. They know how this must make you feel. They decided that sending a representative on their behalf would be best as, over the years, you have failed to back off of your efforts in finding them."

Jeva expected nothing like this. Her eyes swelled with tears. This was like a nightmare coming to pass. She wanted someone to pinch her.

"I can't believe this," Jeva said, rising up from the bench.

"Please, sit down, Ms. Price," the gentleman said. "I just have a couple more items to go over."

"I've heard enough," Jeva said as she began to storm off.

"Please, Ms. Price," the gentleman said, grabbing the envelope off of the bench and going after her. "This is from your parents. Please take it."

Jeva took the envelope from the gentleman's hand. "At least they were kind enough to send pictures," Jeva sarcastically remarked. She looked inside the envelope and found a very thick stack of brand-new crisp one-hundred-dollar bills.

"This is really crazy," Jeva said angrily. "A payoff? I'm their firstborn, for Christ sakes!"

"Please take it," he said calmly, set on finishing his monologue. "By now you should have received a document from United City Bank . . . the document that pertains to a trust fund set up under your name. This trust will allow you to live a more than comfortable life."

"I don't get it," Jeva said. "What's the catch?"

"There is no catch, only a stipulation," he said. "You must agree to relinquish your search to find your birth parents. As I stated before, they have no desire to associate with you. As your parents, though, they do wish for you to have a comfortable life. That's why they have made these arrangements for you. Just make sure you have read over the material carefully, especially the disclaimer, which you are required to have notarized. Keep in mind that any breach on your part will result in your paying back the monies put up, and possibly a lawsuit against you."

"Did they give you any other instructions?" Jeva asked.

"Like what?" he asked, confused.

"Like, for you to take note of what color my hair is and my eyes; how tall I am; how do I wear my hair?" Jeva began to cry. "If I have a pretty smile? Don't they want you to be able to ramble off particulars to them about me?"

"I'm sorry, Ms. Price," the gentleman said as he walked away.

"Don't they even want to know if they have grandchildren from me?"

"There's plenty in that envelope and the trust to take care of any existing and future children you might have. Good day, Ms. Price."

At this point Jeva didn't want someone to just walk up to her and pinch her, she wanted them to shake her. She had to be sleeping. This had to be a nightmare. She couldn't have waited all of her life for this moment, for such crushing pain.

Jeva stared at the envelope filled with money. She wondered if her parents were perhaps somewhere in the park staring at her. She gazed around to see if anyone looked peculiar. After a few moments Jeva, with envelope in hand, walked over to the trash bin. She dropped the envelope inside the trashcan and watched the lid swing back and forth. She stuffed the wad of hundred-dollar bills that she had taken out of the envelope down in her purse and headed for her car.

Jeva drove home, and as she pulled up to her house she saw Lance standing on the porch. He had just put Heather down for a nap and was waiting on the porch for Jeva when she drove up. Jeva walked to the porch in a zombielike state. She didn't even walk up all five steps to get to where Lance was standing. She stopped and sat down on the first step.

Jeva didn't even have the desire to cry anymore. Hell, her parents were strangers, and had been for almost twenty-nine years. She could survive it. Lance, sensing that things didn't go how Jeva hoped and dreamed they might have, joined his woman on the steps and put his muscular arms around her frail little body. She felt like a corpse in his arms.

"Baby, are you okay?" Lance asked. When he didn't get an answer, he continued to rock her. "What's that?" he asked, referring to the wad of hundred-dollar bills stuffed in her purse.

"I guess it's back–child support." Jeva snickered, still in somewhat of a daze. "They didn't want me, Lance. They didn't want to know me. My own mother and father. All I've ever wanted was to be able to call someone Mommy and Daddy . . . just to be somebody's little girl."

Lance squeezed Jeva even tighter as he kissed her on the forehead and whispered to her, "I'll take care of you, baby. You can call me Daddy."

15

It's a Girl

"Mom and Dad, this is her," Reo said, walking through the front door of his parents' Victorian home, which he had purchased for them. "This is Miss Klarke Taylor."

"It's so good to finally meet you," Mrs. Laroque said, walking over to the door to greet them. She hugged Reo and then gave Klarke a hug and kiss on the cheek. "You have made my son so happy. I've never seen him this happy before. He even comes to church now every Sunday that he's in town. I reckon he's giving thanks to you."

"Oh, Mrs. Laroque," Klarke said, hugging her once again and even tighter.

"Honey," Mr. Laroque said jokingly to his wife as he approached them, "you better be lucky our son set eyes on her before I did or you might have been replaced."

"Oh, Mr. Laroque," Klarke said, hugging him too.

"Klarke, we're so pleased you could drive up to join us this Sunday for friends-and-family day at church," Mrs. Laroque said. "Where are the little ones?"

"They fell asleep on the way. They're out in the car," Klarke said, smiling.

"I'll go carry them in," Reo said.

"It's about time to go," Mrs. Laroque said.

"So why don't you just load them right into that big ole semi of yours? We can all fit in it. There's no need in taking two cars."

Everyone climbed into Reo's Escalade and headed to the church. The service turned out to be lovely. Reverend Sandy discussed fornication and babies being born out of wedlock. She touched upon couples taking vows but not seeing them through to the end. The main lesson was forgiveness, how forgiveness is an ingredient for a successful marriage or any relationship for that matter. Klarke felt like everyone in the church knew Reverend Sandy was preaching to and about her.

The children especially enjoyed Sunday school. Vaughn was really taking to the Christian way of living and wanted to absorb all that she could. She even asked Mrs. Laroque if they had a church in Toledo. Mrs. Laroque promised to ask the Reverend to suggest a nice Baptist church that Klarke could attend with her children in Toledo.

Everything was falling into place far more smoothly than Klarke could have ever visualized. There was only one occurrence she hadn't prepared herself for . . . falling in love.

Reo sat at his computer, frustrated. He tapped his freshly manicured nails on the Kartell Maui table that his computer sat on. The deadline for his next novel was right around the corner and he couldn't figure out how to wrap up the storyline. He was undecided as to whether he wanted to add another twenty thousand words to the story or leave it open for a sequel.

Reo got up from the computer chair and flopped down on the rattan chair that hugged the corner of his study. He let out a sigh of relief when he heard the doorbell ring. It was just the time-out he needed.

Reo exited the study and made his way down the long corridor of his oversize ranch house. He stopped at the rusty, gold-trimmed vintage mirror that hung on the wall to make sure he looked suitable before answering the door. Outside the door stood a young man around twenty years of age, wearing a velour olive-green Outkast jogging suit with white K-Swiss kicks. He was holding a vase with a mixture of beautiful pink-and-white blooms. Three pink balloons wavered above his head, which was adorned with jailhouse braids.

Reo opened the door, leaving the security storm door locked.

"May I help you?" Reo asked.

"Delivery," the young man said in a *duh*-like manner. "I need you to sign for this."

Reo opened the storm door, took the pad the young man handed him, and signed his name. He dug into his wallet and pulled out a dollar bill to tip the young man with.

"Naw, I'm straight, cuz," the young man said, handing him the delivery. "You keep that. I'm going to rob Fifth Third Bank at three o'clock P.M. for some real money."

Reo closed the door behind the sarcastic smart-ass chump. He admired the lovely arrangement, wondering who it could be from.

He pulled out the letter-size envelope that was tucked gently in the flowers. "Congratulations!" was written on the outside of the card. Reo double-checked the delivery ticket to make sure the delivery guy had delivered him the correct item. Reo's name and address was written in the "deliver to" column, so he opened the envelope.

Mr. Reo A. Laroque
5437 Easton Trails
Columbus, OH 54237

RE: CASE No. DR0356852
Dear Mr. Laroque:
    I represent Ms. Meka Tarrant in the above referenced case.
Please read the attached complaint and suit. You or your attor-
ney may file an answer with the Franklin County Court of Do-
mestic Relations or contact me at my office in regards to a
settlement.

Very truly yours,
T.C. Bowens, Esq.

"I think if half of the men in this world got paternity tests done on the kids they've claimed as their own, they would be very surprised at the outcome," Nate said. "Just calm down until you get the results of the paternity test, man."

"Do you know what this shit could do to my life?" Reo said in a rage. "That fucking bitch!"

"Whoa, hold up. She didn't plant a seed in a pot of dirt and grow that baby on her own," Nate said. "Just relax before you say some foul shit that you can't take back, especially if that child does turn out to be yours."

"What am I supposed to tell KAT?" Reo said.

"You tell her the truth. You tell her the truth and you tell her now. Don't drop a bomb on her like it's been dropped on you. If she's the beautiful woman you claim her to be, then she'll understand and she'll be by your side to support you through this drama. It's not like you planned all of this."

"I don't understand why Meka waited so long. Hell, the kid is probably walking now."

"Do the dates match up?" Nate said, looking over the suit papers again.

"Yeah, man. Actually they do. *Fuck!*" Reo shouted.

"Is everything okay in here?" Persia asked, coming out of the kitchen with two glasses of lemonade.

"I'm sorry, Persia. I didn't mean to disrespect your home," Reo said, rubbing a hand over his face.

"Is there anything I can do?" Persia said, setting down the glasses and then putting her hand on Reo's shoulder.

"You can make me understand the game," Reo said putting his head down to his knees as tears filled his eyes.

"The game?" Persia asked, confused.

"The game women play," Reo answered.

"Now I know how Jennifer Lopez feels," Klarke said, stroking her hand down one of the gowns in the dainty little bridal boutique. Klarke, Breezy, and Jeva had passed the shop that sat right outside of Nordstrom in the mall a thousand times. This time Klarke insisted that they stopped in to take a little peek. "I can't believe I'm getting married for a third time, but this one just feels so different."

"He hasn't even asked you to marry him yet," Jeva said, exasperated. "And you got me and Breezy up in some bridal shop. You're going to jinx yourself, girl. Remember when I did the same thing the year I thought Lance was going to propose to me on Valentine's Day?"

"Girl, you even started getting quotes on invitations and writing out your guest list." Breezy laughed.

"But I can feel it coming," Klarke said in a dreamy tone. "I know that he's going to ask me to marry him. And to think I almost fucked up everything when I thought I might have gotten myself pregnant by Evan."

"Can you imagine having to explain that little white baby to Reo?" Breezy asked, poking out her lips and rolling her neck. "You would have died if your period hadn't come."

"Well, that little white baby would have been a product of something that took place before you and Reo even met face-to-face," Jeva said.

"I know, but still, who wants to start a relationship with someone only to find out that there will be a new addition to the relationship? I mean, come on. Remember when that girl told Hydrant that she thought her five-year-old child was his? Him and Breezy fought about it until the paternity test came back verifying that he wasn't the father. I think it's different when you get into a relationship knowing that the person has x number of children versus finding out after the fact."

"Well, I love kids. So something like that wouldn't matter to me," Jeva said, throwing her hands up.

"Yeah, well," Klarke said in a carefree manner, grabbing the gown she had been admiring off of the rack, "I don't have to worry about that now."

Klarke held the dress up and stared at it. It was a snow-white beaded-and-lace tube gown.

"Excuse me," Klarke said to one of the store clerks. "May I try this on?"

"Certainly," the clerk responded as she led Klarke into the fitting room.

"Make sure you come out so we can see what you look like," Breezy shouted.

"I can't believe that she is trying on a white gown," Jeva said, feeling more than just a little jealous.

"There is no force greater than the will to get even," Reo's attorney said to him. "Revenge is the mother of all."

"So, are you saying I should just give her two million dollars just like that?"

"Reo, the DNA test results conclusively prove that the baby is, without a doubt, yours."

Reo shook his head, feeling dazed. "I'm just going to go over there and talk some sense into Meka."

"You know I've advised you against doing so."

"Well, now that I know that the baby is mine I have to communicate with her. It's my child."

"For two million dollars you can walk away," the attorney said. "That has been your thing all along, that you've wanted a way out. We could probably even talk them down to one million. By agreeing to her terms you can buy your way out of parenthood. You can leave that part of your life behind. When the child turns eighteen, we can't prevent her seeking you out, but for now, this buys you years to build a new life."

"I don't know," Reo said, unsure.

"It's up to you. It's unfortunate that men are put in these positions every day. You can't stop a woman from having an abortion and you can't stop her from having the baby. Your entire life is affected by the decision she makes."

"I can't believe this is happening to me," Reo said again.

"Well, just think about it for a few days, but you're going to have to get back to me soon. She could have a change of heart and decide she wants three million or that she wants you to be the father of the year."

"I'll give you a call in a couple of days," Reo said, standing up.

"Just keep in mind," the attorney said, "you have the golden opportunity to buy your way out of a situation that you had no control over."

"You're wrong on that one," Reo said, staring into his attorney's eyes. "I could have controlled my dick and kept it in my pants."

"Thanks for coming over, Dad," Reo said as he and Mr. Laroque sat down on the couch. Reo tossed one of three gold raffia cushions that decorated the couch out of his father's way so he could sit more comfortably.

"Well, it sounded urgent when you called me," Mr. Laroque said.

"I have a problem, Pops." Reo sighed.

"Women trouble, huh?"

Reo took a deep breath. "It's Meka."

"Meka. I haven't heard that name in a long time."

"She had a baby, Dad. My baby."

"Son!"

"I know, Dad. She kept the pregnancy from me. I had no idea. I just found out myself."

"But why?" Mr. Laroque asked.

"This is why," Reo said, handing his father the paternity suit papers.

"She's lost her mind!" Mr. Laroque exclaimed. "You're not going to sell the rights to your child!"

Reo looked away and then looked back at his father.

"Son, you didn't," Mr. Laroque said, his face filled with shock and disappointment.

"No, Dad. Not yet anyhow."

"I can't believe you are even considering such a thing."

"Dad, do you have any idea what it would do to my life right now to bring Meka back into it? Meka and a baby?"

"*Your* baby. Your baby, son. What's Klarke say about all of this?"

"Nothing," Reo said once again, lowering his head.

"You mean you haven't told her? That poor girl."

"Well, I didn't want to tell her if that baby wasn't even mine. I didn't want to get her all worked up over nothing."

"Tell her, boy. You mark my words, not telling her would be one of the worse things you could do."

"I just need to think about everything, Dad. Can you do me a favor and not tell Mom about any of this, not until I make a decision as to what I'm going to do?"

"If that's what you want, son," Mr. Laroque said, standing up from the couch and heading toward the door. "I'll keep it from your momma. You can keep it from Klarke and whomever else you feel like. But you can't keep it from God."

After talking with his father Reo paced the floor for hours. He didn't know what to do about Meka, the baby and, most of all, KAT.

There was no way a baby would fit into the picture of his life with KAT. And there was no way in hell Meka fit into it, either.

Reo searched deep within himself for a solution to his dilemma. The longer he kept the situation from KAT, the harder it would be for her to be understanding. Besides, keeping secrets did nothing for a relationship but hurt it. The last thing Reo wanted to do was hurt KAT. So after hours and hours of soul searching Reo made a decision. He hoped it was the right decision. Just as long as the old cliché, what a person doesn't know won't hurt them, was true, then everything would work out just fine.

16.

The World Is Mine

"We've gotta stop meeting like this," Reo said as he sat down at the barstool next to Klarke at Club 504. A local entertainer, Middle Child, was about to perform. It would be her last performance in Columbus for a while as she had just signed a record deal with a major label.

Comedian Steven G was emceeing that night, and had just commented on the fine woman sitting alone at the bar—Klarke.

"I'm sorry that my meeting with my attorney kept me from being here on time. Have you been waiting long?" Reo asked.

"That's okay," Klarke said. "I'm sure you'll make it up to me, and you can start by buying me a drink."

"Bartender," Reo said, "another Shirley Temple for the lady, please."

"Make that a glass of Passion Alizé with ice," Klarke said. "What's wrong with you? Don't you know that when a man is buying a lady a drink we upgrade? Besides, I want to get a nice buzz. That way you can take advantage of me." She smiled.

"Light on the ice and heavy on the Passion," Reo said to the bartender.

"To answer your question, I've only been waiting here about fifteen minutes or so."

"How was the drive? Did you run into any traffic?"

"My drive was fine. There was an accident coming in off of Twenty-three, but other than that, everything was smooth."

"We're putting far too many miles on our vehicles with all of this driving back and forth."

"Am I not worth it, Mr. Laroque?"

"Oh, you're plenty worth it, but I was thinking next time we meet somewhere different. Let's fly to a destination and meet there. You know, save some mileage and prolong those warranties."

"And where do you have in mind?" Klarke asked.

"Las Vegas."

"I've never been there before," Klarke said as the bartender set her drink in front of her.

"Don't worry. I've been there a couple of times. I'll be your tour guide," Reo said as he lifted Klarke's drink from the napkin, sprinkled salt on the napkin, and placed the drink back down. "We'll start off by checking into the Rio hotel. We can get massages, enjoy the sauna, and then hit the strip. We can check out Rodman's club, get married, eat at a seafood buffet, and of course, gamble."

Klarke sat her drink down calmly, and tried to reassure herself that she wasn't hearing things. She was almost certain Reo had slipped in a marriage proposal. This is what she had hoped for. This was the climax and conclusion of a well-thought-out script, all rolled into one.

The feeling of finally getting the proposal was nothing like she thought it would be. Where in the hell were all of the warm emotions that were taking over her body and mind coming from? This shit felt like love, true love. She was speechless and couldn't even bring herself to look up from her drink at Reo.

"Baby, what's wrong?" Reo asked, wrapping his hand gently around the back of Klarke's neck and wiping her tear with his thumb. "Don't cry. I want you to be my everything. I want to look in the mirror and see you, the man you've made me."

Reo reached into his pocket and rolled a ring down to Klarke, then took her drink and stole a sip. Klarke captured the ring in the cup of her hand as it made its way past her. She gasped at its beauty. The ring hosted tapered baguettes on each side of the band. The cut was perfection. The color and clarity were crisp, and the carats totaled seven.

"Baby, I know you've been through a lot," Reo said in a low, deeply emotional tone. "But I love the woman that life has made you into. I love you. I wanna be more than your man. I want to be your everything."

This was one of those times in a person's life where the devil is on the left shoulder and the angel is on the right. The devil was throwing confetti and humming the wedding song, while the angel was kneeled in prayer asking God to give Klarke the heart to tell Reo how she had manipulated him to this point.

Yes, a marriage proposal was exactly what she wanted, but she never imagined she would feel so bad about it.

She had fallen in love with Reo. She slipped the ring on her finger and turned to him with a smile. "When do we leave for Vegas?"

Reo's face broke out in a wide grin and he slid his arm around her and kissed her until she couldn't breathe. When he finally let her up for air he shouted, "Champagne for everybody! She said yes!"

The patrons clapped and shouted their congratulations. Middle Child stopped the song she was singing and serenaded them with a song selection titled "I Feel You," declaring the future Mr. and Mrs. Reo Laroque.

Three months after accepting Reo's proposal, Klarke was still on cloud nine. She had counted the days to their Vegas wedding date. It seemed like it took forever, but the big day was finally right around the corner.

Nothing could have made Klarke happier than the fact that she was on a plane to marry the most loving man in the world. The kids were thrilled. If her children hadn't loved him, then she wouldn't have been able to go through with it. But Reo treated them as if they were his very own.

Vaughn was especially excited about her new family. When Klarke asked for her blessings in the marriage, Vaughn only had one stipulation, and that was that Klarke promised that no one would break up their family this time. This was a promise that Klarke was glad to make.

Their first day in Vegas was awesome. Klarke had never been pampered so much in her life. Reo had arranged for them to receive the deluxe spa package, which included Swedish massages, facials, manicures, pedicures, lunch, use of the steam room, and aromatherapy showers. That night Reo saw to it that Klarke had dinner at the Top of the World Restaurant that Breezy had bragged about so much.

The next day was their wedding day. Klarke stayed up the night before staring at the ceiling while Reo stared into the night sky.

They each were pondering over their own dirty little secrets, secrets that could mean the difference between the beginning of a new relationship with one another or its end. But they were determined. The taunting thoughts of the night before didn't keep either of them from the intentions of going ahead with their wedding vows.

Reo got up at the crack of dawn to shower and prepare himself for his wedding day.

Klarke was up shortly after. She prayed the entire time she was in the shower. She thanked God for Reo and asked him to understand her deceptive means in gaining Reo's love. Her tears mixed with the water streaming down her face. How crazy was it for her to ask God to forgive her for a wrong she planned to do ahead of time? But she knew that if Reo wanted to marry her then it was part of God's will. Maybe telling him the whole truth was the right thing to do after all.

Klarke rinsed the soap off of her body and wrapped herself in one of the thick cotton English robes the hotel had provided. Klarke called out to Reo but there was no response. Where was he? She needed to tell him now before she chickened out. She assumed he must have stepped out of the room for a moment.

Klarke stared at the long silver evening gown that was hanging in the closet. She had purchased the gown years ago because it was on sale for 50 percent off. It had been in her closet for ages without an occasion to be worn. Since she wasn't having a big church wedding, where she would be seen by her friends and family, she had decided against going all out on a bridal gown, figuring the evening gown would suffice. It looked as though the gown wouldn't have its occasion after all.

Klarke walked away and headed toward the bed, where she discovered a snow-white beaded-lace tube wedding gown laying across the bed. It was the identical dress she had tried on in the bridal boutique with Jeva and Breezy. Klarke couldn't believe her eyes and had to pinch her own self to make sure she wasn't dreaming.

Beside the dress lay a card and a single red rose, hosted by a stem and some baby's breath. Klarke picked up the card and read it:

> *I hear it's bad luck to see the bride*
> *before the wedding, so I'll meet you*
> *in the chapel in an hour.*

> *P.S. A little bird told me you admired this dress.*
> *And you might want to check the closet*
> *for the matching slippers, Cinderella.*

Klarke was ecstatic. Reo was her prince, her knight in shining armor, her everything. There was no way she was confessing now. She was Reo's and Reo was hers. If she had to live with the lie so they could be happy together, then so be it.

Once Klarke got dressed and put her makeup on, she clipped the red rose and baby's breath and pinned it in her hair with a hair comb. She felt like the most beautiful bride in the world as she made her way to the chapel. She had never felt so loved before. She had never loved a man like she loved Reo.

When Klarke entered the chapel she couldn't believe her eyes. Not only was the decor of white sheer heavenly, but the cathedral ceiling was to die for. There was a stunning baby grand piano with a crystal candlabra filled with gold candles.

But the most stunning detail, which left Klarke breathless, was the sight of Jeva and her daughter Heather, Lance, Breezy, Vaughn, HJ, Mr. and Mrs. Laroque, Nate, Persia, and of course, Reo.

Klarke almost fell over, she got so weak in the knees.

Reo had flown in everyone close to them to share in their union. Breezy, Jeva, and Persia were each in tangerine matching gowns. HJ was in a black tux holding a ring pillow. Vaughn was in a beautiful tangerine junior bridesmaid's gown, while Jeva's daughter was in a cute, lacy, sheer white dress holding a basket of tangerine rose petals. Mrs. Laroque was in a lovely cream suit, and all of the men were in black tuxedos.

No one would have known this was Klarke's third marriage by the way she boohooed throughout the brief ceremony. One would have thought she would have been a pro at it by now.

Not to take anything away from how she felt about Harris and Rawling, but this time nothing or no one was going to keep her from living happily ever after. Nothing and no one!

"So, the son of a bitch decides he's going to run off and get married to live happily ever after?" Meka shouted, slamming down a magazine that had reported on the details of Reo's wedding. "I can't believe this is happening!"

"This doesn't affect our case at all," Meka's attorney said, handing her the settlement papers. "All you have to do is sign right here on the dotted line next to where Reo signed and all of this will be over. You'll be one-point-five million dollars richer."

The attorney's words couldn't soothe Meka, nor could the idea of her being a made millionaire. Deep down inside, Meka was hoping that once Reo found out he had a child that he would come back begging to be in her life again. His marriage eliminated any chance of that happening.

Money was no longer a leading contender in Meka's fight to get to Reo. Love was taking over, perhaps tainted with a little jealousy. Meka realized that she had never actually stopped loving Reo. It had been anger that had kept her from telling him how she really felt about him. Pride had kept her from apologizing for not sticking by his side.

Now, Meka wanted her man back.

"To hell with these papers," Meka said. "I'm not letting that son of a bitch off that easy."

"What are you talking about?" Meka's attorney said, wide-eyed. "We've won. Don't you get it? You're getting exactly what you wanted."

"No, I'm not. He won. He wants me out of his life forever. He doesn't want me or his baby."

"I know how you must feel," Meka's attorney said soothingly. "It will pass."

"No, it won't pass. I won't let it," Meka said, grabbing her jacket and purse, leaving the papers behind free of her signature.

"Now you wait a damn minute," Meka's attorney said, grabbing her arm. "I've worked very hard on this case, forever. You can't just walk away from it now. Do you know how much time I've invested for your greedy ass?"

Infuriated, Meka snatched her arm from her attorney's grip and sucker-punched her dead in the nose. Meka watched her fall to the floor while blood oozed from her nose. "Bill me," Meka said, storming out of the office.

Reo and Klarke decided that they would keep both of their homes until they had a new one built for them and the children. In the meantime, Reo would commute back and forth from Columbus to Toledo. Of course he spent most of his time in Toledo with Klarke and the children.

Reo always made sure he was in Toledo whenever it was Vaughn and HJ's week with Klarke. By the time Reo would arrive in Toledo on Sundays, the children were normally already home. On this particular Sunday Harris kept them late because he had tickets for the Universal Soul Circus.

"How long before the kids come home?" Reo asked Klarke as the two put together a five-thousand-piece puzzle at the dining room table.

"I'm not sure. Why?" she asked absently.

"Because I want to make a baby," Reo said smiling.

"Boy, you are so crazy," Klarke said, pushing Reo off of her and planting a puzzle piece in its place.

"I'm serious. Let's make a baby, a little girl."

Reo stood up, picked Klarke up, and carried her over to the chaise longue. He began kissing her passionately while unzipping her pants. Klarke tore Reo's shirt off of him and began kissing his chest and licking his nipples.

"Oh shit," Reo moaned as he slid inside her. "You are so wet."

Feeling him inside her reminded Klarke of an Arrested Development song titled "Natural." Tears slipped down her cheeks. She was deep inside Reo's love.

"Oh, yes," she cried, pulling Reo even deeper inside of her.

As Reo pumped in and out of Klarke, he lifted her shirt up over her neck and removed her bra. With each thrust he watched her titties jiggle and erotic expressions move across her face.

Although Reo and Klarke had made love many times, it always felt like the first time. Reo always came quick round one, but he was always up for it during round two.

"I love you, baby!" Reo said as his penis jerked semen inside of her vagina. "I would die for you."

"Oh, you feel so good!" Klarke screamed as she placed her feet behind Reo's neck and allowed her pussy to stroke up to his belly button and down to his upper thighs as she released her own passion juices.

"I really do love you, Klarke," Reo said.

Reo rarely called her anything but KAT. Klarke just looked at him and said, "I love you, too."

A knock on the door jolted them both to their feet.

"Vaughn must have left her key," she whispered.

The two were in a race to get their clothes on. Reo went over to the kitchen sink to wash his hands as Klarke answered the door.

Standing there was a woman with her hair pulled back in a bun. She had on a white blouse with some navy khakis and a black leather jacket. She had a diaper bag over her left shoulder along with a duffel bag. In her right arm was a baby. "Is Reo available?" the woman asked with a fake smile.

"May I tell him who's here for him?" Klarke asked with a per-plexed look on her face.

"Tell him it's his baby's momma," the woman said.

Reo had raced to the door as soon as he heard Meka's voice. His heart almost stopped beating when he saw her standing there with the baby.

Before he could say anything Meka handed him the baby and left the bags at his feet.

"How come you look so surprised?" Meka asked Reo as if everything was just okey-dokey. "Did you really think I'd take your two million dollars in order for me and my child to stay out of your life?"

Reo looked up at Klarke, who just stared in shock.

"KAT, let me explain," Reo said desperately.

"Oh, she doesn't know about our baby, Reo?" Meka asked with a rehearsed surprise look on her face. "Even after the paternity test proved she was yours you still didn't let the Mrs. in on your nasty little secret?"

"Why are you doing this?" Reo asked Meka.

"No, why are *you* doing this?" Meka said, holding back her tears.

Just then Harris's car pulled up. Vaughn and HJ, followed by Harris, walked slowly up the walkway, sensing the tension in the air.

"Is everything okay, Klarke?" Harris asked.

"Sure, yeah . . . uhh, I'll call you," Klarke said.

Taking the hint, Harris kissed the kids good-bye and left.

"Come on, kids," Klarke said. "Let's go upstairs."

HJ proceeded to go up the steps, but Vaughn wasn't going anywhere until she got some answers.

"Whose baby?" Vaughn asked.

"These your stepkids?" Meka asked Reo, who didn't reply. "Well, this here is your new baby stepsister," she told Vaughn.

"Is that true, Mom?" Vaughn asked in shock.

"Go upstairs with your brother," Klarke repeated.

"Oh, no, honey, I'm leaving. You all feel free to continue playing house. But it looks like you have a new addition to your little family," Meka said, rubbing her nose against the baby's as she began to coo. "Mommy loves you and she'll see you in a couple of weeks."

"A couple of weeks!" Reo shouted, startling the baby and making her cry. "Meka, you can't just abandon her!"

"Why not?" Meka said walking away. "You were willing to."

The baby's wailing filled the house. Reo stood there rocking her, hoping it would make her shut up.

"Here," Klarke said reaching for the baby. She was at a complete loss for words. She couldn't believe Reo had kept such an immense secret from her. Klarke was more disappointed in Reo than she was angry. The fact that she had her own dirty little secret is what forced Klarke to grin and bear it. "Let me take her. Vaughn, look in those bags and see if there is any milk. I bet she's hungry."

Vaughn stood staring at the baby with pure malice.

"Did you hear me, Vaughn?" Klarke asked. "Look and see if the baby has any bottles."

Vaughn proceeded to do as she was told. "There are bottles in this bag," Vaughn said carrying them over to the refrigerator. "Do you want me to warm one?"

"Yeah," Klarke answered. "Put it in the microwave for forty seconds. Make sure you shake it up really well afterwards."

"So, you got a little girl," Vaughn said to Reo as she followed her mother's instructions.

Reo couldn't even look up at Vaughn. He simply nodded. Vaughn's shoulders slumped. Reo could tell she was disappointed.

"What's her name?" Vaughn asked, pretending to give a damn.

Reo looked at Klarke as she shrugged her shoulders in ignorance at him.

For the rest of the evening Klarke tended to the baby, and she and Reo never spoke about the situation. For one reason, they didn't want the children to overhear, and for another, neither knew what to say.

"We'll have to go out and buy a crib first thing in the morning," Klarke said as she lay down in the bed next to Reo and pulled the cover over her body.

She had just placed the baby in a bassinet, which she had re-trieved from the attic, at the foot of their bed. It had belonged to HJ when he was a baby.

"Yeah, along with some other stuff," Reo replied, as if he was already exhausted from baby shopping.

"I'll make a list. I'll check the attic again to see what else I might have of Vaughn's and HJ's from when they were babies." Klarke climbed into bed, kissed Reo good night, then rolled over as if everything was normal.

Reo lay down and pulled the cover over himself. He and Klarke just lay there, listening to each other breathe.

"Why are you doing this?" Reo suddenly asked her.

"Doing what?" Klarke asked softly.

"Acting like some strange woman didn't come to your doorstep today and drop off a kid."

"Some strange woman didn't just come to my doorstep and drop off a kid. The mother of your child gave you your daughter."

"You know what I mean, KAT," Reo said.

"No, I don't!" she exclaimed, sitting up. "What do you want me to do, Reo? Send you and your child packing?"

Reo sat up too. "I want you to be mad. Hell, I'm mad and it's my baby," Reo said, his voice waking the baby from her sleep and causing her to cry. "Damn it, not again."

"What do you want me to do, Reo?" she asked again as she got out of bed, went over to the bassinet, and picked up the baby. "Do you want me to tell you how godforsaken awful you are for even thinking about paying Meka off? You want me to yell, scream, and cry? Well, that's not going to happen. You'll have to get your punishment from a higher authority on this one," Klarke said as she turned to walk out of the room, hoping that a warm bottle would put the baby back to sleep.

"I'll get her," Reo said, stopping her. He walked over to her and took the small bundle, who opened her bright sparkling eyes. She cooed and melted Reo right then and there. And right at that moment he could never imagine not wanting such a beautiful child in his life. He still couldn't overlook the hell having her in his life would bring, and Klarke couldn't overlook it either, but they could get through this. Their love was stronger than Meka's hate. They could get through this . . . somehow.

17

Happily Ever After

Jeva's twenty-ninth birthday was less than two weeks away when Lance decided he would have a small get-together to celebrate. Time was of the essence and he didn't know a thing about throwing parties so he relied upon the baby-sitter, Cassie, to arrange everything for him.

"Does Jeva like seafood?" Cassie asked Lance as she handed him a bottle of beer. Lance sat on Cassie's new three-piece, brown-and-tan tweed living-room set, which she had just purchased on credit, and started watching TV.

"Yeah, shrimp. Order shrimp for the bash. Run baby! Run baby! Run baby run. Yeah, that's what I'm talking about!" Lance exclaimed as he jumped up, almost turning over the oval glass living-room table. He always got excited when the chosen running back for his fantasy football league scored a touchdown.

"Damn you, Lance. You trying to get me kicked out of my place?" Cassie said between her teeth.

"Son of a bitch. The coach needs to trade that bum right there," Lance said, ignoring Cassie's comment.

"Lance, I swear to God if you holler one more time. My neighbor next door would just love to call the cops on me for disturbing the peace. These walls are paper thin and she's always complaining about the noise my kids make running up and down the steps. Management wouldn't hesitate putting me out, and do you have any idea how long the waiting list is for a four-bedroom down at the housing authority?"

"This is how you watch football, girl," Lance said to Cassie. "Now let a nigga be."

Since the incident with her parents went down, Jeva hadn't been herself. She had been consistently late for work and missing deadlines. This week she missed two days straight without even calling in. Her boss wanted to fire her ass, but Patty, his personal assistant, covered for Jeva. She took the heat by saying that Jeva had told her she was taking a couple of vacation days but that she must have forgotten to log them in and forward the notice to him.

Ironically enough, Jeva's boss had planned on assigning her a high-profile photography shoot that would have taken her to Jamaica. But instead of showing up for work, she stayed home in bed.

Jeva hadn't neglected work because of the money her parents had provided her with. Jeva actually enjoyed taking pictures. This was such a low point in her life right now that finding joy in her work wouldn't even have replenished her spirits.

Patty was pretty cool. She was only nineteen but always thought quick on her feet. Her uncle, Jeva's boss, hired her right out of high school. No matter what the circumstance, she had always had Jeva's back. For example, one time Lance stayed out all night and hadn't made it back home by the time Jeva needed to leave for work. Jeva had paged him on 911 until his pager was full, and of course he wasn't answering his cell phone. It was the fourth time over a two-month period that he had done this.

Jeva had run out of excuses to tell her boss. She had already used the one about her alarm clock not going off—twice, as a matter of fact. She had, too, exhausted the one about her daughter being sick. The month before that she told them the car wouldn't start. Of course she always told Patty the truth.

Jeva's inconsistency with work was the main reason why most of the time Jeva's boss only gave her local assignments. He didn't want to risk her screwing up a big money-making shoot.

On this occasion when Jeva failed to call, Patty handled it for her once again. She told her uncle that she was supposed to pick Jeva up, but couldn't find her house and didn't have her cell phone on her. Her uncle, catching on to Patty's loyalty to Jeva, asked, "Well, couldn't you have stopped at a pay phone to call her?"

"I didn't have her phone number on me, and besides, no way was I stopping at a pay phone on that side of town," Patty said, throwing in that retort just in case her uncle tried to drill her with something like she should have called information.

Patty knew she had to warn Jeva that her uncle was on the warpath. In addition, Patty had run out of excuses. It was time Jeva got her shit together.

"Hello," Jeva said, answering the phone.

"May I speak with Jeva?" Patty asked.

"Speaking," Jeva replied.

"I understand if you don't want your job, but now you are jeopardizing mine, not to mention my relationship with my uncle."

"Oh, Patty. I'm sorry," Jeva said. "You have no idea what I've been going through."

"You're right. I don't, and that's because you haven't even bothered to call in to let me know what's going on with you."

"I apologize, Patty. I really do. I'll be in Monday," Jeva said.

"Well, I won't. I'll be in Jamaica," Patty said.

"What's in Jamaica?" Jeva questioned.

"A gig that would have been yours if you had carried your ass into work!"

"Get dressed, I'm coming to take you out," Breezy ordered Jeva over the phone.

"Oh, Breezy, not today. I'm trying to rest and the phone has been ringing off the hook. I'm not up to it."

"You haven't been up to anything lately. Look, I know how you must feel."

"You couldn't possibly. Why do people always feel as though they have to say that? You have a mother you can go see every day if you wanted. Your father may be locked up, but at least you can communicate with him."

"Leave my father out of this," Breezy said in a sharp tone.

"Well, you know what I mean," Jeva said, brushing Breezy off.

"No, I don't know. I don't know about half of anything when it comes to you."

"Well, what half is it that you don't understand, the white half or the Hispanic half? Perhaps I can enlighten you," Jeva said, getting bold.

"Just fuck it, Jeva!" Breezy said, throwing her hands up on the situation.

"No, Bria, fuck you."

Jeva slammed down the phone and hunched over and began bawling. She couldn't believe she had just talked to her best friend that way when all she was trying to do was get her out of the house and cheer her up. She was only trying to do what best friends are supposed to do . . . be there for her.

She waited a couple of minutes before picking up the phone to call Breezy back. When she did she didn't even have to dial the number. Breezy was sitting on the phone. She must have been calling her back at the same time.

"Hello," Jeva said.

"Hello," Breezy responded.

"Breezy, I'm so sorry. I didn't mean to act so nasty. I know you're just trying to help."

"Look, just squash it," Breezy replied to Jeva. "It's Friday, and if you're going to play hooky from work on a Friday you might as well make it worth it. Get up and get dressed. Fuck window shopping. We're going to make a purchase."

"Girl, I'm raggedy," Jeva said. "I don't know if I can even make myself look presentable enough to leave this house."

"Then that's just one more thing we can do. Let's go to the salon and get our hair and nails did. You know that Cinnabon shop is right next door. We can hit them up afterwards."

"Okay, say no more," Jeva said.

"We're about to pull a Julia Roberts. We walking out of that mall looking brand new. New clothes, hair, shoes, the works. You with me?"

"I'm with you, girl," Jeva agreed.

"All right, I'll be there in about an hour," Breezy said.

"Okay, I'll be waiting," Jeva said. "And Breezy . . ."

"Yeah, girl."

"Thank you."

After a day full of shopping Jeva was speechless when she walked into the living room to some of her closest friends yelling "Surprise!" She hadn't suspected a thing. She couldn't believe the girls hadn't slipped up and revealed information about the surprise party.

"Thank you, guys. I can't believe neither of you peeped a word about this. You two usually can't plan anything and keep it a secret," Jeva said to Klarke and Breezy.

"Hey, you've got your man to thank for this one. We didn't have anything to do with planning this party," Klarke said.

"You mean to tell me Lance put all of this together himself?" Jeva asked.

"Yes indeed," Lance said, creeping up behind her and planting an intoxicating kiss on her neck. "You have your husband-to-be to thank for this here engagement party."

Jeva's mouth dropped open. She looked at Klarke and Breezy, and they each shrugged their shoulders to insinuate that they had no idea what was going on.

"Excuse me, everybody, excuse me," Lance said, tapping a spoon from the cocktail sauce against the crystal serving platter the shrimp was on. "I have an announcement to make. I know some of you thought this was a party to celebrate Jeva's birthday, but I lied. It's actually an engagement party. The only problem is that I left out one minor detail."

Lance pulled a small black velvet box from his pants pocket. "I forgot to pop the question. So without further ado . . ." Lance dropped to one knee and opened the box. Jeva admired the contents of the box, which was a three-carat marquis molded into a platinum band. Her eyes filled with tears of joy as she looked up at Klarke and Breezy, who each placed dark sunglasses on their faces and then yelled, "Gotcha."

Everyone in the room giggled with excitement as they waited for this production to play out.

"Jeva, will you be my wifey?" Lance asked.

"What kind of silly question is that? Yes, baby! I'll be your wifey."

Jeva was almost in hysterics. She cried with so much joy. She felt like she was Snow White and had just been brought out of a deep sleep by the kiss from her prince.

Of course Klarke and Breezy were happy for Jeva, too. They hated the fact that Jeva was going to be Lance's wife—they felt that she could do better—but as long as Jeva was happy, that's all that mattered to them.

The golden rule of not bashing one another's men didn't keep Klarke and Breezy from ridiculing Lance among each other.

"I just can't believe Lance finally proposed to her," Klarke said.

"It's a Boyz N the Hood pity proposal," Breezy said as she and Klarke began to laugh. "Him proposing was about the only thing that was going to pull her out of the slump she's been in. They'll probably be engaged until little Heather graduates college."

"Do you really think she'll fall for his game again?" Klarke asked Breezy.

"Girl, Lance is like alcohol to Jeva," Breezy said. "He impairs her judgment."

"Well, at least we know what Lance has been doing with all of the money he supposedly makes," Klarke said. "That ring is gorgeous."

"Girl, please. You know somebody's Grandmama is laying in an alley somewhere with her ring finger missing."

The two toasted their champagne glasses and laughed so hard it was almost rude. Everyone's attention turned to the two of them, from across every corner of the room. Once they noticed that all eyes were on them, they settled down and Breezy raised her champagne glass to the entire room in toast.

Almost all the guests eventually made their way over to Jeva to congratulate her and to look at the stunning stone. Last but not least, Reo sought the opportunity to bid his best wishes to her.

"Congratulations. I wish you and Lance the very best. I wish you as much happiness as KAT and I share."

"Thank you Reo. Thank you very much," Jeva said, giving Reo a nice warm hug. "Oh, I must look a mess. I've got makeup running all down my face."

"Next time you might want to try Mary Kay," Reo suggested, trying to make a joke.

"Huh?"

"Oh, nothing," Reo said as he took a sip of his champagne.

"I can't believe this," Cassie said to Lance in hysterics. "I can't believe you actually just proposed to her. What were you thinking?"

"Shhh," Lance said as he locked the bathroom door, securing both him and Cassie inside. "Do you want her to hear you?"

"Shhh, my ass. There's a party going on downstairs in the name of your engagement. You even had me plan it," Cassie said. "Oh my God, how could I be so stupid? Here I thought I was planning a birthday party for the woman I baby-sit for, and I'm planning my man's engagement party to another woman."

"I'm not your man. I'm her man. It's you I have to sneak

around with, not her. You're the other woman, so get that straight," Lance said angrily.

As Cassie began to cry Lance did the best he could to comfort her by taking her into his arms and rubbing her head. He was quite sincere. He had feelings for Cassie and didn't enjoy seeing her hurt.

"Baby, you know this has nothing to do with the way I feel about you," Lance assured Cassie.

"Then what do you call what you just gave Jeva, a fashion ring? At least that's what you told me you were getting her for her birthday. Lance, do you love her?"

"Yes, I mean, we're raising a kid together."

"I can't believe this," Cassie said.

"But I'm in love with you. There's a difference. Cassie, just trust me on this one. It's not going to change anything you and I have. You know it's only going to make it better in the end. Trust me on this one."

Cassie pulled away from Lance and wiped her tears. "Yeah, well, just make sure you pay the bill every month for that ring you got her from Bedrock on credit in my name!" Cassie exclaimed as she exited the bathroom to rejoin the party.

Lance sat down on the toilet and sighed a sigh of relief. Just then Breezy entered the bathroom. "Hey Lance, what's crackalackin?"

"Oh, Breezy, hey. Uhhh, nothing. I'm good. Everything is good."

"Is Ms. Cassie good?" Breezy asked sharply.

"What, huh?" Lance stuttered.

Breezy glared at Lance, then turned to close the bathroom door.

"Look, nigga, locking a door keeps people out. It doesn't keep people from hearing what's going on behind the locked door."

"Not today, Breezy," Lance said getting up and barging past her. "Not today."

Breezy grabbed Lance by the arm. "You tell her or I will. I think it will be best coming from you."

"Yeah, right," Lance continued for the door. "I don't know what you're talking about."

"Hey, that's my best friend and I'll be damned if I'm going to let her marry you after what I just heard between you and Cassie. Jeva can choose to get caught up in this make-believe bullshit world you try to keep her in, but this is taking it too far. I stay out of my girls' business. I've never been one to run to them like a Channel Two news reporter, but I can't let this go down, Lance."

"You fucking hypocrite. I didn't see you racing to tell Jeva shit when it was you and I talking behind locked bathroom doors. Or have you forgotten about that?" Lance said as he walked up to Breezy, putting his arms around her waist. "What's the matter? You miss Daddy? You jealous it ain't you no more?"

"First of all, that was a long time ago, Lance, over three years ago to be exact. I had only known Jeva a couple of months. We were just associates then. Now we're girls. My relationship with Jeva back then was nothing like it is now."

"Well, once you and Jeva's relationship started to become what it is, why didn't you tell her then?"

Breezy stared at him in disgust. She wished she had never slept with Lance. It should have never happened. When Breezy showed up at the house for Jeva only to find that she had gone into work to pick up some extra hours, she should have left immediately. But no, she had to sit and make small talk with Lance. She just had to have that glass of wine. She just had to have that chocolate hairy-chest hunk of a man.

She just couldn't resist. It was his fault. He should have never answered the door with no shirt on. He should have never answered the door with those boxer shorts on with his johnson just wagging in front of Breezy. That was like waving raw meat in front of a hungry pit bull.

As the saying goes, one thing led to another and Lance was tossin' it up. He had gotten on his knees, picked Breezy up and placed her legs over his shoulders, and sucked her clit like a poisonous snake had just bitten it and he was trying to save her life.

By the time Lance got finished with his rescue technique, Breezy's pussy was ripe. At first she just climbed on top of Lance with the intentions of only grinding on his rock-hard dick. They both kept whispering to each other that the act they were committing was wrong and that they couldn't go all the way. So she just grinded Lance by stroking her pussy lips and swollen clit along his penis. He had gotten her so wet and it was feeling so good that they both could have cum from just grinding. But about a minute before they both reached their climax, Lance pushed her off of him and onto the floor, where he dove into her stuff and pumped until they both screamed in ecstasy.

"Look, Lance," Breezy said, "it was only one time."

"Oh, so that's why you trippin'? Are you mad that it was only one time and you didn't get seconds?"

"Oh, please, boy, you know I could still have you to this day if I wanted. I'm the one who made sure it never happened again. You were like a dog in heat, always sniffing at my ass every time Jeva turned her head. Listen to myself. I sound ridiculous." Breezy pushed Lance off of her and headed for the door.

"Okay, I'll tell her," Lance said sincerely.

"When?" Breezy said in a demanding tone.

"Right after I tell her about us. What do you think that's going to do to poor little Jeva, your best friend?" Lance said, smiling coldly.

Breezy paused. What could she say? Lance had her right where he wanted her. There was no way she ever wanted Jeva to find out that she had been betrayed by someone else who was supposed to love her.

"You are so lucky that my heat ain't out in my trunk. I would make a trip outside just for you. I swear, I hate you so much right now, I would pump your shit with lead and wouldn't mind spending the rest of my life in the joint for first-degree murder."

Lance grabbed Breezy and pulled her close to him. She was once again face-to-face with his masculine hairy chest that his knockoff Coogie sweater showed off. The same chest that had gotten her in trouble years ago.

"Oh, baby, you know that would never happen," he said, nibbling on Breezy's ear. "Any half-decent attorney would say in your defense that it was a crime of passion. You'd only be charged with manslaughter at the very least. But a real good attorney, hell, he'll cop a plea and you'll be locked up no more than five to seven years at the most. Either way it goes, I guess that would be hard for you. I know how you like a good fuck no matter whose man's dick it is."

Lance stuck his tongue in Breezy's mouth and for two seconds she was tempted. Then she pushed him away. He grinned at her mischievously as he left the bathroom. He knew he had the W.

Breezy closed the bathroom door, then slid down it. She was so angry, yet there was nothing she could do about it. She sat there and cried. She cried hard.

Jeva frazzled her brain with wedding preparations. She had always wanted a spring wedding and the season was right around the corner. There was no way in hell she was going to wait for another year to roll around to get married. She knew she had to hurry and confirm every detail. After all, she now had the money to make it happen.

Lance was no help at all. Every time Jeva asked his opinion he would just tell her that whatever she wanted was fine with him.

"I want this to be our wedding, not just mine," Jeva said to Lance.

"I just want all of your dreams to finally come true," Lance said, kissing Jeva and caressing her bootie with his hands.

"They have," Jeva said, kissing Lance back. "They have."

Jeva got down on her knees, unzipped Lance's pants, and pulled out his penis. She began licking the shaft in preparation for the blowjob of a lifetime.

"Oh, yeah, baby, that's right," Lance moaned. "Take good care of your man. I'll take good care of you."

As Lance's penis pumped against Jeva's jaw the feeling got him to talking mad shit.

"Oh, yeah, Daddy gonna take care of you. Just think, you don't have to tire yourself with some nine-to-five anymore. We're gonna take exotic trips all over the world."

"Umm, Daddy," Jeva moaned as she swirled Lance's saliva covered penis all over her face.

"We gonna invest the money from that trust fund of yours and flip it four times over. Then we're going to fuck on a bed of money. We'll be like Whitney and Bobby." Lance laughed as he grabbed Jeva by the back of her head and rammed her head harder onto his vessel. "Umm, and after you make Daddy cum down your throat, I'm gonna finally nut my baby son up inside that tightass pussy."

"What trust fund?" Jeva asked as she gripped Lance's dick in her hand.

"You know, the one you told me your parents set up for you. Now come on, baby, don't stop."

"Lance, I never told you about any trust fund."

"Yes, you did. You must have or else how would I know about it?" Lance attempted to shove his penis back in Jeva's mouth, but she pushed herself away from him and rose from up off her knees.

She knew she hadn't mentioned the trust fund to Lance. She deliberately withheld the information as a surprise wedding gift. She would offer Lance something no other woman could, the opportunity to never have to work for someone else as long as he lived.

"No, I didn't, Lance. I know for a fact I didn't. How do you know about my trust fund?"

Lance had no answer for Jeva. He began to sweat and silently cursed himself.

"Never mind that trust fund, anyway. It's not important."

"Obviously it is. It's important enough for you to play dumb about it. I want to know, Lance, how did you find out about it?"

"It's nothing really, Jeva, but damn, if you insist."

"I insist," Jeva said, patiently waiting for Lance's explanation.

"I opened the letter from Welford before you did. I was curious. I know how you are and I just wanted to know ahead of time what I was going to have to deal with. I wanted to prepare myself to be there for you."

"I still don't understand. That letter didn't say anything about money or my parents not showing up."

"There was a second letter, from a bank. I opened it. I read about the trust and the terms. Then I resealed it the same way I had done with the letter from the agency."

"You opened my mail. You read my personal mail and then resealed it like nothing," Jeva said.

"It wasn't like that at all."

"Just stop it!" Jeva said putting her hands over her ears and sitting down on the Popason chair in their living room. "You knew they weren't going to be at the park. You knew my parents were going to be a no-show and you let me walk out that door into one of my worst nightmares. So Lance, who is it you're marrying, me or the trust fund?"

"Jeva, you know I love you. You deserved it. I knew you would have never gone to that park first and experienced the fact that your parents didn't want to have anything to do with you. If you had known beforehand what was going to happen, you would have ruined everything, and you deserved that money."

"I just needed that little something to push me over the edge, huh, Lance? Did you really feel as though I deserved the money, or was it you who deserved it?" Jeva asked. "Was that your payoff for putting up with me for all of these years?"

"I swear, it's not like that at all," Lance said.

"Once again, I was going to be your fool. Only this time I was going to take vows committing to be your fool for the rest of my life."

"Please listen to me, baby. Jeva, you know me," Lance said, getting down on one knee at Jeva's lap. "I love you so much. I want you, Jeva, to be my wifey. I want to have a son with you. I want all of this with or without a trust fund. Jeva, baby, you know me."

After listening to Lance state his case, Jeva put her hands on top of his. She viciously pushed them off of her knees.

"Oh, stop it with that goddamn wifey shit," Jeva said, mugging Lance in the forehead with her index finger. "I know you, all right. I know that you are a low-down dirty bastard. You're trash."

"I'm trash! When I met you, you didn't know who you were nor did you have a hole in the ground to shit in," Lance said to Jeva. "You were dancing in a club like some whore. I saved you!"

"There are worse things than being a stripper," Jeva said.

"Like what?" Lance asked.

"Like being broke, which is what you are. Now get the fuck out."

"This is my house. This muthafucker is in my name."

"Oh, you're right," Jeva said. "Then I'm getting the fuck out. Me and Heather are gone."

"Am I supposed to cry? We both know that Heather isn't my daughter. You were already pregnant when I first met your ass and put that fifty down your G-string. I'm the one who agreed to your little insurance scam, remember? If it wasn't for me signing that fucking birth certificate knowing damn well that baby wasn't mine, Heather, *your* daughter, wouldn't have health insurance to this day. So while you are at it, throw me back all those fucking premiums that got pulled out of my paycheck," Lance yelled.

"Fine," Jeva said, blowing it off like it was nothing.

"You damn right it's fine. Knowing how you felt growing up not knowing who your own parents were, you still decided to make your daughter go through the same experience. And for what, Jeva? A lousy medical bill. So make sure when you go crying to your little girlfriends you tell them that piece of truth. Tell them how you cried and begged me to pretend to the world that I was the father of your child and how you said we'd take it to our graves. Tell them how any trick you might have turned could have resulted in the birth of that baby. But I stepped up to the plate and made sure that baby was taken care of. Didn't your momma tell you about a thing called welfare, Medicaid? Oh, that's right, you didn't have a momma. She didn't want your ass and neither do I."

Jeva lifted her chin proudly. "I know you're trying to break me down. You're trying to break me down like you've done our entire relationship. But right now, at this very moment, I know that there is no way you ever loved my child or me. To say all of those things you just said, you couldn't have possibly ever loved us. People try to use the excuse that they say things out of anger and don't really mean it. All the while, it's just the opposite. Anger gives people the courage to tell the truth. But you know what, Lance?" Jeva asked. "I guess that's why it doesn't hurt for me to leave. Walking away from you, for good, feels nothing like I've ever thought it would. You always take credit for saving me and I'll give you that, Lance. You did save me. You saved me from a lifestyle that would have led me God knows where. It felt good to be saved, to be wanted. But you know what's funny? Being with the person that saved me hurt like hell. I'd often find myself weighing the odds. All the lies, the games, and the arguing, it's taught me so much." Tears slipped down her cheeks. "And what's so ironic is that out of everything, the good and the bad alike, I've learned to love myself. I've done nothing but hurt myself by being with you, so I'm convinced my days will be real cool without you. I'm crying right now because I'm happy, believe it or not. This is what it feels like to finally love myself. Besides knowing that God loves me, this is the greatest love of all. And out of all the people in my life, Lance, I have you to thank for it. So, thank you."

Lance sneered at her speech. "It's easy for you to walk away, huh? Then walk, bitch. I'm giving you the entire weekend to get your shit and walk," Lance said, slamming the door behind him, causing the picture of him and Jeva that was hanging on the wall to fall off and shatter.

Jeva just stood there, looking at the closed door. She looked around the house at everything she and Lance had shared and realized that she wanted nothing. All she wanted was to pack an overnight bag for her and her child and never return. She walked over to the CD player and fumbled through the collection of CDs. She put on Ashanti's "Foolish" and pressed the repeat button. Even if it had to play the entire weekend, she wanted that song to be the one Lance heard when he walked through that door and found her gone.

Jeva felt as though the finest hotel was more appropriate than the nearest; after all, she could afford it now. Jeva thought if anything ever happened between her and Lance she'd wallow for weeks in self-pity, but surprisingly, she didn't. She decided she would take Heather and herself on a little shopping spree.

Jeva looked up limousines in the yellow pages and arranged for one to pick them up the next morning from the hotel. They would spend the entire day going from mall to mall. Their last stop was an exclusive day spa. While her daughter was entertained in the child-care facility, Jeva got a makeover and purchased an obscene amount of cosmetics and perfumes. Her head full of straight black hair was now a head full of luscious curly locks with blonde highlights. Jeva wore herself out with all the indulging. Her next luxury would be a new car.

Fuck Lance! Fuck her parents and fuck the fairytale. It was time for Jeva to start living happily ever after in the real world.

18

Cry of the Wolf

Breezy was awakened abruptly from her sleep by a blood-curdling howl. Her heart slammed in her chest. Afraid to move, she lay frozen in her bed until she heard another scream.

Breezy slowly scooted to the edge of her bed and reached over to pull her gun from the nightstand. She cocked it and crept out of the bed. She unlocked her bedroom door and went into the hallway. Once again she heard the howl and determined that it was coming from her father's bedroom.

Her father had been released from prison only two weeks ago and was staying with her.

As Breezy opened the door to her father's room she could hear some movement and moans. She switched on the light to find her father thrashing in his sleep.

"Dad. Daddy," Breezy said as she shook her father in an effort to wake him from his sleep. "Daddy, wake up. You're having a nightmare. Dad, please wake up."

Breezy could see that her father had also been crying. Traces of tears had seeped from his eyes and formed a puddle in his ear pit. He was flinching as if he were having a seizure.

Breezy shook her father, trying to wake him. All of a sudden Mr. Williams got up and grabbed Breezy around the throat. Frantically Breezy tried to peel her father's hands from around her neck. She tried to scream "Daddy!" hoping her father would snap out of his fit and come to. But his hands tightened around her throat until there was no hope for air. He had locked in Breezy's voice with the power of his grip.

Breezy's instincts were to fight, which included hitting her father with the gun, until it came down to her last breath, and if all else failed, she'd blow her father's brains out. During the struggle Breezy lost grip of the gun and it fell to the floor and underneath the bed. She began bashing her father's head with her closed fist in an attempt to wake him. He finally opened his eyes and became aware of what was happening.

He snatched his hands from around Breezy's neck and Breezy fell back, choking and gasping violently.

"Baby, I'm sorry. I'm so sorry," Mr. Williams said as he ran into the guest bathroom to get Breezy some water. When he returned with the water Breezy had caught her breath. "Baby, Daddy is so sorry. I was having another nightmare. Daddy's sorry."

This was the third nightmare that week. This one, though, was the worst. On occasion Breezy had heard her father whimpering in his sleep, but never had he cried out so painfully. Breezy thought this time an intruder was attacking him, which is the reason she had retrieved her gun.

"It's okay, Dad. It's okay," Breezy said, massaging her neck, now bruised with the imprint of her father's fingers.

Breezy took a sip of the water and watched her father bury his head in his hands and cry. She could only imagine the pain he had gone through all of those years in prison. She had wondered, but never asked, if he had been raped, beaten, or abused. She had cried many nights at the mere thought of her father being thrown into a dark cell, nude, left to live in his own feces for days or even weeks. She knew some of her unasked concerns were where his nightmares derived from. The more nightmares Breezy's father continued to have, the more Breezy's conscience ate away at her.

"Jeva, I need to talk to you," Breezy said as she pounded on Jeva's hotel door. Jeva and her daughter had been staying at an extended-stay hotel while Jeva house-hunted.

Jeva opened the door, a frown of concern on her face. "Shhh, Heather's asleep. Now Breezy, what's wrong? What's going on?" Breezy blew right pass her and began pacing the floor.

"I can't do it anymore, Jeva. I can't live with this any longer. I have to tell my father or I'm going to kill myself."

"Look, Breezy. Just calm down and talk to me. I'm here for you. I'm here for you, girl," Jeva said as she squeezed Breezy, who was weeping frantically in her arms.

Jeva had never seen Breezy so vulnerable. She sat frozen stiff as Breezy exposed a lie she had lived with for the past fifteen years. The lie that had led to her father's incarceration.

For two hours Breezy told Jeva of how the boy she accused of raping her never actually raped her. The sex that took place between them had been consensual.

Growing up, Breezy's parents were hard but fair with her. Church and school were the only activities she was permitted to engage in. Extracurricular activities at school were thought to be a negative influence, so Breezy was never allowed to join the track team, cheerleading squad, or anything of that nature. Dating was absolutely out of the question.

Breezy's parents had sacrificed, and had forced her to sacrifice, everything in order for her to attend college. Breezy earned a partial scholarship at a university out of state. In the midst of getting accustomed to dorm life she went buck wild. Breezy was free at last from her parents' clutches and virginal way of life.

It hadn't been long before Breezy found herself knocked up. She had been only eighteen and a freshman in college. Breezy didn't know how she was going to explain her condition to her parents. She made the mistake of sharing her pregnancy with her father. When Breezy saw the disappointment in her father's eyes there was no way she could allow herself to live with being the cause of it. For the first time in her life she witnessed her father cry. Before Breezy could catch the lie she told her father, it had made its way through her lips.

Judge attended Breezy's college on a full football scholarship. He was also studying pre-law. His teammates had given him the nickname of Judge because he was the only football player who dreamed more about being a Supreme Court Justice than an NFL star. Football was Judge's mistress. Law was his true love.

Judge was the most ambitious boy Breezy had ever met. He loved football, the law, and God. Unfortunately for the both of them, his strong love of God didn't keep him from loving sex outside of marriage.

What turned Breezy on the most was the fact that when she met him, Judge, like herself, was a virgin. For a couple of months they kissed and fondled, but that was as far as Judge would go. He wouldn't even allow Breezy to suck his dick. He believed oral sex was sex and was still a form of fornication. Breezy, being Breezy, just wouldn't let up.

One evening, in celebration of Judge leading his team to the championship, Breezy lucked up on a drunken Judge at a party that was taking place at one of his teammate's homes. Judge rarely drank, if at all, but on that night he had gotten pretty full.

Breezy lured him to one of the bedrooms just to *talk*. Words led to kisses, kisses led to fondling, and fondling led to some oral acts and finally to full-blown intercourse.

Breezy had branded Judge with her pussy. He was going to be hers forever. Hell, if he didn't get drafted into the NFL, without a doubt, Judge would serve as a Supreme Court Justice someday. It was Breezy's mission to make sure she would be right there by his side.

Getting pregnant hadn't been part of the plan. Breezy was too ashamed to even tell Judge of her condition, but she needed help. She had to tell someone.

Breezy and her father had always been close, closer than the average father-and-daughter relationship. Mr. Williams had always been Breezy's best friend. She knew her father would never judge her, and that no matter what situation she got herself into he would always love her. That is why she decided to go to her father and ask for his help. She needed money for an abortion and had no where else to turn.

Had she been forewarned of the dissatisfaction and repugnance that would form within her father, she would have opted to use a hanger to rid her body of her unborn. She couldn't have guessed her father would gun down Judge.

Ironically, a few days after Breezy found out she was pregnant she miscarried the baby. By that time, she had already apprised her father of the life-altering mendacity.

"Breezy, you have to tell him," Jeva pleaded.

"I know. I know I do," Breezy cried.

"It's going to be hard for both you and your father, but you owe him that much. You owe it to yourself."

"Whoever came up with that fucked up cliché about it being better late than never," Breezy said wiping her tears, "never had to do anything remotely comparable to what I'm about to have to do."

"Dad, I'm home!" Breezy shouted as she came through the door. "Dad, where are you? I need to talk to you."

Breezy went into the kitchen to see if her father was there. When she didn't find him there she checked her father's bedroom. His clothes were laid out on the bed and she could hear the shower water running from the connected guest bath. The bathroom door was cracked, so Breezy went back into the living room.

Breezy sat down on the couch and turned on the television with the remote. She hoped that her father would hurry out of the shower before she lost the courage to tell him the truth about the rape. She twiddled her fingers, closed her eyes, and asked God for the strength to go through with the confession.

After about fifteen minutes of waiting, which seemed like forever to Breezy, who was becoming even more of a nervous wreck, she decided to go into her room to get the family photo album. She thought it would make things easier if she and her dad could reminisce over some happier times.

Breezy went to her bedroom and pulled several old photo albums from underneath her bed as well as a shoebox full of letters her dad had written her over the years. She noticed that her answering machine message light was on. It displayed that she had five messages, but when she went to play them, they were all hang-up calls.

"Hmm, that's strange. It ain't nobody but Guy's wife," she said as she piled the photo album and shoebox in her arms and headed out of her room. All of a sudden the coldest chill went through her body. She stopped in her tracks and the contents of her arms fell to the floor. She rushed to the guest room and called for her father. She knocked on the guest bath door and called for him again, but there was still no answer. She pushed the door that was partially cracked open only to find her father lying on the bathroom floor in a pool of blood, his fist clenched around his bath towel.

"What do we got, Sams?" the heavyset detective said to Sams, the rookie investigator on the scene, as he ducked under the crime-scene tape strapped across Breezy's front door.

"Oh, Detective Edwards," Sams replied. "A fatal gunshot wound to the head. It looks as though the victim might have startled an intruder."

"Who discovered the body?" Detective Edwards asked Sams.

"The victim's daughter. She's right there," Sams pointed. "The one in the middle."

"I know this must be difficult for you," Detective Edwards said as he walked over to Breezy, "but there are just a couple of questions I need to ask you that might help us find your father's killer."

Breezy didn't reply. She just sat on the couch crying as Klarke and Jeva attempted to comfort her.

"Your father's been out of prison for a little over a month now?" Detective Edwards continued as he looked down at his notepad.

"Why don't you ask her questions you don't already know the answers to?" Klarke said, glaring up at him.

"And you are?" Detective Edwards asked Klarke.

"Klarke Taylor, her best friend," Klarke said, still not used to using her married name.

"Do you own a gun?" Detective Edwards asked Breezy, totally ignoring Klarke's inquiry.

"Uhh, yes," Breezy answered, dazed. "A nine-millimeter."

"Where do you keep it?"

"Nightstand drawer, my bedroom," Breezy answered as the detective signaled Sams to go check it out.

"Now think about it really hard, Ms. Williams. Is there anyone, anyone at all, who might want to see your father dead?"

"For crying out loud," Klarke interrupted again. "Don't you think if she knew the answer to that she would have told you all about it two hours ago? The man was in jail for murdering her rapist. Why don't you go have a look at some of the members in his family and see if they weren't out for a little sweet taste of revenge?"

"Miss Taylor, is it?" Detective Edwards asked.

"Actually, I'm recently married, it's Mrs. Laroque," Klarke responded.

"Well, Mrs. Laroque, we're already looking into that as a possible scenario. Now would you be so kind as to let me do my job here?" Just then Sams came out of Breezy's bedroom, shaking his head in the negative—Breezy's gun wasn't in the nightstand. "Ms. Williams, it looks like we're going to need to ask you a few more questions down at the station."

"Oh, no, you don't," Jeva said, clutching Breezy's arm. "I've seen *Law and Order*. You're not taking her anywhere. You want us to think you are taking her just to inquire about a few innocent questions and the next thing we know we'll be putting money on her books."

"Jeva, Klarke," Breezy snapped, "I think it will be best if I go with the detective."

"Fine," Klarke said. "If that's what you want. Let's go. Jeva and I are right behind you."

"No," Breezy said. "I'll go alone."

Breezy had been down at the station for almost twelve hours. She had been asked thousands of questions, some a hundred times over, only to keep giving the same answers. She was tired. She just wanted to mourn the loss of her father. Already she missed him painfully.

"I'll ask you again, Ms. Williams," Detective Edwards said. "What did you do with your gun after you shot and killed your father?"

"How many times do I have to tell you?" Breezy screamed. "I didn't kill my father! Please, Mr. Edwards. Why won't you believe me?"

"I want to believe you. I want to help you, but you have to help me first. Just tell me the truth. Your father was having one of those nightmares you were telling me about. You thought something was wrong. You went into his room just like you had done before, with your gun in hand. It's not your fault you shot him. You had to protect yourself. You didn't know what your father was capable of. You had to kill him. It was him or you."

"No, no, no! I swear I didn't do it. That's not what happened," Breezy cried.

"Then it was an accident," Detective Edwards played. "If it was an accident then you don't have anything to worry about."

"Traces of gunpowder on Ms. Williams is negative," Sams said as he poked his head through the door.

"Can I go home now?" Breezy cried.

"Not until you tell me who you had kill your father," Detective Edwards said. "Who did you give your gun to? Ms. Williams, you were the only one in the home. You are the only one who can tell us what happened."

"Detective Edwards," Sams said. "Can I see you out here for a moment?"

"Sure," Detective Edwards said, scooting a notepad and a pencil in front of Breezy. "I'll be back, Ms. Williams. In the meantime I want you write down all the details of how you set up the murder of your father."

Breezy threw the notepad and pencil at the door that closed behind Detective Edwards.

"We don't have anything but a missing gun on her, huh, Sams?" Detective Edwards asked. "That and the fact that nothing was stolen and there was no sign of a break-in. I just have a hunch about the daughter."

"Actually, I just got a call from one of the investigators at the scene. A nine-millimeter was found under the bed in the victim's bedroom," Sams said. "It's being sent to the lab to be tested. Lieutenant Ross says we can hold her on the suspicion that her gun is the murder weapon and perhaps fluff up our other suspicions, but you know how he is. He'll only give us seventy-two hours to find hard evidence that could convict her. If we come up with nothing, then we have to let her go for now until more evidence against her develops. What do you want to do?"

Detective Edwards looked at Breezy, who was pacing back and forth, through the two-way mirror. He could see she was tired and worn out. He had asked her every question there was to ask her and yet nothing she said struck a guilty cord with the detective.

"She's not represented by counsel and she hasn't asked for a lawyer," Detective Edwards said in a conniving tone.

"Yet," Sams quickly added, "a senior law school student would know that we really don't have anything factual against her."

Detective Edwards thought for a moment before saying, "we'll just have to take that chance. Let's book her."

Klarke, Reo, and Jeva looked like three angels standing side by side as Breezy walked outside of the Lucas County jail. It had been a long seventy-two hours.

When Breezy reached the three of them they all put their arms around her.

"This wasn't exactly what I had in mind when I said I wanted a gated community lifestyle," Breezy said.

The three drove Breezy home. When Breezy walked into her apartment she was greeted by tossed and broken furniture. Furniture had been turned over and some seized as evidence. There were shattered picture frames and broken drawers. The Lucas County Police Department had no mercy in their search of Breezy's home for evidence. Nothing was worth salvaging.

Her father's blood had dried and seeped into the cracks of the bathroom floor tiles. Breezy fixed up a concoction of baking soda and water and scrubbed away the blood.

When Breezy arrived back at work her desk had been cleared and her nametag had been removed from her office door. Supposedly she was being terminated for no-show call. Her arrest had been on every six o'clock news channel so she was certain her place of employment knew of the ordeal she had to contend with. She knew this same ordeal was the true reason behind her being fired. She was too drained to try to even fight it. She loaded her belongings into her car and never looked back.

A tip had been phoned in to Detective Edwards, putting Guy at the scene of the crime on the night Breezy's father was murdered. The female caller stated that Guy had mentioned something about an attempt to shut up his mistress, only to have his plot interrupted by an unexpected occupant, Mr. Williams. Supposedly Guy had contacted the caller's boyfriend in hopes of hiring him to finish the job. Detective Edwards felt that the call might have had some validity to it so he got his brother, Judge Thomas Edwards, to issue a warrant to search Guy's vehicle and home. Lo and behold, traces of Mr. William's blood were found on Guy's car steering wheel and on an article of Guy's clothing that was retrieved from his home.

"So, what do you have to say for yourself?" Detective Edwards said to Guy as he sat down at the table in the interrogation room.

"I don't have shit to say until my attorney gets here," Guy responded as he slammed his cuffed hands down on the table. "You sons of bitches better get prepared for the lawsuit of your lives."

"No, you better get prepared to spend the rest of your life in jail. As a matter of fact, I'll help you prepare," Detective Edwards said as he threw a tube of Vaseline at Guy. "I sometimes get chapped lips, but I figure you're going to be needing this far more than me."

Detective Edwards began to laugh, and Guy went ballistic. Guards had to come into the interrogation room and settle him down.

"Now, are you ready to talk? I can't help you unless you talk to me. You can wait for your attorney in CB7 with bootie-snatchin' Bill if you like," Detective Edwards said.

"Fuck you!" Guy shouted. "This is bullshit."

"No, fuck you. And that's just what's about to happen if you don't start talking. Now did I hear you say you would like to waive your right to an attorney and tell me why traces of the victim's blood were found on your steering wheel and on the sleeve of one of your shirts?" Detective Edwards roared, becoming highly frustrated.

"Listen, I'm telling you the truth. I don't know how anybody's blood got anywhere. I was with my wife the night of the murder. I already told you that. She's my alibi. Call her and ask her."

"Oh, I don't think you want me to do that." Detective Edwards snickered.

"Call her and you'll see for yourself, you fat son of a bitch!"

"For your information your wife is in the next room, and her story ain't matching up with yours."

"Quit bullshitting with me, detective. You wanted me to be straight with you, well, don't insult me by playing games with me."

"Oh, you think I'm playing games?" Detective Edwards said as he pulled out a tape recorder and hit the play button.

Guy almost shit his pants when he heard what sounded like his wife's voice spilling out information about his relationship with Breezy. His wife stated that Guy told her that, after the incident with the cell phone call, he was going to take care of Breezy once and for all. She went on to give blow-by-blow details of how she herself suspected her husband of the crime. Guy's wife danced around vouching for his whereabouts the night of the murder.

"So just tell me the truth," Detective Edwards said after hitting the stop button only a quarter way through Guy's wife's spill. "We already have another witness, a neighbor, who heard you break in Ms. Williams's door one night. This witness says prior to the door being bashed in she saw a heated argument take place between you and Ms. Williams."

"This is bullshit!" Guy yelled.

"Your fingerprints are all over the apartment, not to mention the blood evidence. So tell me, are you ready to make a deal now?" Detective Edwards asked. "I can have the district attorney here in no time."

Guy was denied bond. The evidence that continued to pile up against him was a guaranteed conviction. His lawyer begged him to take a plea, but he refused as he maintained his innocence.

When his lawyers attempt to point the finger at Breezy failed, Guy quickly started talking deals, but by this time the DA had him by the balls and had called off all deals.

Once she was certain that Guy was going to be convicted, his wife decided to visit him at the downtown jail, where he was being held while awaiting the outcome of his trial.

"Was the pussy worth all of this, you cheating bastard?" Guy's wife asked as she sat down her small, slender frame.

"Baby, why are you doing this to me? How the fuck you going to put a block on the phone so that my calls don't go through?" Guy inquired.

"It doesn't feel too good to be played, now does it?" his wife asked.

"Baby, honey, this is much more serious than an infidelity. Is that why you telling the cops all that bullshit? You trying to get back at me? Okay, baby, you win. I'm sorry. I'm a sorry-ass bastard. Now come on. You've got to tell them the truth."

"Truth? Since when do you know anything about the truth, Guy? Look, I'm not here to tell you how much I love you and how I'm going to see to it that you get out of here. I'm not even going to bullshit you like that. I just wanted you to know that divorce papers are being drawn and the kids and I are going to Arizona to visit with my parents for a while."

"What?" Guy yelled. "Baby, please. Come on now."

"You look so cute when you beg," his wife said. "Reminds me of the sweet young man I married. It's a shame how some cute little pups can grow up to be big ugly dawgs."

"Fucking bitch!" Guy mumbled under his breath.

"I'll be that," his wife said, jumping up. "I'll be a fucking bitch. But I'm a free bitch. You, you're behind bars for God knows how long. You jeopardized everything for a piece of ass. How did it feel when that detective told you they found the victim's blood on your steering wheel and on your shirt? You felt like someone was playing you, didn't you? Good, because now you know how it feels. I'm sorry things turned out this way. It wasn't supposed to be the old man, but when there's interference and one doesn't have a plan B, shit happens. One sometimes has to make do with the situation at hand."

"You fucking set me up!" Guy began to yell hysterically. "You fucking set me up! Who was it? Who did you get to do the deed? I know you didn't have the guts. Was is that little pretty muthafucker who lives next door? Do you think I don't know about the two of you creeping back and forth across the lawn every afternoon while I'm out breaking my back at the job. Or is it his son? Yeah, you nasty ho, I know about him, too. It's funny how some little girls grow up to be women and others grow up to be hoes."

The guards had to run over and subdue Guy. He started going crazy. Once they finally got him settled down, tears of complete detestation for his wife rolled down his face. He was breathing as if he had just run a marathon.

"How could you do this to me?" Guy pleaded with his wife. "Why, why are you doing this to me, baby?"

"Why am I doing this to you? I gave you fifteen years, most of my youth, and all of my adult years. I gave you beautiful children, washed your nasty drawers, and this is how you pay me back, by running around keeping some tramp on the side. She's not even as fine as me, Guy," his wife scolded. "I had been faithful to you for all those years until you started playing me like an idiot. I had needs, too. But just remember, you started it, Guy, and I'm finishing it."

"You'll burn in hell for this," Guy said as the guards began to haul him away.

"Was it worth it, Guy?" his wife repeated while the guards carried Guy away. "Oh, Guy, just one more thing. This Bria, Ms. Williams person, she's a little thick for your taste, isn't she? That picture of her in the wooden frame with her name engraved on it . . . well, let me just say that you could have done better."

19

Son of Satan

There was a loud banging on the door. Klarke and Reo both sat up in the bed.

"Damn!" Reo said wiping his eyes. "Who is that?"

"I don't know," Klarke said, looking at the clock that read 9:00 A.M.

Vaughn suddenly burst through their bedroom door.

"Mom, Reo," Vaughn said in a panic. "There's police everywhere!"

Klarke and Reo both jumped up out of bed and hurried to put on something decent. Klarke threw on a long pink satin robe. Reo grabbed a dark blue, plaid pajama shirt that was hanging over the footboard of the bed. It matched the pajama pants he was wearing.

The two, followed by Vaughn, couldn't get down the steps quickly enough, each stumbling over one another.

Reo made it to the door first. He opened it to find four officers and a swarm of police cars.

"May I help you?" Reo asked, puzzled.

"Yes," one of the officers replied. "We're responding to a nine-one-one call we received from your neighbor. Do you mind if we check in the back, your swimming pool?"

"Sure," Reo said with a perplexed look on his face. He moved out of the way and let the officers inside. Klarke led the officers to the back patio door and opened it for them. Reo, Klarke, and Vaughn followed the officers out to the back patio. What they saw was wrenching.

The police taped off the swimming pool area of Klarke's home. It had been two hours since they had responded to the neighbor's 911 call. The neighbor had reported seeing what appeared to be a small child floating facedown in the pool.

"I don't understand! I don't understand!" Reo cried.

Several officers had to restrain him as he tried to go after the deceased baby. He completely lost his mind as he watched his lifeless baby girl being dragged out of the pool.

"Oh, baby. Oh, my God," Klarke said trying to comfort him.

Nothing anyone could do at that point could calm Reo down. He finally fell to the patio ground. The officers released him into Klarke's arms. She knelt beside him and hugged his head close to her bosom as tears slipped down her cheeks.

"I'm so sorry, baby, I'm so sorry," Klarke said over and over again.

"I don't understand. I don't understand how this happened. My baby girl," Reo said, clinging to her. "It hurts, KAT. It hurts."

Vaughn and HJ were in the kitchen awaiting the arrival of their father. Vaughn was hugging HJ tightly as he tried to understand the entire scene.

"Everything is going to be all right," Vaughn said rubbing HJ's head. "Everything is going to be all right."

The police officers had asked if there was anywhere the children could go to get them away from the tragic scene. Vaughn suggested their father be phoned. She read her father's phone number to the female officer, who called, explained the situation to Harris, and asked him to come pick up the children.

The police asked Vaughn and HJ a few questions while they waited for their father. Neither Vaughn nor HJ had any knowledge of how the baby might have drowned in the pool.

"The baby is dead, isn't she?" Vaughn asked the female officer. "Is there any way they can make her come alive again? I mean dead is dead, right?" Just then Harris came through the front door.

"Vaughn, HJ, are you all right?" Harris asked, hurrying over to them and hugging them tightly.

"Yes, Daddy," HJ said. "The baby couldn't swim."

Through the sliding patio doors Harris could see Klarke holding Reo. He headed toward them but was stopped by an officer.

"I'm sorry, sir, but you're going to have to stay inside," the officer said with his hand across Harris's chest. "And you are?"

"I'm Harris Bradshaw, the children's father," he said, pointing to Vaughn and HJ. "I just wanted to let Klarke know I was taking them with me."

"Wait right here. I'll go tell her," the officer said, walking over to Klarke. Klarke looked up at Harris as the officer pointed to Harris. Klarke nodded her head that it was okay for Harris to take the children.

"Come on, kids. Let's go," Harris said.

"Sir, could I get you to write down your name, address, and phone number?" the female officer asked. "We might have a few more questions to ask the children."

Harris wrote his information down and handed it to the officer.

"Sir," the officer said before Harris and the children headed out of the door, "this is the card of the detective who will be leading this case. If the children say anything to you that might be helpful, please give him a call anytime. His cell phone number is on the back of the card."

By this time Klarke had managed to finally bring Reo to his feet. A police officer noticed that she could barely handle Reo's weight and assisted her in getting him into the house and sitting him down on the couch.

"Can somebody just tell me why?" Reo said distraught. "I don't understand. I don't understand."

Klarke's heart was broken as she witnessed her strong husband melt down. She tried to empathize by imagining if it had been one of her own children and knew that there would be nothing she could do to ease that kind of pain. "Oh, God!" Reo exclaimed. "Has anyone called Meka yet?"

"A six-month-old baby didn't just hop out of her crib and decide to take a swim," an officer said to Klarke and Reo as they sat hand in hand. The officers had been drilling them on the last time they had each been with the baby. They had even called Vaughn and HJ to ask them questions before finally sending an officer over to Harris's house to question them in person.

Meka arrived with her mother and one of her sisters shortly after Reo's mother and father had arrived to the house.

"You bitch," Meka yelled as she lunged at Klarke. "What did you do to my baby? What did you do?"

Everyone hurried to hold Meka back. Reo grabbed her and held her tight as they each cried an ocean of tears.

"Reo, my baby," Meka cried. "Please, where's my baby?"

"I'm so sorry," Reo said. "I'm so sorry."

The two clutched each other and embraced. The emotions were so heavy that there wasn't a dry eye in the room. Even the huskiest officer was in tears. There was something about the death of a child, an unexplainable death at that, that tormented one's soul.

"How'd she get in the pool, Reo?" Meka asked. "How did my baby girl end up in that woman's pool?"

"I don't know," Reo answered. "I don't understand."

"Were you that afraid that my daughter would put a dent in your happily-ever-after life with him?" Meka said to Klarke, referring to Reo. "Were you afraid there wouldn't be enough room in his heart left for you, or enough money left in his bank account, you greedy bitch? I know your kind."

Meka again launched herself at Klarke. Meka's angry words to her cut like a knife. She didn't blame Meka, though. She, too, would be just as devastated if it had been a child from her own womb. She was, in fact, hurting deeply too.

"I didn't know where else to go," Klarke said, standing on Harris's porch.

Meka and her family as well as Reo's parents were staying at the Clarion hotel for the night. Officers and the media had swarmed Klarke's home until she couldn't bear to stay there.

Klarke wanted desperately to be by her husband's side, but she knew he wanted to mourn with his family and the mother of his child. Meka was already blaming Klarke, so she knew her being there would have only made things worse.

Both Jeva and Breezy offered for Klarke to stay with them, but

Klarke wanted to be with her children. She hadn't even thought about calling Harris to ask if her camping out there would have been a problem.

"As long as I have a roof over my head," Harris said, "you always have someplace to go. Come inside, Klarke."

"Where are the kids?" she asked.

"Asleep," Harris answered. "It's having a strong impact on Vaughn. I've never seen her this way before. This whole thing is just surreal."

"Harris, I don't know what happened. Words can't explain how confusing this all is to me."

"Klarke, you don't have to explain yourself to me. I know you. The truth will make itself known."

"I hope so, Harris. You should have seen how Meka, the baby's mother, came after me. And I could see it in everyone's eyes. I could see it, Harris." Klarke cried. "Everyone in that room felt the same way she did."

"She blames you?" Harris asked.

"Yes, but I swear to God, Harris, I would never—"

"Shhhh," Harris said, holding Klarke tightly. "You don't have to say it. I know the kind of woman you are, Klarke, and it's not the kind of woman who is capable of killing a baby, or anyone, for that matter."

"Now all I have to do is convince the rest of the world of that," Klarke said in a hopeless tone.

"Look at me," Harris said, pulling Klarke's face close to his. "Anyone who knows you knows you're not capable of such an act."

"I shouldn't be dumping my load on you. I know you are still trying to cope with Tionne's death. How are you dealing, Harris?"

"Oh, man. I might as well had been the one who put that rope around her neck because I feel as though I took the life out of her."

"How can you say that?" Klarke asked. "You took great care of Tionne. She had everything she wanted."

"Except for me," Harris said sadly. "For some reason I never could give her all of me."

Klarke and Harris sat there looking into each other's eyes. Harris's support was exactly what Klarke needed at that very moment. The two moved closer together until their lips just barely touched. Harris proceeded to stick his tongue into Klarke's mouth, but she pulled away.

"I better go call Reo," Klarke said as she got up to make her call, leaving Harris alone on the couch.

20

Love or Money

"I'm supposed to be your friend and I feel so useless," Jeva said to Klarke as they strolled through the mall, along with Breezy. "I see your pain and there's nothing I can do to ease it. Same goes to you, Breezy."

"You just being my friend, being by my side," Klarke said to Jeva, "is enough for me. That's all I need right now."

"Ditto, girl," Breezy added.

"Why are we bothering with this mall today?" Jeva inquired.

"With all the crap that's going on in our lives," Breezy added, "we're at the fucking mall. Typical women."

"Breezy's right," Jeva said. "Klarke, do you really think it looks good for you to be cruising the mall while your husband is mourning the loss of his child?"

"What can I do, Jeva?" Klarke asked. "Meka wants my head on a platter. Reo and his parents are spending all of their time with Meka and her family. I have to let Reo deal with this the way he needs to. Do you think I don't want to be by my husband's side? This is just all one big mess. Once again a dream come true has turned into a nightmare."

"My life is in shambles too, girl," Breezy said, "but you know I got your back."

"Did you find another job yet?" Jeva asked Breezy.

"Nah, but I'm looking," Breezy replied. "That unemployment check don't even cover my Hudson's charge card bill."

"Hey, isn't that the guy from your company Christmas party?" Jeva asked Klarke.

Klarke looked across the mallway only to see Evan. He was looking casually fine and laughing it up with some woman who was clinging to his arm.

"That's my boss," Klarke said surprised. "I mean my ex-boss."

"Who's that woman he's with?" Breezy asked. "Klarke, she looks just like you."

Evan spotted the threesome staring at him and walked over to them with a comforting smile.

"Hello, Evan," Klarke said.

"Oh, Klarke," he said embracing her. "How are you?"

Klarke looked over Evan's shoulder at the woman who did seem to hold an uncanny resemblance to her. She couldn't help but notice the shiny engagement ring on the woman's finger.

"Klarke, this is Aliyah," Evan said.

"Pleased to meet you, Klarke," Aliyah said. "You are right, Evan. She and I do look as though we could be twin sisters."

Klarke smiled, then turned her attention back to Evan and reacquainted him with Jeva and Breezy.

"How are things at Kemble and Steiner?" Klarke asked.

"Not the same since we lost our number-one executive accounts representative," Evan said. "I just want you to know that when everything blows over, and I know it will, your desk will be waiting for you."

"Can it be waiting for me inside of an office this time instead of a cubicle?" Klarke smiled. "I mean, come on, I'm an executive accounts rep, for pete's sake."

"You got it," Evan said. "It's really good to see you, Klarke."

"It's good seeing you, too."

Evan kissed Klarke on the cheek, nodded at Jeva and Breezy, and walked away.

"You must have put it on him, girl," Breezy said. "He must crave chocolate now."

"Y'all stupid," Klarke said.

"Hell, you could have just kept screwing the boss and got what you wanted out of life," Breezy said.

"Is that what you think this is about?" Klarke said. "I love Reo. Loving him wasn't part of any plan."

"That's not what she means, Klarke," Jeva said. "Come on now, y'all. Each other is all we have right now. We almost lost Breezy to the system and now Klarke is up to bat. We need each other now to lean on more than ever."

"Jeva's right," Breezy said. "I don't know what I would have done without you all."

"Klarke, do you really think they might try to pin this on you?" Jeva asked.

"I don't know, baby," Klarke said putting her arm around Jeva. "All I know is that Reo and I have been made out to be like the Ramseys. You know, I never had been able to sympathize with that family until now."

"Reo ought to make a book about our lives," Breezy said.

"Yeah, it would be a guaranteed bestseller all over the world," Jeva said.

"I'm scared," Klarke said out of nowhere. "I'm scared."

The girls all hugged each other as if they had been college room-mates and were packing up to go their separate ways. Their lives had all done a 360-degree turn. Although Jeva was starting to find comfort and love within herself, she could hardly bask in the glory of her new days as she watched her best friends' lives become ruin.

"Will you guys say a prayer for me?" Klarke asked Jeva and Breezy.

"Sure," they said.

"I mean right now," Klarke said.

"Right here in the middle of the mall?" Breezy asked.

Just then a girl in a low-cut open-back halter top with painted-on tight jeans walked by. She was sporting three-inch heels and an up-do with spritz spit curls hanging down.

"If she ain't embarrassed to walk through the mall looking like that," Breezy said, "then we sure shouldn't be embarrassed to bow our head in the name of the Lord in the mall."

The girls laughed as they bowed their heads in prayer.

"I don't have nothing," Breezy wailed as she stacked boxes of her belongings, which consisted of some clothing and a few personal items. Breezy had been unable to maintain her bills and had received an eviction notice. Jeva was helping her pack.

All the high spirit that made Breezy who she was had been lost. She didn't go out and seek another job as was stipulated for receiving unemployment compensation benefits.

"I can't believe I'm moving back home with my mother. I'm thirty years old. That's thirty years of my life wasted, gone. I had to beg her, but I don't have anywhere else to go. I wish I had my daddy," Breezy cried.

"I'll take care of you. We can be roommates—you, Heather, and me. We'll need a big house, compliments of my birth parents of course." Jeva smiled. "There's nothing more I'd like than to live happily ever after with my best friend."

Breezy hugged Jeva. She loved her so much. She knew she didn't deserve Jeva's friendship or financial support, not with the secret of betrayal she had kept from her. But with Lance out of her life Jeva would never have to know the truth.

The more Breezy thought about it, after all she had jeopardized and lost, she wasn't going to make the same mistake twice. No amount of money or lifestyle in the world was worth spending years torturing herself with lies. Nothing was worth robbing herself of quality of life with a clear conscience. Besides, she feared God wouldn't be willing to forgive her for the same deliberate mistake. Even if telling Jeva about her and Lance meant that she'd have to live the rest of her life in a homeless shelter, she had to tell her the truth.

"Jeva, you've really been there for me and I really do appreciate you for that," Breezy said. "I know I don't show it. I know it seems like I'm always coming down hard on you. It's just that you are always so easygoing with life. I wish I could be that way. It makes me jealous sometimes. I get angry. I get mad for not being able to be more like you in a sense."

Breezy paused and then looked up at Jeva. "I need to tell you something. After you listen to what I'm about to say, if you decide never to be my friend again, I'm just thankful for all this time I've been fortunate enough to have you in my life. You've always had my back." Breezy began to sob.

"Breezy, what are you trying to tell me?" Jeva asked.

"It's about Lance," Breezy said putting her head down.

"Breezy, you know what? You don't even have to go there,"

Jeva said, putting her index finger over Breezy's lips to shush her. "Like you told Lance yourself, a locked door only keeps people out. It doesn't keep them from hearing what's going on on the other side of that door. I know. I know about you and Lance."

Breezy couldn't believe Jeva had overheard her and Lance's conversation and had never said one word about it. She couldn't believe Jeva remained such a good friend to her knowing how she had backstabbed her by sleeping with Lance. Breezy broke down.

"I don't understand," Breezy said, shaking her head.

"Lance was a man, a sorry man at that. Not that I didn't love him, and not that hearing you two discuss your fling didn't hurt like hell. Do you know how hard it was to go back down to that party with a smile on my face after hearing that my best friend had slept with my fiancé? When I wasn't smiling I was crying. Not because I was elated with the fact that I was about to become this happy bride, but because I was absolutely beside myself," Jeva said as she caught a couple of tears from making their way down her face.

"Then I don't understand why you stayed with him, knowing . . . and why you remained my friend."

"It's like you told Klarke, she had the fairy tale once and chose to give it up. Well, I wanted it and I was willing to compromise everything, including myself, to have that fairy tale and to hold on to it at all cost. I didn't want to be like Klarke and Harris."

"So you would have married Lance and pretended that everything was just fine?" Breezy asked.

"Isn't that what a fairy tale is . . . pretending in a make-believe world?"

"I love you so much, Jeva," Breezy said, hugging her and rubbing her fingers through her hair.

"I love you too. You know that," Jeva responded.

Breezy pulled away from Jeva and looked into her eyes. She didn't know why she was so blessed to have such a beautiful person in her life. Filled with emotion she kissed Jeva softly on the lips. Jeva sat there, shy.

"I'm sorry," Breezy said, pulling away. "I don't know why I just did that."

"It's okay," Jeva said, putting her hand on Breezy's shoulder. "It's okay."

Breezy kissed her again, only this time it was a much welcomed and bracing kiss.

21

Seek and Ye Shall Find

"Miss Taylor. I mean, Mrs. Laroque," Detective Edwards said. "So we meet again, and under similar circumstances."

"Detective Edwards," Klarke acknowledged.

"Mr. and Mrs. Laroque," the detective said to Reo and Klarke, who entered his office arm-in-arm. "Please have a seat."

"Thank you," Reo said as he and Klarke sat down.

Although this was Reo and Klarke's third time being questioned about the death of the baby, it was Detective Edwards's first stab at them. Each time the questions were the same, only worded differently. It was obvious Detective Edwards's goal was to now catch Reo and Klarke in some type of lie. Reo and Klarke had been questioned both together and individually in an attempt to find incriminating flaws in their stories.

"So can the two of you start by telling me the last time you each saw the deceased alive?"

Reo broke down at the thought of his child being labeled *deceased*. It broke his heart.

"She was in our bed with us," Klarke said. "At about ten

o'clock that night we took her into the spare room and put her in her crib."

"We," Detective Edwards said. "The both of you walked her into the room."

"No, it was just me," Klarke answered.

"I see," Detective Edwards said. "About how long would you say Mrs. Laroque was absent from the bedroom when she left to put your daughter in her crib, Mr. Laroque?"

"I don't know, about ten or fifteen minutes or so," Reo said. "She went downstairs to get something to drink."

"I noticed the minirefrigerator in your bedroom was fully stocked," Detective Edwards said.

"I wanted water," Klarke said in a defensive tone.

"There are Dixie cups next to the bathroom sink in your master bedroom private bath," Detective Edwards drilled.

"I wanted ice water," Klarke added.

"So did Mrs. Laroque come up with a glass of ice water?" Detective Edwards asked Reo.

"I drank it downstairs," Klarke interfered. "There wasn't any need to bring an empty glass upstairs."

"After your wife left the room with your daughter at ten o'clock P.M.," Detective Edwards asked Reo, "when was the next time you saw your daughter?"

"Being pulled out of the pool." Reo cried.

Detective Edwards supplied Reo with a box of Kleenex and continued his questioning.

"Let's see, prior to Mrs. Laroque you were Miss Taylor. Is that correct?" Detective Edwards asked Klarke.

"Correct," Klarke responded.

"And prior to that you were Mrs. Rawling Davis, and before

that you were Mrs. Harris Bradshaw. So Taylor is your maiden name, correct?"

"Correct," Klarke said, looking at Reo, who was quickly becoming enlightened on some minor details of Klarke's history.

"Where are you employed?" Detective Edwards asked Klarke.

"I'm not," she responded.

"Oh, yeah, I see, you were formerly employed at Kemble and Steiner Printing, is that correct?"

"For a short period, yes."

"Two and a half years, if you want to call that short," Detective Edwards said.

Klarke could all of a sudden hear her heart beat. There was absolutely no way out of the heated brew she was about to find herself boiling in.

"Kemble and Steiner," Reo interrupted. "You were the accounts rep. My publisher uses Kemble and Steiner to print my books. I used them when I self-published. Your picture was on the Web site. I remember seeing it when I was researching and getting printing quotes."

"Pardon me," Detective Edwards said, looking back and forth at Klarke and Reo. "Am I missing something here?"

"Detective, I think I'm the one who's missing something," Reo said. "Klarke, what's going on?"

"I can explain, Reo, but not now. Let's answer the detective's questions first. We'll talk at home," Klarke said as her eyes began to water. Right then and there Reo released her hand from his. Right then and there she knew she had lost him.

"A deliberate stranger," Reo said. "That e-mail was on purpose. You deliberately planned all of this. Your company has my personal information in their records. I can't believe it. What did you do, research me? I bet you probably studied every article that was ever written about me." The look on Klarke's face confirmed his suspicions.

"Hmmm, articles," Detective Edwards added. "I guess that would explain this box we found in the attic of your Toledo home."

Detective Edwards pulled a Xerox box from underneath the table and placed it on the table. Klarke's eyes bulged. Detective Edwards proceeded to empty the contents of the box onto the middle of the table. There were several clippings from magazines and newspapers. Reo picked up a videotape that was labeled "Reo Laroque television interview." The tape was dated two months before Reo had ever even met Klarke.

Reo stood up and buried his face in the palms of his hands. It was as if the room was spinning around while his body was still. All of the thoughts going through his head had to be impossible, Reo prayed. There was no way the scenario forming in his scrambled brain could have been played out against him by the woman he trusted with his heart.

"Please tell me this is all a coincidence, please, Klarke."

"Mr. Laroque, can I get you something to drink?" the detective asked, seeing that Reo was becoming a little woozy.

"No, no, detective," Reo said finding his seat again.

He looked up at Klarke with shame, humiliation, and embarrassment. She read everything he was thinking about her in his eyes. She looked away from Reo. She was weakening, not even finding enough strength to look him in his face.

"Reo, it's not like that at all," Klarke said. "I swear I love you. I swear my love for you was not part of the plan. It's real. Come on, Reo, it's me, KAT."

"I gave you that name. Don't you use that fucking name." Reo paced. "So is it true? Did you deliberately seek me out? Look at me, damn it. Did you?"

Klarke looked up at Reo without saying a word. Her actions said it all. The detective was on cloud nine as he watched what felt like an episode of the *The Practice* play out before him.

"I can't believe it. You set me up," Reo said.

"Please, Reo, you're my husband now. I know you know I love you. I know you feel this shit."

"Oh, you love me, do you? And so does every other bitch out for my bank. *Fuck!* How could I have been so stupid? I should have known. I mean, when you e-mailed me that picture. I knew I knew you from somewhere. I knew I had seen you before."

Klarke's stomach began to turn with the world. She placed her hand over her mouth and began to gag. Detective Edwards quickly retrieved the trash pail for her. Just as he placed it in front of her she threw up her entire breakfast.

"I'm the one who needs to be puking," Reo said to Klarke. "You make me sick."

"Would you two like a moment alone?" Detective Edwards asked.

"Yes," Klarke said while at the same time Reo replied, "No."

"Continue your questioning please, Detective," Reo said. "I'd like to finish up here so I can go to Mrs. Lar . . . I mean, Miss Taylor's home and pack up my things."

The detective went over his notepad and proceeded with his questioning.

"Your first marriage ended because your husband was unfaithful," Detective Edwards asked Klarke.

"That's one of the reasons," Klarke said.

"Well, in your divorce decree it's the only reason stated. Your former husband, Mr. Bradshaw, committed adultery with his cousin?"

"She wasn't his blood cousin," Klarke said.

"I'm sure Mr. Bradshaw would be proud that you are defending him. But anyway . . . so the scenario with Reo having a child come into your life was like déjà vu, huh."

"I don't know what you're talking about, Detective," Klarke said.

"Your first husband, didn't he have a child outside of your marriage that you had to play mommy to?"

"I know what you're trying to do, Detective, and you're wrong. I heard about the million-dollar life insurance policy Meka had on the baby. It's all over the news. Why don't you go badger her?"

"I can't listen to this," Reo said.

"Don't you want to get to the bottom of this?" Detective Edwards asked, checking his cell phone, which had just vibrated.

"This is Detective Edwards," he said in a professional tone.

"Detective Edwards. My name is Harris Bradshaw," Harris said quickly. "I don't know if you know who I am, but I—"

"Of course I know who you are," Detective Edwards said, cutting Harris off, glancing over at Klarke. "How ironic you should phone me. Your ex-wife and I were just speaking of you. She's with me now."

"Klarke is there, with you!" Harris said excitedly.

"Yes, as a matter of—"

"May I speak with her please?" Harris said in an almost begging tone.

"Sure. One moment," the detective said, handing his cell phone to Klarke.

"Hello," Klarke said, puzzled.

"Klarke, it's me, Harris," Harris said, frenzied and speaking quickly. "I'm here with Vaughn and, and . . ."

Harris couldn't catch his breath.

"Harris, calm down. Just calm down and tell me what's the matter with Vaughn."

Klarke listened intensely as Harris rambled on and on. She advised Harris that she was on her way to his house and to just stay calm until she arrived. Klarke then ended the call and handed Detective Edwards his cell phone back. Detective Edwards spoke hellos into the receiver only to find that the line was dead.

"I've got to go," Klarke said, jumping up.

"I still have quite a few more questions," Detective Edwards said.

"Then they'll just have to wait. It's my daughter," Klarke said as she began to become panicked and impatient. "Unless you're arresting me I'm leaving. I have to get to my daughter."

"Calm down, Mrs. Laroque," Detective Edwards said. "I'm going to have to ask you not to leave town. You either, Mr. Laroque."

"I need to go home," Reo replied. "Home in Columbus. I promise not to leave the state, Detective, but I've got to get home. I need to be with my family and my daughter's mother."

"Please understand, Mr. Laroque, if we have to join forces with the Columbus Police Department to keep you under surveillance, we will."

"Do what you have to do, Detective," Reo said. "Just find out what happened to my daughter."

Klarke felt in her heart that this moment in that interrogation room would be the last time Reo would be by her side and on her side. Without her husband, her other half, her equal, Klarke felt as though it was her against the world.

. . .

"God comes up with mysterious ways to humble folks," Nate said to Persia as they stood in the dining room at Meka's parents' home. Reo had just finished praying in the nursery with Meka when he joined Nate and Persia.

"How you doing, man?" Nate asked Reo.

"Not good, but I'm trying to hang in there."

"How's Meka?"

"Terrible. She says she doesn't blame me, but I blame myself. I didn't even want to have anything to do with that baby at first." Reo began to cry.

"Don't do this to yourself, man," Nate said. "None of that matters. What does matter is that you came around and did the right thing."

"I was forced to do the right thing, but not on my own will. God is punishing me," Reo said.

"Don't put this on God, son," Meka's mother said, entering the dining room. "Always keep in mind that there was another angel with spiritual force thrown out of the heavens. Satan is an attention-getter, son. He's always competing with the Lord. Don't blame the Lord for Satan's work."

"I'm so sorry," Reo said, hugging Meka's mother.

"We don't blame you. We know that you didn't have anything to do with this. It was all her. Now just stay strong while the police do their business," Meka's mother said, kissing Reo on the forehead and walking away.

Reo was a little affected by the remark Meka's mother made blaming Klarke. Nate could sense this.

"You don't think she did it, do you, man?" Nate asked. "I mean, black people don't do that kind of stuff."

"That's what everybody said before the sniper incident, too," Reo responded.

"You claim to know this woman. You've spoken of her as if you two share the same heart. Do you believe she's capable of something this heinous?"

"There's a lot I didn't think she was capable of, Nate."

"You're avoiding answering the question," Nate replied.

"I mean, Nate, people do things all of the time that they, or the people who know them, would have never thought they were capable of doing in a million years. Circumstance and option are a muthafuck."

Detective Edwards was surprised to see Klarke return for questioning escorted by her attorney. He wasn't surprised at all that Reo wasn't with her.

"Tell it to me straight, Gary," Klarke's attorney said to Detective Edwards. "What do you have on my client?"

"It's mainly circumstantial, but it will hold. Especially our Xerox box full of documentation your client was keeping on her husband. I think a sympathetic jury will see it as premeditation," Detective Edwards said. "Your client is looking at the death penalty."

Detective Edwards went over the evidence with a fine-toothed comb with Klarke's attorney. He detailed how Klarke's character would be shot to hell by just mentioning the scheme that she concocted to gain the attention of Reo and his bank account.

"Here you go, Edwards," Sams said, handing him a piece of paper.

"Here's our warrant for your client's arrest right here," Detective Edwards said to Klarke's attorney. "The grand jury has indicted her."

"Don't worry," Klarke's attorney said to her incoherent client. "Mrs. Laroque, are you okay?"

By the time Klarke regained consciousness several people were standing over her. The shock of hearing that she was going to be officially charged with the murder of the baby was unbearable. Her attorney got Klarke to her feet and made sure that she was okay.

"Mrs. Laroque," Detective Edwards said. "I'm sorry we have to do this now, but you have been charged by the State of Ohio with the murder of the deceased child. This is very serious. As you know, you face the death penalty. Help us now with the details and we'll see about a life sentence."

Klarke looked at her attorney, still slightly disoriented, while her Miranda rights were read. Her attorney's expression showed agreement with Detective Edwards.

"May I talk to my client alone for a few moments?" Klarke's attorney said.

"Sure," Detective Edwards said, clearing the room.

"Mrs. Laroque, everything is circumstantial, so if you know anything at this point, if you can recall any single incident that might support a claim of innocence, now is the time to reveal it."

"I don't understand what they want from me," Klarke said.

"They want a guilty plea to spare your life."

"If I plead guilty, then what?" Klarke asked. "Will the case be closed forever?"

"Yes, but you will be spending the rest of your life behind bars. Do you know what happens behind bars to people who commit crimes against children?"

"Do you know what happens to children behind bars?" Klarke asked.

"I don't get it, Mrs. Laroque," her attorney said.

"Do you have any children?" Klarke asked.

"Excuse me?" Klarke's attorney said.

"Do you have any fucking children?" Klarke yelled.

"No," her attorney replied.

"Then you'll never understand."

Klarke entered her guilty plea like a true soldier. She didn't stutter or hesitate as Meka, Reo, and their families pierced her body with their eyes. Klarke didn't even break down and cry when she saw Meka snuggled tightly in Reo's arms as he comforted her pain.

All Klarke could think about were her children, who she made Harris promise would not be in the courtroom to witness their mother being sentenced to live the remainder of her natural life behind bars.

22

Echoes of Thunder

Klarke lay in her cell in disbelief. She couldn't believe for the rest of her life freedom would be a former companion. She tried to think positive thoughts. She thought of what a good father Harris was, and what a good father Reo would be to their baby, who she would give birth to in a few months. Finding out she was pregnant while in jail was devastating, but Klarke still managed to think of every positive thing about her being incarcerated that she could. Although positive thoughts weren't going to change the scenario, negative ones would have only made it worse.

Throughout the hearing and her court appearances, Klarke had pretended not to see Harris in the courtroom. At each court appearance, unlike Breezy and Jeva, who sat directly behind Klarke, he sat in the back of the courtroom, pulling out his handkerchief every now and then to wipe his tears. He never set out to make eye contact with her anyway. He couldn't bear seeing the mother of his children shackled in a prison uniform. After receiving her life sentence, though, Harris made it a point to visit

Klarke before she was transferred from the county jail to the women's penitentiary.

"You always did look good in orange," Harris said. Klarke laughed to keep from crying. The laughter almost turned to tears, but she fought them off.

"My babies. How are they?" Klarke asked.

"Good."

"You're lying."

"Huh?" Harris said.

"Harris, you're lying. I know when I'm being lied to now. I guess I've been doing so much of it myself lately."

"HJ hates the world and Vaughn cries herself to sleep. Then she wakes up crying," Harris said, starting to break down.

"Don't do that, damn it. Don't do it." Klarke said once again, fighting back tears.

"She'll pull through it. She's strong, remember? Like a sunflower."

"I don't, Klarke. I don't know if this is the right thing to do."

"Harris, don't," Klarke said, cutting him off.

"You're no killer, Klarke."

"And neither is our daughter," Klarke affirmed. "Look Harris, let's not do this. I'm here. The case is closed. I copped a plea and I'm here."

"You call that a plea? You're in here the rest of your life."

"Yeah, but I could have gotten the electric chair."

"But you don't belong here and we both know it. Hell, I've done worse things in my life than you've ever done."

"Why do people on the outside always say that to a locked-up convict? That shit ain't soothing. I'm in here, damn it, and you're out there. There are two types of people in this world, those who get caught and those who don't. No matter which one of those people you turn out to be, you just live with it. Let me live with it, Harris. For the sake of our daughter let me live with this. Whether I take the fall or not, either way it goes I lose my daughter. Just walk away from this."

Klarke looked around at the guards to see if any of them was dipping in on her conversation with Harris.

"I'm just trying to help. I have to help. This is my entire fault. If I had ever thought for one minute this is how things would end up, I swear to God . . ."

"Harris, this is not your fault," Klarke assured him.

"Do you know what Vaughn said to me, Klarke? She said, 'Daddy, you used to call me your favorite girl, then when you and Tionne had another daughter I became *one* of your favorite girls.' She said, 'Daddy, Reo called me his favorite girl, too.'"

"Don't do this to yourself, Harris, and I mean it. Where is the strong man I knew years ago?" Klarke asked.

"He's slowly being chiseled away." Harris spoke in the third person. "He keeps losing the women he loves."

"You're on the outside. You're all our children have to get them through this now, to get them through life. You have to be strong. It will make my days in here a lot easier knowing that you are out there being strong for our children."

Up until now Klarke had not shed a tear, but she could no longer hold them in. The tears flowed like the rhythm to a favorite song. She cried hard, the sniffing, the snorting, the snot, the works. She cried a lifetime worth of tears.

"Oh, baby, I'm so sorry," Harris gulped as he accepted her invitation to cry. "What the fuck happened?"

"You tell me."

Harris couldn't even look at Klarke. There was something else causing his tears. There was something deep-rooted that he could no longer contain.

"This is all my fault. You wouldn't even be here. You would have never met that Reo and you would have never had to scheme in order to get a man to take care of you."

"Damn it, will you stop it? I made my own choices, Harris. You act as if you put a collar around my neck and walked me through life."

"Rawling. He was a decoy, Klarke," Harris said. "It was an arrangement. That's all it was. Who knew it would lead to this?"

"Okay, I'm getting confused. Harris, what are you saying? Harris, what did you do?" Klarke asked, not sure if she truly wanted to know the answer.

"I met Rawling out one night. A couple of dudes from work and I had gone to Club Diamond, and Rawling was in there with a few friends of his own. One of the guys I was with knew one of the guys he was with, so we all congregated. We got to drinking and talking and your name came up. I started talking about my ex, you. When I said your name he mentioned that he had a student in his class named Klarke. It didn't take us long to realize it was you."

Harris could hardly speak he was so choked up, but somehow he managed to continue.

"It was just talk at first. I wasn't serious, but then Rawling called me on it. It just seemed so harmless at the time. I would give him money to pursue you. The two of you would get married, he would decide that marriage wasn't for him and file for an annulment. I would be free of my debt to you. No more alimony payments."

. . .

"She is one fine woman," Rawling muttered to Harris. "I must admit, I've wanted to tutor her ass several times. How did an old cat like you get a woman like Klarke?"

"Yeah, she is fine, huh? But she ain't two thousand dollar-a-month fine." Harris took a sip of his Beefeaters and Coke as he glared at the chocolate piece of ass that was slowly bouncing down to him. The okay-looking dancer dropped her ass to the black marble floor. It was the same floor that had enticed Harris to install marble under the bar at the home he had purchased for Klarke and the children. The dancer stretched her legs from underneath her into a split. She popped her pussy in the air, pulled her g-string to the side and separated her pussy lips with her fingers. Harris was overly generous when he planted Abe's face on her coochie, considering he noticed what he thought might have been a vaginal wart.

"Is child support included in that?" Rawling asked.

"I wish it were," Harris replied.

"Damn, now I see why them rich white men be killing their hoes. Exes are some costly muthafuckers."

"It would cost more for me to have her killed. I'll settle for paying someone to marry her."

"Too bad OJ didn't think more like you."

"OJ didn't have nothing to do with that, man."

"Oh, you really think so?"

"I know so. It's public record . . . not guilty. The legal system is a godsend when it's jailing black folk. But all of a sudden it needs to be reevaluated when it's setting them free."

"We are surrounded by naked women and we are sitting here talking about a big-ass ashy dude." The two couldn't help but laugh and seal it with a high-five.

"You're crazy," Harris said.

"I'm crazy. Hey, man, you are the one acting like Robert Redford, making indecent proposals and shit," Rawling said to Harris.

"I know, but I wasn't serious. I don't expect you to marry Klarke."

"Why not? Women do it all the time. They running around marrying these little African dudes for fifteen thousand dollar minimum to keep the little bastards in the country."

"I guess it's no different from back in the day when young men knew they were going to get money for marrying a girl. A dowry," Harris said.

"It could have worked. It would have taken a little time. You know how women are after a breakup? They love telling a brotha they just got out of a relationship, that the timing is bad, they need time for themselves, et cetera. It's hard to break that wall down. I was liable to charge you another five grand for that alone. I am a fine muthafucker though. It probably wouldn't have taken too long."

Rawling drank the last sip from his beer, pulled $30 out of his wallet, and laid it on the bar. "I have an early class to teach tomorrow so I guess I better hit the road. It was nice meeting you, Harris, man."

"Yeah, you too, man. Take it easy." Harris stared at his glass momentarily before turning toward the exit door to summon Rawling. "Hey Rawling!" Harris's voice barely made it over the Drawz version of "Thin Line Between Love and Hate" that was pounding from the jukebox. "Let me buy you just one more drink."

Klarke was speechless. She had no words for the brick Harris had just busted her upside her head with.

"How much?"

"What?"

"How much did you pay him? Never mind. Because you know

what? No amount of money in the world is worth being in here."

"Baby, I'm going to get you out of here. I'm going make shit right. I owe you. I'll get the best lawyer money can buy," Harris continued. "We'll find a loophole, or some technicality to get you off. We'll appeal. Maybe Jeva and Breezy might have an idea."

"No!" Klarke interrupted. You are not to talk to Jeva or Breezy about anything."

"They are your best friends."

"Vaughn is my daughter. The fewer people who have to take this to the grave, the less we have to worry."

"Then I'll get you out of here on my own."

"You're talking crazy, Harris. I made a plea; there is no appeal. You know there is nothing you can do for me now. This is me for the rest of my natural life, remember. I'm begging you to leave this alone. Now we both already talked about it and agreed that this was the best thing. Don't get pussy on me, Harris. Think of our daughter. Would you really want to see her here instead of me?"

Klarke faded away as a vision of Vaughn wearing an orange jailhouse jumpsuit appeared before Harris. He couldn't imagine his baby girl being locked up like an animal, but by the same token he hated the fact that Klarke would be.

"I'm the sacrificial lamb. This is how the story ends, Harris." Klarke cried. "Now you focus on raising your three children. You make sure they want for nothing, do you hear?"

"Time," the guard said as her butchlike body hovered over Klarke.

"Remember, Harris . . . shhh," Klarke said, putting her index finger over her lips.

The guard tapped Klarke on the shoulder and Klarke stood up. Handcuffs were returned to Klarke's wrists and she was escorted to the door.

Harris was losing, forever, another woman he loved. He didn't care who saw him bawling like a baby. Reality was whipping his ass as he watched Klarke being walked away in shackles.

As the guard signaled for the door to be buzzed open Klarke turned around and looked at Harris. With her hands in cuffs she raised them to her mouth and this time placed both of her index fingers over her lips. "Shhh," Klarke whispered as tears rolled down her face. "Shhh."

Hey you,

It's been a while, eleven months and two days to be exact. I know because that's how long I've been locked up in this place.

I've been doing a lot of thinking in here. It's not like I have anything better to do. I've come to the conclusion that most people who tell a person they would die for them are full of shit. What is it with society thinking they have to say what a person wants to hear? To die for someone you would have to love them unconditionally. Every love is conditional, with the exception of God's, Jesus', and a mother's love. Just know that if ever someone tells you they would die for you that it's more than likely a lie. They probably don't mean for it to be a lie, but it is, in fact, a lie with good intentions behind it.

Is there really such a thing as a good lie? I mean, some people will lie about the weather outside. They'll tell you the sun is shining with the sound of rain and echoes of thunder in the background.

A lie makes a long story short. I guess that's why men lie to women . . . why women lie to men . . . why people lie to each other. But it's funny how a person will pick the hell out of the truth, huh? Tell someone a lie and they are more apt to roll with it. Lying is hard work, though. Do you know how much energy you drain your body of and how much stress you put it through in order to tell a lie? On top of that you have to store the lie in a memory bank so that you don't slip up in the future. A born liar dies a liar.

But you know something? Sometimes lies save lives. The truth hurts, so a lie is kind of like a Band-Aid on life. It covers up some foul-ass acts.

I know you have no idea what I'm trying to say. You probably think this is a bunch of jail talk. Well, that's okay. This letter wasn't meant to heal you. It was meant to free me—my mind, anyway.

I'm hoping you don't see that this letter is from me and toss it out with the garbage before reading it. I know I agreed to let you live your life and raise our child as you see fit without any interference, so I promise I will never contact you again in any form.

You know . . . this doesn't hurt as bad as I thought it would. The entire time I was carrying our child I always knew that it would never know who its natural mother is (look who's waiving the rights to their child now). You are a good man and I know you will raise the baby to be a wonderful human being. I have no worries. Therefore I can sleep at night and live with myself for the decision I have made.

So I guess, in short, I just want to say thank you in advance. Until next lifetime, when our souls mate, I'll love you always!

KAT

As Reo finished reading the letter tears rolled down his face. He was deeply moved by Klarke's words, but still he could not let go of the fact that his baby daughter had been caught in the crossfire of her love for him.

With all of his heart, Reo knew that Klarke truly loved him in spite of her cunning means of gaining his love in return. Reo was now forced to close the book on what he thought was going to be a romance novel. He was left to raise his and Klarke's son alone.

Reo read Klarke's letter over and over again. Finally he was interrupted by a small cry whimpering through the baby monitor.

"Daddy's coming," Reo said as he carried the letter over to the garbage can. His life with Klarke, the good times, flashed before his eyes. It was those good times that reminded him of the good in Klarke, the good that their child would most likely inherit. Reo folded the letter and decided to place it inside his pants pocket.

Once he made it to the nursery, he picked his son up out of the crib and looked into his sparkling eyes that were so full of life. He had eyes like his mother.

Reo walked over to the Noah's Ark trunk next to the baby's crib. He removed the small hand-carved elephant from on top of it. It was the same elephant he had given Klarke on their first date. Inside the trunk was a picture of him and HJ with the clown at HJ's birthday party, and the paper Vaughn had written about him for school. Reo placed inside the trunk the letter Klarke had written him, with the intent of perhaps one day, maybe, sharing with his son stories about the person whose eyes he had inherited.

Reading Group Guide

1. Were you able to identify with Klarke? If so, to what extent? Do you believe Klarke did what she felt she had to do as a mother to protect her daughter?

2. Which character did you enjoy the most? Why?

3. If there were to be a sequel, what issues would you like to be addressed? And which character, if any, could you do without returning? Why?

4. Was Reo realistic? Could you imagine Reo being the perfect soul mate for Klarke as you read the story? Do you feel Reo should have stood by Klarke's side to the end despite the fact that she pleaded guilty to the murder of his baby?

5. Who do you think killed the baby and why?

6. Were you satisfied with the outcome of the book, or were you starving for more?

7. Do you feel as though karma played a role in anyone's outcome? Please explain.

8. Does the author set herself apart from other writers in this particular genre? If yes, how? If no, why not?

9. What is your take on family values and its relation to a) Klarke's choice to protect her child?, b) Reo's initial choice to forgo his rights as a father?, c) Jeva accepting money over knowing her birth parents' true identities?